The Way I've Heard It Should Be

Rachel Cullen

To my husband Doug, for always believing in me.

This is a work of fiction. Names, characters, places and incidents are of the author's imagination or, if real, are used fictitiously.

Prologue - Olivia

If someone had told me 10 years ago that the highlight of my week would be a tennis match with 3 other suburban moms, I would have told them they were crazy. In fact, I would have told this person that they had no idea what they were talking about and obviously knew nothing about me.

10 years ago, I was one of the most sought after marketing executives in Manhattan; working 80-hour weeks and traveling 3 weeks a month. The highlight of my week was a great meal with my new husband, and thanks to his travel schedule and expense accounts, those meals were often in Paris, London or Dubai.

So how did I get here?

It couldn't have happened overnight. It must have been a slow transition from successful businesswoman whose blackberry buzzed with urgent messages day and night...to mother of two whose iPhone is only in great demand to schedule playdates and be handed off to pacify screaming children.

Don't get me wrong, it isn't all bad; in fact, most of the time it's incredible.   It's just those days when I remember that I used to be a different person, and I look around and realize that no one from my current life even knows that other person ever existed.
But now I wish I had left the 'other me' alone, because maybe if I hadn't gone looking for her, I wouldn't be in the mess I'm in now.

Chapter 1 - Olivia

"Julie, let's go, we're running late." I say, as I run around the kitchen trying to clean up after breakfast, finish making Julie's school lunch and make my coffee. I wonder if this statement would carry more weight with my 5-year old daughter if I didn't yell this at least 20 times a day.

"I'm coming mommy, but I need to get Piggy dressed or she'll be cold at school," yells Julie from her room. I don't even know where to begin my response to this. Do I remind her (again) that she cannot bring toys to kindergarten? Do I tell her that even if Piggy could come to kindergarten, she certainly does not need clothes, seeing as she is a stuffed pig? Or do I just yell even louder that we are going to be really late for school if she doesn't come downstairs? I don't have time to ponder my options much longer, because the next thing I hear is a giant splash followed by shrieks.

"My milk, my milk," screams Elizabeth as her cup plummets from the counter onto the floor. There go any chances of us being on time this morning.

***

Eventually we do make it out the door and find ourselves in the drop-off line at Rye Day School where I drop off 3-year old Elizabeth and 5-year old Julie for half and full days of school respectively. It is only 8:30am, but I feel as if I have already done more than some people do in an entire day and I am tempted to go home and take a nap, but of course that isn't on today's schedule.

I now have 3 hours before I pick-up Elizabeth and I have carefully choreographed what I will do with my time. I check the running to-do list I keep on my iPhone to make sure I am not missing some crucial activity for the day; and almost more importantly I make sure there isn't anything that is easy for me to add and then cross off the list – that feeling of accomplishment a reminder of my former self.

After a quick trip to the gym, the pharmacy and the dry cleaners, I head to a local coffee shop in town to meet my friend Gretchen for coffee and to hear how things are going with her husband - last time I saw her they were not going well.

We are meeting at Lucy's Coffee Shop. It is my favorite restaurant in town and the antithesis of Starbucks. It's not that I have anything against Starbucks, and in my 'past life' I was quite possibly one of their best customers. But there is something transformative that happens when I walk into Lucy's that doesn't happen anywhere else. I love the smell of freshly baked pastries and roasting coffee, the large windows that let the light spill in, and the mix of farmhouse pine tables and club chairs that means there is never a bad seat in the house.

Lucy's Coffee Shop is just one of the many things I love about this town. Rye is a small town in Westchester. It is an affluent town made up mostly of people who commute into Manhattan for work, but still want to live the idyllic suburban life – which is why we moved here six years ago. It is a beautiful town along the Long Island

Sound, with dozens of estates well over $10 million, but less than 25 miles from the center of Manhattan – easy to see how it is an appealing destination, at least for those who can afford it.

To be honest, I wasn't that caught up in the prestige of the town when we moved here. We found a house that we liked, the commute was great, and the schools were good. My husband Charlie and I nodded each time the realtor talked about how great the schools were and it felt like we had passed some sort of test. I was only 5 months pregnant with Julie when we bought our house, but I felt like we were already behind when I met my first Westchester Tiger Mom.

***

"Olivia, over here," Gretchen calls as I walk in the door. The smell of coffee and buttery goodness welcomes me and the warmth of Lucy's shop warms me inside and out. I didn't realize how much I was looking forward to being here until right this minute. I know I am meant to be here to lend an ear to Gretchen, but I could use some adult conversation as well.

As I walk over to the table, Gretchen stands up to give me a big hug, not just one of those quick kisses on the cheeks that seem to have become the trend these days. I am fortunate to have a lot of friends at this point in my life, but I only have a few close friends, and Gretchen is definitely one of my closest.

Gretchen is 41, two years older than I am, and she is an attractive woman, but she doesn't turn heads the way our friend Laura does. She is 5 foot 6 with brown hair and brown eyes. She dresses well, but nothing outlandish or attention grabbing. Today she is wearing dark skinny jeans (probably size 8 from The Gap) and a cashmere hoodie with little brown ankle boots. I think she looks great and totally appropriate for meeting a friend for morning coffee, but I have had this conversation with Charlie before and I know he thinks she is a little plain and has said, "she would be a lot hotter if she put more effort into it." This annoys me on many levels, but mostly I think he is just comparing her to Laura – but more on that later.

I take off my coat and get comfortable. I know we will only have about an hour before we have to go back to the real world, but I want to enjoy every moment of it.

"So, how are you? What's going on?" Gretchen says. "I'm fine, nothing new, tell me about you," I reply - the standard ping-pong game that starts all of our conversations.

Gretchen gives me a sad smile and says, "honestly, things aren't great. Alan and I had a huge fight last night. I don't think the kids heard anything, but we were yelling at each other for hours – it wasn't like our usual bickering, this time neither of us was willing to give in or let it go."

I nod for her to go on. "Alan is miserable at work, he is putting in more hours than before, but since he didn't get the promotion a few months ago, it doesn't seem like it is going to pay off like he thought it would."

"I'm sorry he's having a tough time," I say "but why is that your fault? It's not like you are sitting around doing nothing. You work too and you take care of the kids."

"That's what we were fighting about," Gretchen replies. "It started because of a schedule conflict for next week about who could take Ethan to a soccer game on Wednesday night, but then it was like all of our pent-up frustrations came out and we were dredging up things that had happened years ago and throwing them at each other like boulders."

"So how did you leave it?" I ask her.

Gretchen looks at me and starts laughing, "he slept on the couch!! Can you believe it?! It was like a movie or a really bad sit-com. I didn't think people did that in real life, but he grabbed his pillow and a blanket and he announced that he would be sleeping on the couch – almost like he was reading a script. I know I shouldn't be laughing, I should be crying, but it's so ridiculous."

I reach over and put my hand on top of her hand and give it a little squeeze. "It's going to be fine sweetie," I say. "People have fights all the time. It's just part of marriage, you're both going to be fine."

The waitress finally comes over to take our order. I think she has been hovering in the corner and waiting for a good time to interrupt. It's a quiet morning here at Lucy's and unfortunately she probably heard more of our conversation than either we or she desired.

Gretchen and I both order skim lattes and I ask for mine in a to-go cup, realizing that by the time she brings the coffee, I won't have too much time before I have to leave.

The conversation turns toward lighter topics for the rest of our time together. I know that we aren't done talking about Alan or the problems that seem to be brewing in their marriage, but Gretchen seems to feel better after getting a little bit off of her chest and we only have a short time left to discuss important topics - our children and any new gossip about people we know in town.

A few minutes later I am laughing so hard I am almost in tears as Gretchen finishes telling me a story about one of the moms who yelled at her for blocking her driveway at school pick-up. Gretchen's impression is priceless, "and there she is waiting for me by my car with her hands on her hips. She said she had measured and I was blocking her driveway by 3 inches. She threatened to call the police if I did it again. I apologized profusely and said I was leaving immediately so that she could move her car. And then she tells me that she isn't going anywhere that afternoon, it's just a matter of principle."

I don't know how it is already 11:15, but I need to get back into a faster gear or I will never get back to school on time. Gretchen and I say our good-byes and I promise that she can call or text me at any hour of the day or night if she needs to talk; but we both know that with our busy lives it could be weeks before we get the chance to talk again about anything of significance. I will see Gretchen at school pick-up this afternoon and then probably 5 more times this week at the grocery store or gymnastics class or at a school meeting (the beauty of

.g in such a small town), but we will just wave and
.out hello and then go back to our own worlds.

Chapter 2 – Laura

"What time do you want the children to be ready this evening?" Jody asks.

"I would like them dressed and ready by 6. Please make sure they've eaten before they get dressed so they don't spill anything. I put a bag of new clothes in each of their rooms, so they can pick what they want to wear – except for Cameron – I already picked his outfit and it's on the changing table in his room," I tell Jody in my best bossy, but still friendly, tone.

Jody has only been here as one of the nannies for 3 weeks now and I'm hoping she lasts longer than some of the previous nannies. I know my friends think it is ridiculous that I have 2 nannies (and a housekeeper), but I don't think they understand the full extent of my time commitments.

To be honest, sometimes I don't even understand where all of my time goes. And if you had asked me 10 years ago, where I saw myself at age 35, I could never have imagined that this would be my life. Some days I have to pinch myself to believe that this is all real; but with each passing year I get more and more used to this life and it is almost impossible to remember anything else.

It's not quite a rags-to-riches story; I wouldn't qualify for my own book deal, but I definitely grew up a world away from here.

I grew up in southern New Jersey in a middle-class family with 3 brothers, my dad was a plumber and my mom was a blackjack dealer at a casino in Atlantic City.

My parents doted on me from an early age, either because I was the only girl or because I was incredibly pretty. I know most people don't like to say that about themselves and self-deprecation seems to be much more widely accepted than self-confidence, but this happens to be true – I am exceptionally pretty. My mom started me in pageants as soon as I could walk and I kept going until I was a teenager – I won everything I entered except for Miss New Jersey; and once I lost that one, I was done for good.

I had a little bit too much fun in high school, but somehow still managed to get into Rutgers and graduate with a degree in communications. After a couple of years working in Manhattan and living in a 2 bedroom-apartment with 6 girls, I decided that I wanted more for myself and I made it my mission to find it.

It was mostly luck that Michael and I met in the bar that Thursday night. I had been at The Campbell Apartment every night that week after work, and I was beginning to think I needed a new plan, but then Michael sat down next to me and the rest is history. Well, it wasn't quite that easy, but that's how the story has evolved. In reality, Michael was dating someone else and he had been meaning to break up with her, but he said meeting me that night was all the incentive he needed.

I was used to men being attracted to me, and I liked having that type of control. It was a rare evening if I didn't get to pick exactly who I wanted to talk to in the bar and then decide if I wanted something more to come of it. Before I met Michael I had not dated anyone seriously for several months because I didn't want to waste my time on the wrong guy.

When I met Michael I knew he was 'the one'. I don't mean that in the corny way some of my friends mean it when they say it. I didn't get a strange feeling or go weak in the knees or anything like that. I knew he was the one for me because he was exactly who I pictured myself marrying. He fit the physical profile – he was handsome, tall and athletic – he even played lacrosse in college. He fit the work profile – he went to Harvard for undergrad and his MBA and had a great job at Goldman Sachs. And he fit the social profile – he was from a prominent family in Boston, the kind with really old money that had a house on Nantucket and sent holiday cards that were so perfect they looked airbrushed.

Although this wasn't how I had grown up, I had spent the past 2 years living in the city and learning about people like this and I knew that I wanted to be one of those people.
Luckily I was on my game that night and Michael was hooked by the end of the evening. He broke up with his girlfriend the next day and after that it was a dating whirlwind. We saw each other almost every night, even if it was at 2am when he finished up at work. There were weekend trips to Napa and Barbados and day trips to Boston and Atlantic City to meet the families.

10 months after we met, Michael took me to Nantucket for the weekend. It was April, so it was still chilly and way too cold to go in the water, but no one else wanted to be there, so we had his family's house to ourselves.

We went for a walk on the beach all bundled up and then Michael stopped walking and bent down on one knee and took a red Cartier box out of his pocket. Inside was a 3-carat Asscher cut ring in platinum – worth more than my father made in a year – and Michael asked me to marry him.

I know that I set out on a mission to find someone like Michael, but by the time he proposed, I really had fallen in love with him, and not just with the life I knew he could provide. It took both of our families some time to accept the engagement. Michael's family had an exceptionally hard time getting used to the idea, since they all thought I was just a fling and Michael would come to his senses and choose a more appropriate wife – ideally someone with the same pedigree who could trace her ancestors back to the Mayflower.

However, after ten years and four children, I think everyone has accepted that I am here to stay and I can barely remember what my life was like before Michael.

***

My attention shifts back toward the party we are hosting tonight and all of the things that still need to be done before the guests arrive.

I head into the kitchen to check with Claudia, my housekeeper. Although we are using caterers tonight, I still need a lot of help from Claudia to make sure everything gets done.

"Hi Claudia. How's everything going? Have you heard from the caterers yet? Did they confirm what time they will be here?"

"Don't worry Mrs. Bates, I just spoke to them and they will be here in an hour. The guests won't be here until 7, so we should have plenty of time. Will Mr. Bates be arriving with the guests?" Claudia asks.

Sometimes I still think it's funny how formal Claudia insists on being with me. Unlike Jody, Claudia has been with us forever – since we moved into the house the year we got married, but she insists on addressing us as Mr. and Mrs. Bates.

"Michael will be arriving with the guests. Most of them are coming directly from the office – they are taking black cars from the city, and then the spouses will arrive separately on their own. I think the final count now is 20 people." I give Claudia this information as I start to walk out of the kitchen and head up the back staircase to the master bedroom. I know Claudia has everything under control and I still have so much to do, that I don't have time to stand over her shoulder and watch her work.

I walk through the master bedroom and into my closet to change into workout clothes. I didn't have a workout scheduled for today, but luckily John was available when I texted him half an hour ago with an emergency. I think a quick training session will help relax me before the party and will also make sure my dress looks flawless. I put most of the pressure on myself, but the parties I throw for Michael's colleagues and clients are always so extravagant and unique so we are constantly raising the bar. I don't know what my guests are expecting tonight, but they are definitely expecting something bigger and better than before, and I do not want to disappoint.

***

I almost threw-up twice, but for me that's the sign of a really good workout; and at $200 an hour, I think John earned every penny today.

I decide to check in on Jody and the kids before I go get ready. The kids will only make a brief appearance at the party tonight, but I want to make sure Jody knows how I want them dressed and how long to keep them at the party before she needs to take them back upstairs. I also hope that Jody knows how to be invisible in plain site – this is a big night for Jody, hopefully she does well or she'll be looking for a new job soon, and I can't bear to think about going through that again.

I know that even my closest friends, Gretchen and Olivia, don't understand my life and I can't complain to them about my nanny problems or the other pressures I have been feeling recently. They think I live a fairy-tale life. I laugh along with them when they make jokes about me, "Princess Laura in her Castle – ha-ha." But even though this is everything I have ever thought I wanted, it doesn't mean it's easy.

I hear the laughter and screams coming from the twins' room, Avery and Emma are identical twin girls, age 6, and even though we have 8 bedrooms, they insist on sharing a room – my joke is that they actually share a brain. I change my mind about going to check on them and I turn around in the hall and head back to the master bedroom before the twins or either of my other children see me.

I turn on the shower and start to mentally prepare myself for the evening, like an athlete psyching herself up for the big game. And then it happens. Just like it always does. Although later on, I'll swear that I don't remember doing it. Especially because I swore that I wasn't going to do it again. I walk over to the linen closet and reach behind the stack of towels to the back corner and feel around with my hand until my fingers touch the bottle. I guess I thought that if I put it further back there last time, than I wouldn't find it the next time.

I already feel my breathing slowing down as I close my hand around the prescription bottle and pull it out of the cabinet, past all of the towels – careful not to scrape my knuckles like I did before. I open the bottle and shake two of the pills into my hand and then swallow them quickly without water – the faster they are gone and I can put the bottle back, the better. I'm already feeling better as I get in to the shower and tell myself that this will be the last time, after this party will be the very last time...

Chapter 3 – Danielle

"Did you have fun last night?" Jim asks, as I shuffle into the bathroom.

"Give me a minute to brush my teeth and open my eyes and then I'll answer you," I tell him.

Jim is in the shower and I assume is already back from at least a 4 mile run, probably a 6 or 7 mile run. He always has so much energy in the morning and then he likes to be in bed by 9pm. I tease him that he is on an old-man schedule; but there is some truth to it. Jim is 45 and I just turned 29. I can stay up until 2am and sleep until 11am every day of the week, but then we would never see each other and I think that would be frowned upon in my new role as suburban wife and step-mom.

"I did have a good time last night," I say loudly over the noise of the shower. "The party was a little overwhelming, especially since I didn't get to see you all night except to wave from across the room. And I think half of the people there were friends with Linda, so they are never going to like me. But there did seem to be some nice women."

"What about Laura? Michael's wife – did you get a chance to talk to her?" Jim asks as he turns off the shower and steps out without his towel.

I take a minute to admire my naked husband. If you didn't know he was 45, you would think he wasn't a day over 30. Unlike most men who work as many hours as he does, he is also crazy about fitness – triathlon crazy. It was one of the things that attracted me to him in the first place. We were working together on a deal and it turned out that we were both training for the same marathon. I couldn't believe that someone in his position (the managing partner of our law firm) also had time to run marathons, but he said that's what kept him sane. And I definitely get to enjoy the benefit of all that exercise and endurance in the bedroom.

"I did meet her. I actually talked to her for a long time. I thought she would be running all over the place since it was her party, but she was so nice. And she invited me to her wine club next week."

"Wine club?" laughs Jim.

"I think it is the women of Rye's answer to book club. She told me that they never even bothered with the pretense of a book."

"Do they talk about the wine? Is it like a wine tasting?" Jim asks.

"No. I think she just said it was wine drinking. Basically her friends get together and drink wine at someone's house once a month."

"And for this they need a club?" Jim laughs again.

"She made it sound quite exclusive. I think I am supposed to be honored just to be invited. Anyway, I told her I would love to go. Hopefully I'll meet some more women in town. Women who didn't know Linda – or better yet, maybe women who didn't like Linda." I laugh and hope that Jim knows I am kidding – well, mostly kidding.

Jim and his ex-wife are now on decent terms after the divorce; it wasn't pretty while they were separated, which is why her friends hate me. She made out quite well in the settlement and is living in a brand-new house in Greenwich and dating a slightly older divorced man. They travel every chance they can get, which is pretty frequently thanks to the custody agreement – and she claims she has never been happier.

"What are your plans for today?" Jim asks as he continues to get dressed. His routine is like clockwork, it is 7:24am and he is putting on his socks. By 7:26 he will be straightening his tie and he will be downstairs and in the car on his way to the train by 7:33.

"I'm going to go for a run soon, and then I am meeting with the decorators again to discuss plans for the changes to the living room and dining room. And then I need to be in Greenwich by 3 to pick up the kids from school." I try to say this last part with a smile.

"Jim, you remember that the kids are here this weekend, right? Do you think you'll be home early today?"

Jim bends down and gives me a long, slow kiss – he tastes like mouthwash and smells like shaving cream, I put my hands on both sides of his face and start to pull him towards me thinking that maybe today he is planning on going in late. He pulls away and smiles, "sorry love, I think we'll have to take a rain check for tonight. I was just letting you know how much I appreciate what you are doing for Megan and Kyle. I know it isn't easy for any of you. And I'll try to be home a little early tonight, but don't count on it."

"Okay. I'll find something fun for us to do." I say, again putting a big smile on my face and hoping it doesn't look like I'm trying too hard.

"I love you!" Jim calls as he walks out of the room.

"I love you too!" I yell back. "Oh, and I'm ovulating today, don't forget!" I yell down the hall.

"Great." Jim yells back. I think that he said it with enthusiasm, or at least that's what I tell myself.

Chapter 4 – Gretchen

Even though I've probably been to Laura's house a hundred times over the last 8 years, I'm still amazed and humbled when I drive up her driveway.

I will never forget the first time I came here. I checked the address on the gate a dozen times against the address I had scrawled on the tiny scrap of paper I had found in my diaper-bag at the new moms playgroup the previous week. After idling at the gate for at least 10 minutes I got up the nerve to ring the buzzer, certain that I had the wrong house, since I had lived in Rye for 3 years and never even knew this private lane existed.

When I rang the buzzer, a very friendly voice with a Jamaican accent answered and said, "Miss Laura is feeding the baby, please come through the gate and down the driveway to the main house and she will be with you in a moment." As I drove up the driveway that day I knew that Laura was going to be different than any of the friends I had made so far.

***

Tonight is our monthly wine club and it is Laura's turn to host. I don't remember exactly how we started the club; but it started shortly after we were all done breast-feeding and our play-groups were getting less frequent and someone had the idea to invite the few moms we liked to get together one night without babies and bring wine, and here we are almost 8 years later. The group has grown and changed over the years, but it's always nice to see everyone once a month and catch up over a few too many glasses of wine.

I am one of the last to arrive; the group is in full swing when I walk in to Laura's living room. I didn't used to be late for everything, I think once upon a time I used to be early for most things – it was probably somewhere between my second and third child that I stopped being on time.

"Gretchen, it's so great to see you!" Laura calls as I walk in. "Grab something to drink and come sit down!" Laura is so much more relaxed than when I host. I would probably be a lot more relaxed if I had a cook and housekeeper and a whole staff to help me get ready and all I had to do was put on my fabulous clothes.

I pour myself a glass of Sauvignon Blanc and take a seat on the couch between Laura and Olivia. I take a big sip from my glass and feel myself start to relax, my shoulders loosen and I sink into Laura's overstuffed Belgian linen sofa.

I try to catch up with the conversation so I can chime in. It sounds like Laura had a big party the other night and Olivia is telling a funny story about something Elizabeth did the other day. "...and then she came downstairs and tells me she's really hot, but somehow I didn't notice that she had on 4 t-shirts and 3 pairs of pants!" Olivia laughs as she takes a sip of wine and everyone laughs along with her.

"I miss that age," I say. "It goes so quickly Olivia. I know everyone says that, but it really is true. Just yesterday Alice was doing cute 3 year old things and now she is a surly 13 year old and I can't seem to do anything right."

"I don't want to know about the future." Olivia says. "I can't imagine them being any bigger, Julie already seems so big and she's just in kindergarten."

"Do you all have children?" a voice asks from the other couch. I look over and see a woman I've never seen before, not just at wine club, but anywhere before.

"Hi, I'm Gretchen, have we met?"

"Oh, so sorry, " says Laura. "Gretchen, this is Danielle. Her husband Jim knows Michael from work. I met her last week and invited her to come tonight. She just moved here and doesn't know many people so I told her she had to come tonight and meet the best ladies in Rye!"

I look over at Danielle and smile. I hadn't noticed her when I came in because I was in a rush and I just wanted to sit down. She looks very young. I can't tell how young, but she can't be older than 32, and she could easily be 25! Just looking at her makes me feel old. She has brown hair cut into a cute pixie cut, that I could never imagine wearing, but it looks great on her. She's wearing a baggy sweater over leggings with little ballet flats, but even the baggy sweater can't hide her figure. The old grumpy lady in me wants to automatically dislike this new, cute young girl, but there is something about the open and eager look on her face that makes me want to give her a hug instead.

"Yes, we all have children." I answer. "Two, three or even four!" I point at Laura as I say "four".

"Do you have kids?" I ask Danielle.

"Kind of," she says. "Well, I have two step-children. I just got married 6 months ago and my husband had children before. They are 14 and 12 years old, so that's a bit of trial by fire. But I really want to have a baby, so hopefully soon I'll know what you guys are talking about." She looks so excited when she talks about having a baby it is clear she knows nothing about it.

Chapter 5 – Olivia

"Ugh," I mutter under my breath.

"What's wrong?" Charlie asks.

"These pants used to have a lot more room and now they barely close," I complain, standing in the middle of our shared walk-in closet, looking around hoping something else will jump off the shelves for me to wear.

Charlie calls out from the bedroom, "Liv, you look great. You're tiny."

"Not as tiny as I used to be. That's what happens when I wear yoga pants every day, when I finally put on pants with a button and a zipper I realize I've gained a few pounds."

"Olivia, I think you look great. Now pick something to wear or we're going to be late." There is a hint of annoyance in his voice as he says this; he doesn't want to be late and I have surpassed his tolerance for talking about my body image issues.

"Okay, okay. I'll be ready in ten minutes," I say, still standing in the middle of the closet, but now only in a bra and underwear, just staring at my clothes.

"I'll go downstairs and check on the sitter, see you in a minute" Charlie says as he walks out of the room. Of course he's ready and it only took him ten minutes from start to finish. He is wearing his Saturday night uniform of jeans, button down and navy blue blazer.

It isn't that Charlie doesn't care about his looks; it's just that he is pretty low maintenance when it comes to his clothes and his appearance. He has been wearing his hair the exact same way since I met him, and other than a couple strands of gray, it's quite impressive that he has the same amount of hair as when we met. He has thick dark brown hair that he wears short and parted on the side. He is always clean-shaven, he will even shave twice in one day if we are going out at night. Sometimes I wonder what it would be like if he had that sexy stubble like all of the celebrities seem to have right now; although I bet it looks better than it feels.

Charlie is also over a foot taller than I am – he is six foot three and I am five foot two. Our height difference is a key topic of conversation when we first meet people; I'm not sure why, but I've come to understand that people are fascinated by how short I am and how tall he is, it seems people feel that short people should marry short people and tall people should marry tall people, so we are violating an unwritten height law with our relationship.

"Liv, are you almost ready?" Charlie calls up from downstairs. "We should leave in five minutes if we want to be there on time."

"Yup, I'm almost ready," I yell down. Which is a big fat lie, since I am standing in the exact same place I was when he left the room. This cannot be that hard. We are just having dinner with Gretchen and Alan, not going to the Oscars, I just need to pick something.

I settle on a pair of black Hudson skinny jeans and a thin v-neck cashmere sweater in a pale turquoise. I may not be the stunning beauty that Laura is, but on days when I'm feeling good enough about myself to admit it, I am rather attractive. And my best feature is my eyes. My eyes are much prettier than Laura's. I have shockingly bright sea-blue-green eyes, almost turquoise; it's hard to remember a day that someone didn't complement me on my eyes. So the turquoise sweater is always a good choice. I grab a pair of tall black Gucci boots that I haven't worn in a while. I glance over at the custom shelves made to hold all of my beautiful high heeled shoes and boots and realize that I haven't worn most of them in a long time; there may actually be a thin layer of dust on them. I think it started to compensate for my height, or maybe it was just a love of beautiful shoes, but I used to be quite the shoe collector- the higher and more expensive, the better. Now I alternate between my sneakers and my hideous, but practical Uggs.

I throw on some chunky David Yurman bracelets and earrings to complete my outfit and try to make it downstairs before Charlie gets even more annoyed.

***

"Well, you look nice," Charlie says as I come down the stairs.

"Thank you." I beam and walk over to give him a kiss. I catch the edge of his cheek with my lips since he is already walking toward the closet to get our coats.

"I'm just going to say goodnight to the girls, I'll be right there. Okay?" I know I am pushing it, but he can't be annoyed with me for wanting to say goodnight to our children, can he?

I hear giggling in the playroom and peek inside. I don't think Julie or Elizabeth would have minded at all if I left without saying good-bye, or even if I left for a week! Taylor is their favorite babysitter and now that she is in college she can't come that often, but she happens to be free tonight. I hope my girls grow up to be like Taylor. She is smart and polite, captain of the field hockey team in high school and plays on the team at Columbia. She lives on campus, but since she is close to home, she comes home a lot on the weekends and sometimes she even comes back to sit for us. Her parents must be proud.

"Julie, Elizabeth – Daddy and I are leaving," I call to the girls. "Can mommy have a hug and a kiss?"

"We're busy mom," Julie says. "I love you. Have a good date with daddy." When did my five-year old turn fifteen? "Okay Julie, I love you," I say and I blow her a kiss.

Luckily Elizabeth isn't too smitten with Taylor to ignore me yet. Elizabeth runs over to me and attacks my legs with a hug. "I love you mommy. I'm going to miss you so much. Will you be back in 5 minutes? 10 minutes? When? Did you tell Taylor about the dark in my room?"

I bend down to give her a proper hug, and almost fall over in my boots trying to balance and hug her at the same time. "Yes sweetie, I told Taylor about the dark in your room and she knows to leave the light on a little bit. We'll be back in a couple of hours, but that really isn't too long, it's about how long it takes to watch a movie." I give her a kiss on the cheek and hug her warm little body in her fuzzy pajamas. I'm almost tempted to go upstairs on put on my pajamas and get ready for cuddles and stories, but not tempted enough. I really am excited for a night out with good food and drinks and adult conversation.

Elizabeth releases her death grip on my legs and Taylor comes over to pick her up and hold her so that I can make my escape.
When I get back to the front hall I can't find Charlie.

"Charlie? Where are you? Charlie?" I call out into the empty hall.

And then I hear the sound of the car's engine running outside. Wow, he really is in a hurry. I wonder if this is all about tonight or if something else is wrong. I hope he's in a better mood at dinner. It's going to be hard enough if Gretchen and Alan aren't doing well, but it will be miserable if we are all fighting.

I make my way outside and see the shiny black Range Rover idling in the driveway waiting for me. I open the door, all smiles, trying to put a fresh start on the evening. "Thanks for warming up the car, sorry I took so long."

Charlie looks over, a little bit surprised. I think he was expecting me to be defensive, not to start off with an apology. "Oh, um, you're welcome. It's not a big deal, I just wanted to get there before them. I don't want Alan to order drinks for me, do you remember what he did last time? This time I'm getting him back."

I laugh as I remember the last time we went out with Gretchen and Alan and the drunken, raucous evening we had. Alan and Charlie were like fraternity boys hazing each other and Gretchen and I just watched them make fools of themselves, but we all had a great time. Maybe tonight would be good for Gretchen and Alan, maybe it was just what they needed – and maybe Charlie and I could use it too.

Chapter 6 – Gretchen

When I walk into the restaurant, I can already see Charlie and Olivia at the table. We're only 15 minutes late, which is pretty good for me these days, but still late. Hopefully they haven't been waiting too long.

Alan is still parking the car, so I give my coat to the coat-check girl and hurry over to the table. I want to whisper something to Olivia before he comes inside.

"Hi Gretchen, you look great," Charlie says as he stands up to give me a hug and a kiss. Charlie is such a nice guy. I think he would say that to anyone, but still it makes me feel good.

"Hi sweetie," Olivia says, "have a seat."

I don't think they have been here that long, but they are already almost done with their first drinks and they definitely seem relaxed – I wish I were that relaxed.

"Liv, can I talk to you for just a second?" I say, as I grab her arm and draw her ear toward me like we were in third grade telling secrets on the playground.

I lower my voice and keep my eyes on the door as I whisper quickly, "everything is okay right now with Alan. It's not perfect, but we're fine. Please, please don't mention anything about what I told you before or act like anything is weird, okay?"

"Of course I won't!" Liv whispers back. "I would never say anything. I didn't even say anything to Charlie. I'm glad everything is fine. I'll just pretend like you never told me anything." She says as she squeezes my hand.

I feel a cold hand on my shoulder and look up to see Alan standing behind me. "What are you ladies whispering about? Are you talking about me?" Alan laughs.

"I'm pretty sure they were talking about me," Charlie says as he stands up to shake Alan's hand. "Good to see you buddy. How've you been? It's been too long!"

"I took the liberty of ordering you a drink," Charlie says with a big smile on his face.

Alan pretends to scowl, but it quickly turns into a laugh. "Bottoms up," Alan says as he picks up his drink and takes a large sip. He puts down his glass and coughs, but he is still laughing. "Waiter, I need to order two more drinks," Alan yells out to a man walking by.

It seems that the husbands are settling in for a raucous evening, so Olivia and I can relax and have a good time.

I loved Olivia the moment I met her. It might seem odd to say that about another woman; especially one that you meet at a new parents pre-school night. But there was something magnetic about this tiny woman, with a nine-month pregnant basketball belly, and brilliant turquoise eyes. And then she leaned over and said to me, "do you think they'll find out that I lied on our application? I said my daughter already knew her ABC's and that she is learning French at home. But none of that is true." I laughed so hard all of the other parents and the teacher turned around to stare at us.

I loved Charlie when I met him as well, shortly after Elizabeth was born, but I wasn't sure that Olivia and Alan would get along, and I really wasn't sure that Alan and Charlie would hit it off.

Charlie is your All-American guy's guy, but the polished prep school version. Whereas, Alan is just as smart, if not smarter than Charlie, but rough around the edges. Alan is a writer and editor for the New York Times. He is an intellectual and can go head-to-head with almost anyone on topics ranging from current events to medieval architecture, but the way he goes about it is always a little bit louder and rowdier than any of our other friends. Alan also reminds me of a lumberjack. I would never admit that to anyone, but that's what he looks like. He wears his hair long and a bit shaggy (never time for a haircut), and a few years ago he grew a beard for a contest at work and then decided he liked it, so the beard stayed. He works long hours, and in his free time he would rather read or spend time with the kids, so he hasn't properly exercised in years, which leaves him with the body of a lumberjack as well – although I have always liked that he is cuddly like a teddy bear, I just don't want him to get any cuddlier.

I kept Alan and Charlie away from each other for an unnatural length of time and finally I couldn't come up with any more excuses. I told Olivia that I was worried if they finally met, they would hate each other and it would change our friendship. She assured me I was being ridiculous and so we finally went out to dinner on a double date similar to the one we are on right now and to my absolute shock, Alan and Charlie loved each other. In fact, by the end of that first dinner I was worried that their friendship was stronger than Olivia's and mine!

"So, what's new Liv?" I ask as we settle in with our glasses of wine and open up the menus. I stare intently at the menu even though I will get the seared Ahi Tuna, the same way I do every time we come to this restaurant.

Olivia pretends to study the menu as well. "Not much to report. I've decided that my new least favorite mom task is making lunches. Julie hates everything I pack for her and two-thirds of it comes home in her lunchbox. I don't know how she's surviving."

I laugh as I respond, "you are a couple months into making lunches for your first child and you already hate it? Ha! You better pace yourself. It's just going to get worse when you have two lunches to make and when their attitudes get worse. Julie is still so cute and nice. Just wait until she's 13 like Alice."

"You won't believe what Alice said to me the other day," I continue, "I was making dinner and she walks into the kitchen and casually tells me that she knows what a blow job is and that it isn't really sex and she thinks it's disgusting, but she knows a girl in her class who did it, and then she grabbed an apple and walked out of the room! I almost fell over from shock. I haven't told Alan yet, I think he would have a heart attack, or send her to a convent, I mean, she's only in 8th grade!"

Olivia's jaw drops as she turns towards me. "Holy shit! And this is a good neighborhood. Can you imagine what happens in the bad neighborhoods? I don't think I'm ready for Julie to leave kindergarten, maybe I'll even send her back to pre-school!"

Olivia takes a large sip from her glass and resumes, "on a totally unrelated topic. Sorry – I need to change the conversation after that or I won't be able to sleep tonight."

"Don't worry," I say, "I don't think I'm going to be able to sleep for the next 10 years, but you shouldn't have to worry about it yet. So what's up?"

"I got an email from my old boss, Chris, the other day. My old firm just opened a new office and they are having a party and he invited me."

"That sounds fun. What's the problem?" I ask Olivia.

"There's no problem, I just haven't seen most of these people in a long time and it feels weird to go, and there are probably a lot of new people I won't even know." Olivia says.

"I think you should go. You had a lot of friends at work and they wouldn't even be able to open a new office if it wasn't for all of the work you did when you were there. It will be good for you. It's also good to keep your options open. I know you want to be home, but if you ever change your mind, it's good to make sure they don't forget you!" I say good-naturedly.

"Oh they could never forget me!" Olivia says loudly as she tosses her hair back and forth over her shoulders. I think the wine is starting to kick in. "Okay, you're right. I'll go. It will be fun. It will be good for me to get out and say hello to my old life for a night, right?"

"Definitely!" I tell her, as we return our attention to our husbands and enjoy the rest of our night out.

Chapter 7 – Danielle

The house is finally quiet after a long weekend with Jim and his kids.

My cell phone rings and interrupts the silence.

"Hi Mom!" I say, trying to imagine what it was like before caller ID when you didn't always know who was calling.

"Hi Sweetie! I was just calling to say hi and see how the weekend went with the kids. Was it as bad as you thought it would be?" my mom asks.

"Jim promises that it will get better as they adjust to me and to our new situation; I can't imagine it getting much worse! Actually Kyle wasn't too bad. I don't think I can ask for much more from a 12-year old boy. He spent most of his time in front of the Xbox, and the rest of his time watching whatever sporting event he could find on TV. Occasionally he got hungry and wandered into the kitchen and rummaged through the fridge and pantry looking for something to eat, but he did seem pleased with the food I had bought and he even complemented me on the "awesome" cookies I made. Jim assured me that this was normal 12-year old boy behavior and I should not be expecting a deep philosophical conversation with Kyle anytime soon."

"That doesn't sound too awful. And Megan?" my mom probes.

"Megan is another story altogether. I remember what it was like to be a 14-year old girl and you know I have been around my fair share of teenage girls, coaching swim-team or as a camp counselor, but Megan may be the bitchiest teenager I've ever met!" I fume.

My mom tries to suppress a laugh, "Dani, I don't think you are allowed to say that about your step-daughter. And you might be looking back with rose colored glasses – you weren't always a joy to be around in high school."

"There is no way I was as awful as she is. I know I wasn't perfect, but she's horrible! I know that Megan is going through a lot with Linda and Jim's divorce and now she has to deal with me, on top of the ongoing drama that comes with being a freshman in high school. But that does not give her the right to be so mean." I say, totally worked up by this point.

"Did you talk to Jim about it?" my mom asks.

"I can't say anything to Jim about it, and he probably wouldn't believe me anyway, because although Megan is nasty, she is quite clever and is able to be completely wicked to me one minute and the second her father shows up she is a completely different person. She has the Jekyll and Hyde act perfected. Anyhow, I don't have to see her again for two weeks and I am going to come up with a plan to make her like me, or I might kill her, I haven't decided yet." I joke.

"I would suggest the former if I get a vote. I don't think you'll fare well in prison," my mom says.

"In the meantime, I have more important things to worry about. I can start taking pregnancy tests tomorrow to see if this month is going to be the month! My period isn't due for another few days, but I bought the tests that said they could tell you 5 days early, and I have a good feeling about this month," I say excitedly.

"Honey, don't get your hopes up already. Just wait and see what happens. And I can't believe that you can find out that early now. Soon you'll be able to find out the minute you have sex," exclaims my mom.

"Mom!! Gross!" I shout, pretending to be disgusted.

"What? You brought it up," she laughs.

My mom and I have always had a very close relationship. I'm from a small, close-knit family originally from Dallas. My dad was in the army, so I was your typical 'Army Brat'. "10 schools in 12 years" is my standard line. That's probably the reason I make friends so easily now, and why I'm so close with my mom. When my dad retired, my parents moved back to Dallas where both my mom and dad are originally from, so although I don't get to see them as often as I would like, I talk to my mom on a daily basis – especially now that I'm home with a lot of time on my hands.

"Is Jim as excited as you are?" she asks.

I pick up a pen and paper and start doodling at the kitchen counter while I answer, "no, I know he isn't as excited as I am. But he knew what he was getting into when he met me. And he has said that it could be fun to do it over again, especially because he thinks he would have more time to be around than he did when Megan and Kyle were babies. I know he'll be really into it as soon as I'm actually pregnant."

He's certainly into the *trying* to get pregnant part of it right now, I think to myself and smile, thinking about the amazing sex we've been having the past several months. Hopefully that part won't stop once I get pregnant – a friend of mine from college told me it is even better when you're pregnant, but I can't imagine the sex being any better than it is right now. I might die if I have an orgasm any more intense than the one I had last night. Oh god, I can't believe I am thinking about sex while talking to my mom, I don't even know what she is saying right now.

"What was that mom, I don't think I heard the last thing you said?" I ask, hoping she doesn't notice when I stopped listening.

"I just asked if Kyle and Megan know that you are planning to have a baby? If they don't like you now, they really aren't going to like you once you tell them about their new half brother or sister," my mom says.

"Thanks for the support mom. No we haven't told them. We aren't going to tell them until I am 13 weeks pregnant. That's when all the books say it is safe to tell people, and that's when we will tell them. And maybe they'll be really excited about it – people love babies." I say hopefully.

"Okay sweetie. Well, let's hope so. I'm not going to have to wait until 13-weeks, am I?" my mom asks.

"Of course not. I'll call you tomorrow after I pee on the stick. I think I should tell Jim first, but you'll probably be more excited, so maybe I'll call you first," I say with a laugh.

"Alright, then I'll talk to you tomorrow. Remember not to get your hopes up. You have to be patient, these things..."

I cut her off, ready to be done with the conversation, "I know mom, I know. I love you, talk to you tomorrow," I say.

"Love you too Dani," she says as she hangs up.

I look down at the drawing I made and notice I've covered the page in babies. I'm not a very good artist, so not everyone would know that these are babies, but they definitely are babies of all shapes and sizes, I think this is a good sign. I feel better after talking to my mom. I'm still not sure what to do about Megan, but I'm not going to think about it right now.

Hmmm, what to do with the rest of my day - Laura said I could give her a call if I needed any advice about town or about the re-decorating. It seems that I need to have kids to make any friends here since I don't have a job now. Well, Laura's my best bet, maybe she wants to critique what the decorator told me, or she can find another room in this already overwhelming 6,000 square foot home to decorate. I hate to admit that Linda had really nice taste, so there isn't that much I want to do, but Jim said he was sure I would want to "put my own signature style on it" – whatever that means.

Chapter 8 – Laura

I wasn't surprised to get Danielle's call this morning, I just had to figure out how to find time to squeeze her in. I imagine she must be very lonely in her new life here in Rye with no kids, no friends and those horrible step-kids. To be honest, I don't actually know the kids that well, but if Megan is anything like her mother, then I feel terrible that Danielle will have to put up with her.

I think most people liked Linda, but I never did. I know Jim cheated on her, which is wrong, but I really can't blame him for it. If I had to come home to Linda every night, I would probably go looking for something else too. And then he goes to work every day and Danielle is just waiting for him; a cute, intelligent, perky 29-year old who thinks the sun shines out of his ass. I don't see how he could resist.

Although if Michael ever did anything like that, I would kill him! But seriously, how could Michael do that when he has me to come home to? I look around and it shocks me how some women will let themselves go after they get married, and then really let themselves go after they have kids – what do they expect their husbands to do?

I know Michael married me because he loved me, but he wasn't just marrying me for my beautiful inner self – he was marrying the whole package, and I owe it to him to keep the whole package looking just as good as it did when we first met, or he's going to go looking somewhere else.

And I know all of those crunchy granola moms at school would be appalled if I ever told them how I really felt, so

I nod along when they tell me that their husbands don't care what they look like anymore and that little Timmy or Billy is the only thing they have time for anymore. I know that it's all bullshit, and they're going to find that out too when they wake up one day and notice their husband is screwing somebody else – just like Linda did.

I'm sure I sound like a bitch, but I worked very hard to have the life I have today and it is pretty much perfect. I look at it the same way someone else would look at a job. You have to work hard at your job or you'll get fired, right? I am not going to get fired from this job and let someone else replace me. So what do I have to do to keep my job? I just need to be the perfect wife, the perfect hostess, have the perfect children, and the perfect home. It's not easy, but it's worth it.

***

I hoped Danielle would be fine meeting up later in the week, but she sounded really lonely, so I suggested she come over for lunch and she could meet one of the other women from the pre-school. I am meeting with Sharon to discuss a school fundraiser and it might be useful for Danielle to get involved if she wants to meet people, and it's never too early to get involved in the school if she's planning on having kids soon.

***

"Danielle, is that you?" I call out from the dining room.

"Yes, it's me. Hi Laura," Danielle answers.

"Come through to the dining room. It's through the second living room," I say as I see her walk hesitantly into the room, "so sorry Claudia had to rush right after she let you in. We're a mess here today. Robin has the morning off today and then Jody woke up sick this morning, so Claudia is watching the children *and* had to make lunch. Please, have a seat, make yourself comfortable," I say as I point to the place set for her.

Danielle looks overwhelmed at the information I have just given her and at her surroundings, "Thanks so much for including me in lunch Laura. I think I might be a little under-dressed, I may have misunderstood..." Danielle falters mid-sentence. Danielle is wearing faded jeans and a light yellow merino wool sweater with silver ballet slippers; she looks fine, but she is definitely underdressed compared to Sharon and me. Sharon is wearing a grey St. John's knit dress and I have on a Marc Jacobs rust colored silk blouse with black Ralph Lauren pants and black Manolo Blahnik heels.

"Nonsense, you're perfect. Sharon and I just took the opportunity to have a ladies lunch, you know, one that didn't involve mac and cheese and chicken nuggets," I laugh. But even as we all laugh, everyone knows that I have never had a lunch that's involved mac and cheese or chicken nuggets.

"Danielle, I'd like you to meet Sharon. She runs fundraising for the school that our children attend, and where Cameron will go next year. Sharon has two children – her daughter Madison attends the school now." I smile at Sharon while I say this last part.

I continue, "Sharon, this is Danielle. She just moved to Rye about 6 months ago. She's married to Jim Walters. They live in that beautiful Tudor over on Oak Street. Danielle's looking to get involved in the town, and although she doesn't have children yet, I thought it would be great if she could get an early start at Rye Day Pre-School. This will get her name moved up on the waiting list," I joke.

Sharon looks at Danielle and gives her a big smile, not revealing that she knows exactly who she is and who she is married to and that she has been talking about Danielle behind her back for months. "Danielle, it's so nice to meet you. We would love to have your help. And Laura mentioned that you used to be a lawyer? You must be a smart cookie! We could definitely use someone like you, although I hope it isn't boring after some of the work you've done in the past," Sharon says with smirk.

"I think our lunch is almost ready!" I quickly chime in. Hoping to diffuse any potential tension and lighten up the mood. Sharon is a good connection to have at the school and in Rye, but I wouldn't want to cross her, even with my standing on the social ladder.

Luckily, Claudia comes in at that moment with our lunch, so the conversation shifts to the meal in front of us.

"This looks great Laura, what is it?" Danielle asks politely

"It's a kale salad with quinoa, avocado, beets and a lemon-dijon vinaigrette. There's some feta cheese on the side if you'd like, but I'm off dairy this week. Would you ladies like sparkling or still water?" I ask.

"Still water is fine for me," Danielle says.

"I'd love sparkling water," Sharon says. "It's really a shame that they stopped offering sparking water at school as a regular option. Madison came home last week and told me that she asked her teacher for sparkling water at snack and was told "no". Can you believe it? I think maybe we could allocate some of the fundraiser money to that, what do you think?" Sharon says as she puts a bite of salad in her mouth.

I take a minute before answering and have to control my eyes so I don't roll them when I answer – luckily the Botox and collagen make eye rolling a little more difficult. "Sharon, I really understand where you are coming from. But I'm not sure we are going to get enough parents that feel the same way. Maybe you could just send a bottle of Perrier with Madison's snack and we could look at the bigger picture?" I say hopefully.

I may have come a long way from my days in South Jersey, but there are still some people and some things about my life that I find utterly ridiculous – Sharon is one of those things.

The rest of lunch continues smoothly and we agree to pursue the always-successful winter carnival for our next fundraiser. As planned, Danielle can help us negotiate contracts with the vendors and Sharon will figure out what everyone else is doing and boss them around. As per usual, I will escape unscathed and host a few more of these planning lunches.

With Jody sick today, I need to take Avery and Emma to swim practice and gymnastics this afternoon. Not that it's that unusual for me to take them to their activities, but usually I bring either Robin or Jody with me. I look at the clock and realize that I have to leave in 15 minutes. I'm a lot more worn out from that lunch and from my 2-

hour Pilates session this morning than I thought I would be. I'm not sure how I am going to get everything done now that I have to spend all afternoon driving the girls around. Unless...and then I go find my purse to make sure they are still in there. I unzip the inner side pocket and then feel around to find the smooth bottle. I open it and pop out two yellow pills and quickly take them before I can have second thoughts. These are the ones that give me a little extra energy. I already feel better. I'm sure I won't need them again, but I already feel like I can make it through the afternoon.

Chapter 9 – Olivia

"You're a slowpoke mom. Why do you have to stop here?" says the voice in the backseat.

"It's a red light, Lizzie. I have to stop at the red lights." I explain calmly, while silently cursing the light and praying it turns to green so we are not late for ballet again this week.

"Mommy's a slowpoke, mommy's a slowpoke," chants Elizabeth.

"No she's not. You're stupid," says Julie casually.

"What did you say?" I snap at her, now annoyed that the light has changed and I have to keep my eyes on the road.

"I said she was stupid," Julie repeats.

"Well, Julie, that is not a word we use in this house and you know that." I say, trying to be calm again.

"I didn't know that. Sophie says it all the time." Julie says.

"Well, Sophie shouldn't say it. But I am not Sophie's mother and I can only make the rules for you and Elizabeth, and I say that we don't use that word." Oh my god. I just heard my mother as I said that. As those last words came out of my mouth I sounded exactly like my mother. What's next, am I going to tell the girls that they shouldn't make ugly faces or they'll "freeze that way"? I have to remember to talk to Gretchen about this and see if it's normal.

As I'm sitting in the parents' viewing room watching the girls' ballet practice, all I can think about is going back to see everyone at work tomorrow night. I've only been gone two and a half years, but it feels like a lifetime. Most of the team is still there, but I know from occasional emails and texts with Chris and Jennifer that there have been a lot of new hires as the firm has expanded. Jennifer swears that it won't be weird for me to be there tomorrow night for the party, but I have had to stop myself at least a dozen times from texting her and telling her that the kids are sick, or that I couldn't get a sitter and just staying home on the couch in my all-too-comfortable yoga pants. Charlie thinks it's a great idea that I'm going and he even promised he would be home in time to put the girls to bed and relieve the sitter, so she isn't there too late. I am going to take advantage of my time in the city and spend most of the afternoon there before the party. I'm going to Drybar to get a blowout before the party and will take some time walking along Madison and doing some shopping without my two helpers tagging along.

I was complaining to Laura that I rarely get into the city anymore even though it is less than 40 minutes on the train (although I can't imagine Laura on a train). And Laura laughed and said that she only goes into the city when she is going for dinner or for shopping, but she doesn't go very often, and most of the women in Rye only go a couple of times a year! The whole reason we moved to Rye was because of how close it was to the greatest city in the world and I might as well be living in Des Moines for all of the advantage I am taking of what Manhattan has to offer.

I peer back into the ballet studio and look at my two beautiful girls. They look angelic in their tiny pink leotards, pink tights, ballet slippers and their hair up in buns. Generally I don't think the girls look that much alike, but dressed like this, Elizabeth does look like a miniature version of Julie. The teacher has them practicing 3rd and 4th positions and going back and forth between the two. Julie has a look of pure determination on her face and is watching herself in the mirror to make sure she is doing it correctly. Elizabeth is standing next to Julie and is only watching what her big sister is doing as she tries to move her own feet and keeps tripping as she does it. The look of awe on Elizabeth's face and the innocence and goodness radiating off of both my children, makes me forget about everything else for a minute. I try to soak it all in, so later on when they are driving me crazy I can come back to this moment and remember why I chose to leave a high-paying, distinguished career and stay home with my children.

***

I stop in the ladies lounge at Saks to touch up my makeup and check my hair. I should have scheduled the blowout immediately before the party, but I didn't plan it that well.

I can't believe I am this nervous about seeing people I used to work with. These are the same people who used to see me at 2am after I had worked an 18-hour day, sweat off all my make-up and had my hair in a ponytail on top of my head. They also saw me when I came back to work 10 weeks after giving birth to Julie, had only lost half of the baby weight and was still wearing maternity clothes and nursing bras under every outfit.

But it's different now. Now they don't see me as their boss or their colleague; I'm not the superwoman who brings in big clients and puts together amazing presentations in half the time in takes everyone else. Now I'm a mom who lives in some town north of the city that half of the people in the office have never heard of. I remember telling a couple of the new associates where I lived and one of the girls said, "oh, Westchester, that's upstate New York, right?"

So tonight I need to show everyone that I am exactly the same person I used to be, only maybe even better. I look in the mirror and give myself a critical assessment. I know that no one in the office is going to look at me the way I am looking at myself, but this 'homecoming' is inexplicably important to me. I'm glad I decided to have my hair done, my shoulder length dirty blonde hair spends most of its time in a bun these days, but when it's styled it frames my heart-shaped face and the color looks more golden honey than dirty blonde. I took more time with my make-up than I usually do, and as usual, the only feature I accentuate are my eyes - I only ever wear a sheer gloss on my lips.

It took me forever to pick my outfit (not a big surprise), but I'm glad I wore the Hugo Boss tangerine-colored knit dress. It's tight enough to show off my small frame, but still professional enough that it won't look out of place at a work event. I dusted off another pair of boots from a few years ago, but they look perfect with the outfit – camel colored Ferragamo knee-high boots with a three and a half inch heel (if I don't wear at least a three-inch heel, I don't have a prayer of looking above anyone's chin.) I stand back to take in the whole look and I am pleased with what I see. I don't think I look 39. And I don't think it looks like I've had two children, nor do I look like I spend most of my time running around in loungewear after two children. Okay, I'm ready, "let's do this," I silently say to my reflection as I turn and walk out the door to revisit my old life.

.

***

"Olivia!!" Jennifer screams, as I walk in the door. She runs over and gives me a huge hug. "You look amazing! How do you look this good when you just had a baby?" she says, twirling me around.

"Thanks Jen, but I didn't *just* have a baby. Remember it's been over 2 years," I laugh.

"Oh same thing," she says. "2 is still a baby, right?" She says. Spoken like someone who has no children. "You have to come see the new space, you're going to die, it's amazing what we've done, you're going to love it!" she says, as she drags my arm and pulls me further into the office.

She isn't wrong. The space is incredible. It looks so different from the old office where we used to work. It is modern and open and full of light.

"What's wrong?" Jennifer asks. "Are you okay?"

"It looks like everything we used to talk about, but here it is right in front of me in wood and metal and brick with real desks and offices, and none of them have my name on them." I answer sadly.

"Oh Liv, I'm sorry. I thought you were going to come in here and gloat about how great it was at home and laugh at us for having no lives." Jennifer says with a sad smile.

"No, no I'm fine. Sorry to be such a downer. Everything is great at home. I love it. I just didn't realize how hard it would be to come back." I lie, because I knew exactly how hard it was going to be, it's all I've thought about.

"Okay, let's get a drink, and I'll introduce you to some of the new people and there must be a ton of people you want to see!" she says enthusiastically, clearly trying to turn the mood around.

"Sounds great! I want to see how everyone has messed everything up without me here," I say and give her a big smile.

The next three hours are a blur. I consume too many drinks and not enough appetizers, but it's great to see everyone and I quickly get over my strop from the beginning of the night and just enjoy being here and catching up with people I haven't seen in a long time.

I grab Jen's arm and pull her aside, "Jen, I'm going to sneak out, I'm so glad I could come. Good luck with the meeting at Pepsi on Friday."

"Are you sure you have to go? It's only 11:30," she says looking at her watch.

"11:30! I can't remember the last time I was out until 11:30 on a Wednesday! Sad, I know," I say as I lean in to give her a hug, "great to see you, please keep in touch!"

As I'm standing waiting for the elevator and checking the emails on my phone, I feel someone come up right behind me. Before I have a chance to turn around, a voice whispers in my ear, "you didn't think you'd really get to leave without saying hi to me, did you?"

I look up and see Chris and my face involuntarily breaks into a huge smile and I give him a big hug, even though I know this means I am going to be even later getting home.

"Were you trying to avoid me tonight?" Chris teases.

"No of course not." I laugh. "You're just too popular. I tried to come say hi, but every time I looked over, you were talking to someone. I finally gave up."

"I'll always make time for you Liv. Especially when it's been so long! Do you want to go grab a drink so we can actually catch up? I'd love to pick your brain on some new issues the firm is facing," Chris says.

"I'd love to, but I really have to get home. Maybe another time?" I suggest.

"Okay. Well, it's my own fault for not making time for you tonight. But I am going to hold you to your offer. Are you free next week?"

"I'm not sure, I'll have to check. Why don't you text me and we can figure it out," I say, knowing that it will be another two years until I hear from Chris again.

"Will do, Olivia. I'll see you next week. And by the way, you look beautiful tonight."

Chapter 10 – Gretchen

I open my eyes and look at the clock – 6:24 – exactly one minutes before my alarm is set to go off. I don't know why I bother with an alarm anymore, my body has been getting up at 6:25 everyday for the past 6 years; but I know I would sleep until 9 on the one morning I forget to set it. I reach over and shut it off so I don't have to listen to the annoying beep of my 15-year old clock radio. It's also the nice wifely thing to do since Alan doesn't get up until 7.

I lay in bed for another minute thinking about my day and mentally prepping myself for what's ahead, maybe this is what an athlete does before a big game? I'm pretty sure any professional athlete would fail miserably if he had to spend a day in my shoes, but I don't see that reality show happening any time soon.

Thursday is one of the three days that I work, in addition to doing all of the things I usually do on the other days. But since I work 'part-time' and I work 'from-home', no one seems to think I have a 'real job.' That's exactly what Natalie said to me the other day, "it's not like you have a real job like Kate's mom." I should go back to work full time and get a nanny like Kate's mom and see how they like it when I am gone from 8 to 7 every day and someone else has to take care of everything for them.

"Mom do I have gym today?" Natalie screams from down the hall. Followed shortly by, "Get out of my room! Mom, Ethan is in my room, get him out of here!"

And with that, my real alarm clock has gone off and it is time to start the day.

I make it back home by 8:45 and have to fight the urge to crawl back into bed, but instead I make another cup of coffee and head into my office.

My house is on a completely different scale from Laura's and it isn't as big or fancy as Olivia's, but it is perfect for our family, and my office is my favorite room in the house. It used to be the kids' playroom when they were little, but now Alice barricades herself in her room most of the time and the toys we do have are downstairs in the basement for Ethan to play with and for Natalie on the rare occasion when she wants to play with toys instead of reading or drawing in the kitchen.

The office is on the first floor of the house, directly off of the kitchen, with windows on 3 sides so it gets great sunlight. When I went back to work part-time two years ago, I picked out a desk, chair, bookshelves, couch and rug at the local antique store, which made it a bargain to decorate and gives the room an artistic feel even though I am doing bookkeeping and accounting work while I'm in here.

I open up my email and start making a list of all the things I need to get done today. An email from Alan pops up on my screen as I am typing:

From: Alan Fields
To: Gretchen Fields

Subject: Tonight
I just remembered I have a dinner tonight with people from the paper. Home late.

Shit. Shit, shit, shit. Of course he would do that. And of course he didn't remember that he wasn't just supposed to be on time tonight, he was supposed to be early. So now instead of starting work, I am going to have to spend the next 15 minutes trying to find a sitter for tonight, so that I can get Alice to her field hockey game and have someone take Natalie to karate and Ethan will just have to come with me.

From: Gretchen Fields
To: Alan Fields

Subject: Re: Tonight
You were supposed to be home early to go watch Alice's game. But don't worry, of course I'll figure it out – I always do…

As I open up my Excel program, I hear a text message on my phone. I should ignore it, but curiosity gets the better of me – I only get a few texts a day, so they are hard to ignore.

Olivia: u there?

Gretchen: I'm here, but working, what is it?

Olivia: can u talk for just a min?

Gretchen: ok

Instantly my phone rings. "Hi! Sorry to bother you, I won't be long," Olivia says.

"It's okay. I have a couple of minutes, but I really need to get some work done, my whole afternoon and evening just imploded," I tell her.

"Oh no, what happened?"

"Never mind, not important. What's going on? Why did you need to talk?" I ask.

"So, you know how I went to that thing for my old firm last night?" Olivia says.

"Oh right! How was it?"

"It was great. So fun to see everyone, and the new office is amazing. I'm actually a little hung-over this morning, but totally worth it!" Olivia laughs.

"So what's wrong?" I say.

"Oh right. So you remember Chris? My old boss? I didn't really get a chance to see him all night and then ran into him as I was leaving. He said he was going to text me and ask me to come into the city next week for drinks, but I thought he was full of crap and I wouldn't hear from him again. Well, I got a text from him 5 minutes ago," Olivia pauses to take a breath.

"Okay, so?" I probe.

"So this is what the text says: "Great to see you last night. Wish I could have seen more of you. I miss you. Can you come meet me next Wed night for a drink after work?" Gretchen, What does that mean?" Olivia almost shouts.

"I don't know. I don't know if it means anything. He was your boss right? Nothing weird ever happened, right? I think he just misses working with you. Didn't you guys work together for like 10 years?" I ask her.

"You're right. Of course you're right. And he's married and has kids. What's wrong with me? So it isn't weird if I have a drink with him? He said he wanted to pick my brain about some problems they were having at the office," Olivia says.

I'm already scrolling through my emails and have moved my attention elsewhere, "I think you are totally reading into his text. He's probably more hung-over than you are and just sent you a quick text. Don't worry about it. Definitely go meet him."

"Okay, thanks Gretchen. I feel a lot better now. I just wrote him back, I'm going to see him next week! Just need to find a sitter because Charlie is out of town," Olivia says.

"Oh crap, Liv. That reminds me, I have to go, I still have to find a sitter for tonight. Talk to you later," I say as I hang up the phone, her problems already a distant memory.

Chapter 11 – Danielle

Three minutes has never taken so long.

I know this is a waste of time and money, since the test yesterday and the day before were both negative, but maybe I was taking them too early, or maybe those weren't good brands.

I am a smart woman. I graduated top of my class from Yale Law school and was an editor of the Yale Law Review. So why can't I understand that I am not pregnant? Taking more or different pregnancy tests is not going to make me pregnant. I really should be able to grasp this, but it's not sinking in.

Maybe it's for the best. When I told Jim last night that the second test was negative he had a hard time concealing his enthusiasm. All he could talk about was this couples' triathlon that he found for us in Hawaii and now that we didn't have to worry about being pregnant we could enter the race. Maybe that would be good, we'll stop trying for the next couple of months and train for this race and that will make Jim really happy and then once the triathlon is over, we can really start trying again – maybe even in Hawaii!

The alarm on my iPhone goes off telling me that 3 minutes are finally over. I glance down at the plastic stick, about to throw it in the trash, when I notice in clear block letters the word "pregnant". That can't be right. Where is the word "not" in front of it? I hold it up to the light, I hold it at an angle, I place it flat on the bathroom counter – no matter how I look at it, the test says the same thing, "pregnant".

You know how you've imagined something happening a million times in your head? You've played out all of the scenarios and you think you know exactly what you will do when it happens? But then it happens and you have no idea what to do.

That's me 45 minutes later clutching my pee-stick, sitting on the floor of the master bathroom still in sweaty workout clothes from my run this morning.

Of course I'm ecstatic. I'm actually pregnant. There's a tiny baby starting to grow inside of me. But those thoughts I had before about Jim aren't going anywhere. I'm sure he'll be happy when I tell him; but he was *really* happy last night at the idea of not having to worry about a baby for the next few months. He seemed so excited about training together and then going to Hawaii together, and he was even more excited that I wanted to do it with him.

***

"What's all this?" Jim asks as he comes in and sees the dining room table set for dinner. "Did I forget an anniversary? Are we still celebrating months?" Jim teases.

"No silly," I say as I walk over and give him a hug and a kiss, "I just thought it would be nice to eat in the dining room for a change."

"Oh, okay" Jim says, but he still looks nervous, "I'm just going to run upstairs and change, I'll be back in a minute."

I never had time to cook when I was working, but I really enjoy cooking, so on the nights when Jim isn't working too late, I cook dinner and we eat together. My plan is to tell him the news somewhere between the main course and dessert; I don't know what morning sickness feels like, but it can't be half as bad as the butterflies I have in my stomach right now.

Jim comes downstairs in jeans and a sweater, "what smells so good? I'm starving."

"It's a vegetable lasagna, but I also made a spinach salad and a flourless chocolate cake" I say with a hint of pride.

"Wow, you've been busy. Are you sure we aren't celebrating anything?" Jim asks.

It's such a lay-up, I should just spit it out right now - come on, say it. But when I open my mouth, all that comes out is, "not that I can think of." Dammit, I suck.

We have a great dinner and enjoy each other's company and the food. In addition to exercise, one of the things we have in common is that we both really like to eat! We work out so much, that we can eat whatever we want. Apparently Linda didn't like to exercise, but she was always struggling with her weight, so she didn't like to have "real food" in the house. Jim loves that I love to cook and eat - another point in my favor.
Jim seems so relaxed tonight, he had a great day at the office and we talk about the case he is working on and he asks my opinion on the case and the people he has working on it (my friends from work) and then we talk

about the race in Hawaii and his face lights up when he starts to outline our training plan.

Now it's 11pm and I am cleaning up in the kitchen and Jim has gone to do a little bit of work in his office before he goes to bed.

The subject just didn't come up tonight. I looked for a good opening, but there didn't seem to be one. Obviously, I will tell him tomorrow...

Chapter 12 - Laura

"I know mom, but we were at your house last year for Thanksgiving. This year we are going to Boston to be with Michael's family," I say to my mom over the phone; I'm already exhausted and we've been on the phone less than 2 minutes.

"Okay, but then you'll come to Jersey for Christmas or should we plan on coming to you?" my mom asks.

I take a deep breath before I answer because I have been dreading this conversation and was hoping to avoid it for another few weeks. Although, since it is already the end of October, it is rather unrealistic to think I could elude her any longer. "Actually mom, we are going away for Christmas."

"Away, what do you mean away? Where are you going? You're spending it with Michael's family *again*?" she asks.

"No, nothing like that. We are going to Turks and Caicos for Christmas. Just the six of us, Michael and I thought it would be nice to go somewhere warm" I tell her, feeling better now that it is finally out in the open.

"So you're just going away? You won't see any family for Christmas? No tree? That doesn't sound much like Christmas to me," my mom scoffs.

"I know mom, but we'll put a tree up before we go and I think the kids will have a great time at the beach; there's a lot for them to do at the resort and it will be nice to get away..." I trail off.

"Well, it doesn't sound nice to me, but I guess you've already decided that's what you're doing. So when *are* we going to see you? I can't remember the last time we saw you and the kids, I think it was in July?"

"No, it can't have been that long. I'm sorry mom, it's just really busy here, it's hard to find a good time to come see you, but I promise we'll find a weekend in January," I say cheerily, January sounding far away.

"Laura this is ridiculous. We live less than 3 hours away and I would like to see my grandchildren and my daughter. You may not have time to come down here, but your father and I can come up and see you - you can't be *that* busy!" My mom says getting worked up.

"Really mom, things are crazy. With four kids and Michael's schedule, it's just so busy, it's hard to explain, but I wouldn't have any time to spend with you and I wouldn't want you to come all this way and feel like you didn't have quality time with me or the kids," I say, my voice getting panicky at the thought of my parents actually coming.

"I don't care if it's quality time, I just want any time. If we aren't going to see you at Thanksgiving or Christmas, then we'll just come up for a few days before then- I'm worried my grandchildren will forget what I look like." I hear papers rustling on her end of the phone. "I just looked in my day-planner and your dad and I are going to come up the first weekend in November. I don't care what you have going on, we'll keep to ourselves, but I know you have room for us and I won't take no for an answer," my mom says definitively.

I'm speechless. I guess I've pushed her off one too many times and now this is what's happened. She's an easy-going person most of the time, and all of her friends talk about what a sweetheart she is, but underneath she's tough as nails.

"Okay mom, I guess that weekend will work." I say knowing that I have been defeated.

"Great sweetheart, I'll let you know when we know what time we think we're going to get there. So glad we worked this out," she says, back in her sugary sweet mom voice.

"Bye Mom," I say, staring off into space as I end the phone call.

Shit. That is not how that call was supposed to go. It's not that I don't love my parents; it's just that I don't really want to *see* my parents. I know that sounds horrible, I realize how that sounds, but they don't fit in with my life here. Every time I see them, the dichotomy becomes more apparent and harder to overcome. They don't understand the children either. They think their activities are ridiculous and therefore they think I am ridiculous for scheduling them in all of these activities and making sure they practice their instruments and study on the weekends.

My dad will laugh and say, "you didn't do any of this and you did okay for yourself, right Laura." And then my mom will add, "they're just children, shouldn't they be outside running around and playing in the dirt – it was good enough for you Laura." Neither of them understanding that I was lucky enough to make it to where I am today despite my mediocre academic upbringing and my hours of playing in the dirt with my brothers while my parents spent their time at the local casino.

And it's worse when they try and talk to Michael, although he never seems to get annoyed by them. My dad will ask Michael how it's going at work and then no matter what Michael says, my dad will say, "that reminds me of a time when..." like it's possible that any hedge fund story could remind my dad of a day at work as a plumber.

They are both good people and they did the best they could raising me, but I have a hard time figuring out how to fit them into this world of affluence.

I head upstairs to see if Cameron is up from his nap yet. I could call for Robin, but with the other 3 at school, this is something I want to do. I know Olivia doesn't think I work as hard as she does because I have help, but she doesn't see me when I'm home at times like these. I'm not sure why Olivia does it all by herself anyhow, I know she has enough money that she could have help – I think she likes the constant activity. She was in charge of everything at work and now she needs to do the same thing at home.

I pop into my bathroom on the way to Cameron's room. As I was walking upstairs I told myself that I didn't need anything, but I'm still a little shaky from that conversation with my mom and it would take the edge off a little bit if I took one pill. I reach back in the cabinet and pull out the bottle and shake two pills into my hand – I meant to take one, but two came out; maybe two would take the edge off even more. I peer into the bottle and notice that there are only 4 more pills left in the bottle – how is that possible? I just refilled this last week. Did I put some of them into the bottle in my purse? I'll have to check later. But I'm going to have to call Dr. Singha this time for a refill, I'll have to check my list, but I don't think I've called him in at least a month.

I swallow the pills with one gulp of water from the bathroom tap and feel the stress start to melt away. I know they can't actually work that quickly, but my body knows help is on the way.

I wander down the hall to Cameron's room ready to cuddle with my little boy as I feel the familiar haze starting to settle in.

Chapter 13 - Olivia

No matter how many times I look at my watch, time does not seem to be moving any faster today. In fact, time seems to be standing still on this early November Wednesday. Frequently I can't find enough time to go to the bathroom, but today I am more excited than I should be to get out of the house for the evening, and so as retribution, the next eight hours will feel like eighty.

***

Slowly but surely, the day moves along: Elizabeth is picked up from school, lunch is made and cleaned up, Julie is picked up from school, snack is made and cleaned up, Barbie's are played with and fought over and cleaned up, Legos are played with and fought over and cleaned up, dinner is made and finally Taylor rings the doorbell.

The chime of the doorbell sounds like the halleluiah chorus. I let Taylor in and I run upstairs to get ready as quickly as possible. I wish I could enjoy the pleasure of getting ready in an empty bathroom without Julie or Elizabeth banging on the shower door or playing with my makeup, but I only have 25 minutes to get ready and make my train into the city in order to meet Chris on time.

I drive into the Rye train station parking lot as my train is pulling in and I have to run to make it before the doors close. I'm glad I opted for riding boots with a lug sole, instead of my usual heels; I would never have made the train if I had to run in any of my other boots, thankfully Chris and I will be sitting most of the night, so it doesn't matter how short I am.

I decided to go more casual with my look tonight; I picked straight-fit jeans and a fitted black v-neck sweater – no need to try too hard. I can't count the number of times Chris and I have had drinks, either alone or with a team, and we've traveled to dozens of cities together, but tonight feels different for some reason. It's probably just because it will be the first time that we have gotten together and he isn't officially my boss, but I'm just excited to talk about the firm and have a conversation that uses my brain where someone genuinely values my opinion.

***

Chris is waiting at the bar when I walk in. He is already half way through his pint of beer and intently reading something on his phone. He reminds me of Charlie, the way he is so absorbed by whatever is on his phone that a bomb could go off next to him and he wouldn't notice. He must not be as absorbed as I thought though, because when I get a couple of feet away, he turns around and smiles at me and then gets up from his stool.

"Olivia, I'm so glad you made it," Chris says as he bends down to envelop me in a hug and puts his phone away in his pocket. Chris isn't quite as tall as Charlie, but he must be at least 6 feet tall, so still a lot bigger than I am. I take a seat on the stool next to him as he sits back down and I catch the bartender's eye.

"I'll have a dirty martini please, extra olives," I tell the bartender.

"Whoa, you're a changed woman. What happened to the Olivia who drinks white wine?" Chris laughs.

"Oh some days I drink wine, but today wine isn't going to cut it – at least not for my first drink," I say just as the bartender puts my giant martini down in front of me. I pull it closer and bend down to take a sip off the top because it is too full to risk picking it up yet.

Once my martini is a little less full, I pick it up and hold it in the air toward Chris, "Cheers! To the good old days!"

"Cheers, Liv!" he says, and takes a drink of his beer.

"So, tell me everything. It was such a blur the other night I didn't get to talk to Jennifer for very long; I felt so old, I can't believe half those kids are actually old enough to have jobs!" I say.

"Overall things are good. We've hired a lot of new people, as you saw the other night, and we're turning away business if you can believe it - nothing big, obviously. But we've gotten really lucky with some recurring clients over the last couple of years and now we can turn away some of the smaller less profitable ones –you know the ones that you and I used to kill ourselves for when we first started out!" Chris is clearly very proud as he tells me how the firm is doing.

"I'm glad to hear it's all going so well. I was kind of hoping you had fallen apart when I left," I say laughing.

"Don't get me wrong. Things are going well, but it isn't the same as it was when you were there" Chris says in a very serious voice. "There are people still there from the original crew, like Jennifer, although she could never replace you; but the new guys just aren't the same, *especially* the kids. Don't get me started on these 25-year olds who think everything should be handed to them on a silver platter and don't know how to work hard. They're not even scared of me – can you believe it?" Chris says to me with a look of disbelief.

"I promise, I was always scared of you," I say flashing him a big smile "in fact, I'm still pretty scared of you," I say pushing his arm playfully.

I go to take a sip of my drink and notice that it's all gone. "Well, we can't have that, can we?" Chris says. "Excuse me, can we have another round over here?" Chris motions to the bartender.

I wouldn't normally have two martinis. In fact, I usually don't even drink one martini – Charlie drinks them and I'll have some of his, but it seemed like a good drink choice tonight; if I'm being honest, I thought it would be cool to order one in front of Chris.

But right now I'm feeling the vodka run through my whole body and it feels great. I'm relaxed, warm, and loving being here and talking with Chris – it feels like Rye is a million miles away.

The bartender brings our next round and this drink tastes much better than my first one – the first one tasted strong, but this one is really smooth. We should probably order something to eat, but I don't want to interrupt the story Chris is telling me about the new Pepsi deal – we can order something to eat later.

"So be honest, do you really like being at home with the kids? Don't you miss work?" Chris asks.

"Is this a recruiting meeting?" I laugh.

"No, I'm serious. I just can't imagine you *not* in meetings all day and running a team and writing presentations and having new clients fall in love with you as you create marketing campaigns for them on-the-spot that are better than anything they've ever seen."

Through the haze of my one and a half martinis, I look up at Chris and as I open my mouth to thank him or defend my choice to be home, I'm not sure which, tears start to well up in my eyes and I can't say anything or I am going to be sitting at the bar sobbing.

"Liv, what's wrong? What did I say?" Chris looks at me bewildered.

"Nothing, nothing. You didn't say anything wrong," I tell him, thankful that the tears have gone almost as quickly as they came. "I hadn't thought about work in a while, and how much I was valued there. I miss that. But you don't need to hear about this, sorry to bore you." I say, trying to regain my composure and steer the conversation elsewhere, but the martinis are making that much harder.

"You're not boring me. And I'm not trying to recruit you, but I wouldn't say no if you wanted to come back," Chris laughs. And then Chris leans over and gives me a big hug. It's different than the hug he gave me when I came in tonight. It's awkward at first, because of how we are sitting, but then I move my shoulder down so my chest is pressed up against his and then it doesn't feel awkward anymore, it feels good. I close my eyes and smell the faint smell of cologne on his neck. Charlie doesn't wear cologne, which I always liked, but Chris smells good, manly.

"Would you two like another round? It looks like those are almost done." The loud voice of the bartender interrupts us and I open my eyes and try desperately to think of something witty to say to Chris as we pull away from each other that would make this less uncomfortable, but nothing comes to mind.

"Nothing else for me," I manage to say to the bartender, "oh wait, actually a large glass of water would be great. " "I'll have one more pint, " Chris says. To me he says, "what? it's just beer, I'm not a heavy drinker like you."

"So, how's the family?" I ask him. It's not witty, but at least it keeps the conversation moving.

"The kids are great. Mason is doing really well. Can you believe he is a freshman in high school?"

"That's not possible! He was 2 when I met you." I say, trying to picture the blonde toddler roaming the halls of high school.

"Crazy, right? He's on the varsity soccer team. Doing great in school. And he has a girlfriend," Chris is beaming as he tells me, ever the proud dad.

"And Grace?" I ask.

"Grace is good. Seventh grade is hard – sorry, but you don't have a lot to look forward to with middle school girls. But she's doing well. She is so smart it kills me. She plays piano, she's trying out for the volleyball team, and maybe even lacrosse! You wouldn't recognize her – she's taller than you!" Chris laughs.

"Well that isn't hard to do. And how's Mary?" I ask.

"She's okay. We're finding a way to be nice to each other for the kids' sake." Chris says, his tone totally changed from before.

"Wait, what do you mean?" I say, wishing I didn't feel so fuzzy.

"Oh shit, I thought you knew. I thought everyone knew. Mary and I got divorced two years ago. It must have been right after you had the baby."

"Oh my god. I'm so sorry. How did I not know that? I'm so sorry Chris." I say, now my head spinning with alcohol and this new information.

"Oh don't be sorry. We had been miserable for a long time. She kept the house in New Jersey and I got a place in the city. I'm in Gramercy, not too far from the office; you'll have to come see it. The kids are with her most of the time because of school, but they're with me in the city most weekends and I promise you, we're all much happier," Chris says and he looks like he means it.

"Oh, well that's great then," I say, not sure what the right thing is to say.

I want to ask him if he is dating anyone, but I'm not sure if I should, and I'm not sure if I want to know the answer – although that's ridiculous, why would I care if he's dating someone? Up until 5 minutes ago I thought he was happily married. And of course I *am* happily married.

***

Sitting in the back of a town car on the way home, I hear the chime on my phone telling me I have a new text. I hope it isn't Taylor, I told her I would be home before midnight and it's only 11:15.

Fortunately, the text is from Chris.

Chris: So good to see u tonight. Have missed u. Can u do dinner next week?

I read the text several times. There's nothing wrong with his text. I have dinner with my friends all the time, that's totally normal.

I text back:

Olivia: Good to see you too. Would love to have dinner. Tuesday good?

I re-read the text exchange and then delete my text and Chris's text from my phone – I know there's nothing wrong with them, but taken out of context, they might be misinterpreted.

Chapter 14 – Danielle

Every morning I wake up and I tell myself that this is going to be the day that I tell Jim the news, and then something happens and there is a reason why this wasn't a good day to tell him. So now here I am two weeks later and it's getting out of hand.

Maybe I'll pull one of the girls aside tonight at wine club and tell them.   Laura convinced me to host wine club this month. Actually I think it was an honor that I was even invited a second time. Someone named Victoria was supposed to host, but she had to cancel at the last minute. Laura told me that it was related to plastic surgery, but she couldn't tell me any more than that.

So tonight I have 12 women coming over for wine club, then this weekend Kyle and Megan are staying here, I am supposed to be kicking my triathlon training into a higher gear, Sharon keeps calling me about contracts for the event at the school and then somewhere in there I need to figure out how to tell my husband (and my mother) that I am pregnant. It's getting harder and harder to keep it from my mom, but I promised myself I would tell Jim first.

Well, I'll tackle this in order. First thing is getting ready for tonight. Laura sent me a list with everything that needs to be done. It's almost as long as any paper I wrote in law school. I read through her mission statement and make my own list to bring with me to the gourmet food and wine shop in the center of town. I've only been in there a few times, but considering how overpriced everything is, hopefully the service is directly proportional to the price.

***

Three hours later I return home with countless bags of groceries, cases of wine, Diptyque candles and armfuls of fresh flowers. It takes four trips to bring everything in from the car and I am exhausted from the trip. Yesterday was the first day I felt more tired than normal, but I chalked it up to a restless night's sleep. However, I am tired again today and I remember that 'fatigue' is a common symptom of the first trimester and at six and a half weeks pregnant; I am definitely in the first trimester.

I'm sure a shower will wake me up. I certainly don't have time to be tired today. Twelve women will be at my house in two hours; most of who are just coming to see what I've changed in the house since Linda moved out and to be able to say that they know the 'home-wrecker' Jim married. Actually, I'm not sure what they call me, but I've learned over the last six months that I am an attraction – like an exotic animal at the zoo. Laura doesn't seem to care at all and I'm not sure about her close friends Gretchen and Olivia, they certainly have been the nicest ones so far.

Getting dressed is still easy - I'm so newly pregnant that none of my clothes fit any differently and I look exactly the same; although, I keep forgetting that it's normal to try and hide it from everyone for the first 3 months, it's just not normal to hide it from your husband.

I pick a pair of cream colored wide-legged pants and a navy cropped sweater that shows about an inch of my stomach, or more when I raise my arms. I'm not going to have too much longer before I can't wear shirts like this anymore, so I might as well wear them now. I've worked so hard to get my body to where it is, at least I can flaunt it in front of these ladies and give them a real reason to hate me.

***

The doorbell rings and I brace myself for the long evening ahead. Jim knows that everyone is here tonight, so he said he would stay at work as late as possible and then come in through the back door when he gets home so he doesn't have to see anyone.

I answer the door and breathe a sigh of relief as I see that Laura is my first guest – I should have known she would be first.

"Hi Laura, you look beautiful," I say to her and genuinely mean it; she may be the most attractive person I have ever met in real life.

"Hi sweetie," Laura says. "How is everything? Are you ready? Do you need any help?"

"I think I'm okay. Thanks for the list you gave me. I think I got everything," I say feeling like I am about to be graded on a test.

"Let me just take a quick look around if that's okay. You met most of these women before, but it's your first time hosting and I don't want to give them any reason not to... well you know..." Laura cuts herself off and then wanders into the dining room and then the living room inspecting everything I worked on all afternoon.

"This looks good, Danielle" Laura says.

"Thanks!" I beam. At the same time pleased with her praise and annoyed with myself for being reduced to caring so much about what she thinks of my hostessing skills. Less than 18 months ago, I was on the partner-track at one of the top law firms in Manhattan and I would have laughed at these middle-aged women getting dressed up on a Thursday night to bitch about their husbands and kids and drink a few too many glasses of wine; but now here I am hoping these women will like me enough to drink my wine and be my friends – life's funny that way.

Everyone arrives shortly thereafter and soon my living room and dining room are filled with women eating and drinking and talking – mostly talking. I'm trying to follow Laura's advice and move around from group to group, say hello, refill drinks and try to pick up on enough of their conversations to add my own perspective.

I wander over to Gretchen and Olivia and perch on the edge of the couch, still clutching my untouched wine glass, and try to find my moment to jump into their discussion.

"So, I saw Chris for drinks last night," Olivia says.

"Oh right, how was that? Did he offer you your job back?" Gretchen asks.

"Not quite, but I think I could go back if I wanted, I'm just not quite ready," Olivia says.

"So, anything else? No good office gossip?" Gretchen probes.

Olivia takes a big sip of her wine before she answers, "nope, not much else to report."

"So anyone need a refill?" I blurt out, looking for my opening into their conversation.

"No, I'm good," says Olivia, "I had a little too much last night, going to take it easy tonight."

"I'll have some more," says Gretchen, "but only if you join me. You need to celebrate a successful night, look around, everyone's having a great time," and then she leans in and whispers, "even the uptight ones over there don't have anything to complain about, and that's rare!"

I raise my glass and toast Gretchen, "cheers" we say, and I take a sip of my wine.

I'm sure a few sips of wine can't hurt the baby at this point, maybe this will help me relax and then I'll finally be able to tell Jim when he comes home tonight. I take another sip of wine and decide that I'm telling Jim tonight – or if not tonight, then definitely tomorrow.

Chapter 15 – Gretchen

I'm running late to meet Olivia for coffee. But it's Monday morning, so running 10 minutes late isn't too bad; and sadly Olivia is probably expecting me to be late.

I pull onto Main Street and can't believe that there is actually an open parking spot right in front of Lucy's, maybe I won't be that late after all.

I park, run inside and easily spot Olivia sitting at a table since Lucy's is totally empty this early on a Monday morning.

"Hi Liv," I say as I walk over to the table and bend down to give her a hug and kiss on the cheek. "How was your weekend?" I ask her as I take off my coat and sit down. It's a beautiful fall morning with most of the leaves still on the trees in brilliant hues of yellow, orange and red, but I needed to wear my field jacket this morning, not the fleece vest I've been wearing for the last couple of weeks – it won't be long before it's heavy coats and gloves every day.

"The weekend was good. You know crazy as usual. Charlie was in Chicago most of last week, so it was good to have him back. We drove up to Westport on Sunday to see Charlie's brother and his wife and kids - fun, but a long day. What about you?" Olivia asks me as she takes a sip of her coffee.

"It flew by, just like they all do. Alan had to work most of the weekend, so I was by myself with the kids for most of it. One field hockey game, two soccer games and one soccer practice – I'm living the dream," I say and smile.

"That sounds terrible! Maybe Julie and Elizabeth won't play any sports and then we'll get to keep our weekends," Olivia groans.

"Nope, it's inevitable. If it isn't soccer or field hockey, it will be dance recitals or chess club. There is no way to avoid your weekends being taken over by your children's activities – unless you don't have children and you're a little late for that," I say and give her a big smug smile.

"Is something wrong? You look distracted. And you keep looking at your phone – are you waiting to hear from someone?" I ask Olivia, slightly worried.

"Oh no, nothing. Not really," she says in a feeble tone.

"That wasn't very convincing, you sure?" I ask her again.

"Everything's mostly fine. Well, not really... So, Charlie and I haven't had sex in three weeks and I don't think either of us really cares. That's a problem right?" Olivia blurts out.

I take a big sip of coffee to give myself a minute to think about how to answer her. "Well, first I'm sure he cares – all men care about sex. And second, sometimes these things happen. He's been traveling, you're both busy and tired, so just have sex tonight. You're thinking too much about it," I tell her, trying to be helpful without sounding like a cheap daytime talk show host.

"So what's the longest you and Alan have ever gone? Not counting being pregnant or when they were babies. Sorry, now I'm thinking about it and I have to know if this is normal," Olivia asks me and is staring intently waiting for my answer.

"Everyone is different..." I start to say.

"Oh shit, that means this isn't normal. So how long?" she pleads.

"Okay, probably two or three days. But calm down," I say as she puts her hand over her eyes to pretend to hide from me, "we have plenty of our own problems, I promise. Sex has just never been one of them. It's one of the few things we always agree on. We can have sex in the middle of a fight and then go right back to fighting. Everyone's different and you and Charlie are fine, don't worry," I say in a soothing voice.

"I am never going to be able to look at Alan the same way now that I know about your wild sex life. How did I not know this?" She asks, "not that I'm glad I know now. I think I could have gone my whole life not knowing that my best friend has sex almost every day after 15 years of marriage. Wow, I might just shoot myself," she says in a tone I can't quite read.

"Hey, you asked!" I remind her. "So you'll do it tonight and then you'll be fine, or are you worried you forgot how?" I say laughing.

"Ha-ha, aren't you funny. I'm going to trust you that Charlie still wants to! I swear he doesn't even look twice at me if I'm standing in the middle of the room naked anymore – I've just become part of the scenery, I'm like the bench at the end of our bed, he walks right by and doesn't even notice," Liv says, her tone has changed from sarcastic to serious.

"I'm sorry Livvy. You're gorgeous, and he knows that. I'm sure he just thinks that you're too busy or that you're not interested either. Maybe let him know how you feel? Or maybe you guys need a night away? Hotel sex is so much better than regular sex," I say trying to lighten the mood.

"You're right, I've got to do something. I'll figure it out. Thanks for listening to me Dr. Ruth" she jokes. "Okay, I've got to run so I can get to the store before I have to pick up Elizabeth, these mornings just fly by."

"Let me know how it goes, I'll be waiting to hear all the juicy details," I tell her, waving my phone at her.

"I'm not telling you anything now that I know about you and Alan, I'll never be able to live up to that!" she yells as she walks out the door.

***

As I'm making dinner later that evening, Alice walks into the kitchen and grabs a carrot from the cutting board where I am chopping vegetables and slumps into a chair at the table.

"Hi love, how was school?" I ask cautiously. Lately every conversation with Alice is a minefield, anything I say can set her off and send her back to the fortress of her room. I don't remember being like this with my parents in 8th grade, but I'm learning that everything was a lot simpler 28 years ago.

"Okay," she mumbles staring down at the table. I want to walk over and push the hair back off of her face and tuck it behind her ears or pull it back into a ponytail so I can see her beautiful face, but I wouldn't dare.

I'm hoping this non-communicative child that has replaced my outgoing, vibrant daughter will be leaving my house soon and the real Alice will return. I've talked to friends with middle school girls and Alice doesn't seem to be any different from their children, but it doesn't make it any easier.

And then it happens.

"Mom, something's wrong," Alice says, and dissolves into tears with her head buried in her arms on the table.

I haven't seen this little girl in a long time, she looks like the 6-year old who fell on her way into school on the first day of first grade. I want to scoop her up and put her on my lap and tell her everything is going to be okay; but I know if I don't handle this the right way she will close back up and I'll miss my chance to help her, and to find out what's so wrong that she's actually come to me with a problem instead of one of her friends.

I slowly make my way over to the table and pull out the chair next to her and then put my arm around her shoulder. Other than a quick peck on the cheek, Alice has not wanted physical contact from either Alan or me in months. It might be my imagination, but she seems to lean closer to me, and she definitely doesn't pull away.

"Can you tell me about it?" I ask her.

Through loud sobs and sniffles I think she says, "You're going to be really mad."

And now I tell her what every parent says and then wishes they hadn't, "I promise I won't be mad, just tell me."

She sits up a little bit in her chair and uses her hands to wipe her eyes and her nose, I desperately fight the urge to get her a tissue or tell her that it's disgusting, because I don't want to lose any momentum.
"We didn't mean for anything to happen. It was just a joke," she says.

"What was?" I ask.

"So, we really didn't think it was going to happen, but this guy took it seriously and now we don't know how to stop him," Alice says, all of the tears gone now, replaced with a new sense of panic.

"What are you talking about? What happened? What guy?" I ask her, starting to get concerned.

"You promise you won't get mad," Alice begs me.

"Fine," I promise, "now tell me what's going on, the whole thing."

"So, it started a few weeks ago. We were sleeping over at Annie's house, remember?" She asks.

"I think so. Who else was there?" I ask her, thinking that I probably want to be writing this down, but I'm pretty sure Alice wouldn't like that.

"It was just me and Annie and Kate. So, anyway... Kelly has been such a bitch lately," she looks at me as she says the last part, unsure how to proceed.

"It's fine, go on," I tell her.

"So, Kelly has been so mean to us recently since she started seeing Ryan. All she cares about is Ryan, and she only wants to spend time with Sidney because she has a boyfriend too, so all they talk about is boys and that day after field hockey practice - by the way mom, Alyssa and Kelly totally suck now because they keep skipping practice and they're not taking it seriously. But anyway, that day after practice, Kelly said that Annie and Kate and I were probably all lesbians because we didn't even like boys and we were having a sleepover and that was 'totally gay'." Alice pauses to take a breath and I am nodding along, but saying nothing, trying to make sure I am keeping up with the middle school soap opera.

"So that night at Annie's house we were really mad at Kelly and we went online and we sort of made a fake dating profile for her," she says, looking at me to see if I understand.

"Go on," I direct her.

"Well, we thought it would be funny to sign her up on match.com and make up crazy stuff about her. It seemed funny at the time."

"Don't you have to be older to go on those sites?" I ask naively.

"Well of course mom, but we just put in a fake birthday for her and said she was 19. And we have a ton of pictures of her, so we uploaded a lot of pictures of her." Alice is nervously playing with her hair as she tells me this.

"What do you mean you uploaded pictures of her? What kinds of pictures?" I'm trying to remain calm, but I'm starting to see where this could be going and I don't like any of the outcomes.

"Um, you know, just pictures," she says and then she sees the look on my face and knows that answer is not sufficient. "So we couldn't put her school picture or her field hockey picture, right? Because she is supposed to be 19, so we had to put pictures where she looked older. So we used some from this summer at the beach and then one of her that Kate took a couple months ago when she was being funny and trying on her sister's clothes and making these weird sexy faces," Alice exhales as she admits this.

"Okay, so you put pictures of your 13-year old friend on a dating site half naked and dressed up in slutty clothes and said she was 19 and you didn't think anything would happen? What did you girls think?" I am fighting to keep my voice level.

"We didn't think. We were just mad at her and it was stupid, I don't know. But that isn't the worst part. So, of course she got about two hundred guys right away who wanted to go out with her, you know because she's so pretty," she tells me while having the nerve to be annoyed by this part of the story. "So we picked two of these guys as her dates and we have been writing back and forth with them for the last two weeks," Alice can't even look at me anymore while she is talking.

"So why are you telling me this now Alice? What happened?"

She starts crying again as she's talking, "you're going to kill me."

"Just tell me, it's always better once it's out in the open."

"Okay, so we really didn't think it was going to come to anything, it was just harmless and these guys didn't really know who she was. But all 3 of us have the username and password and I don't know what happened, but in one of the conversations, somehow we agreed to meet one of the guys," Alice confesses.

"What?!" I practically scream at her.

"I know, it's bad. And we gave him Kelly's address as the real place to meet, so this one guy is going over to her house tomorrow night," she looks up at me finally happy to have the burden off of her 13-year old chest.

I look at Alice and can't find any words to say. I wish I could rewind the clock 15 minutes and go back to when I was annoyed with her for keeping her distance. Now I'm looking at my daughter and can't believe that my child could be in this amount of trouble; or have potentially put another child in this type of danger. How the hell am I supposed to know what to do?

"Alice, how old is this guy?" I ask her. I don't know why this is important, but it's all I can think to ask.

"He says he's 23, but I mean we lied, so maybe he's lying too."

All right - 23. That's not so bad I tell myself, at least he's not a 45-year old pervert.

I give Alice a long stare and then pick up my phone to start making my first phone call of many, as I say, "I can guarantee you aren't going to like any of it, but we have to try to fix this quickly. And *then* I will deal with you."

Chapter 16 – Olivia

"Mommy, you're doing it wrong. You don't drink the tea yet. You have to wait for all the dollies to have tea first!" Elizabeth says disapprovingly.

"Oh, sorry honey. Mommy will wait. Can I have the soup?" I ask.

"Noooo!" Elizabeth yells, "that isn't soup! That's the special sleeping potion I made you. Didn't you hear me? That's not for this game Mommy!"

"Oh right, of course, that's what I meant," I say trying to appease my 3-year old. I am so distracted that I can't even get make-believe right, and she had just about forgiven me for getting her lunch wrong. I could have sworn she asked for grilled cheese in the car, but I must not have been listening and apparently she said ham and cheese. I shouldn't be at the mercy of a toddler, but if I'm not going to bother to listen to her, than why ask her in the first place. She's also used to super-mommy, so apparently she isn't sure what to do with spacey-mommy.

My doubles partner Heather wasn't sure what to do with me this morning either. I was sure tennis would be exactly what I needed to clear my head, but I was a total mess and that *never* happens. I'm always the one everyone depends on, but this morning, I could barely keep track of the score, and I missed shots that I haven't missed in years. I told everyone I was coming down with something, but really I couldn't stop thinking about last night.

Charlie and I finally had sex. And Gretchen was right about Charlie – as soon as I suggested it, he was thrilled and really into it. But every time I closed my eyes, I kept picturing Chris. It was weird at first, but then it was exciting and I just kept my eyes closed and went with it. Afterward, Charlie even commented on how amazing it was and he seemed really proud of himself, but I felt confused and a little guilty.

And now I'm even more conflicted about seeing Chris tonight. I know I should probably text him and cancel. I already had to text him yesterday and change it from dinner to drinks and tell him that I probably only have time for one drink. Actually it doesn't make sense for me to go at all; but I know I won't cancel, especially after last night. All I can think about is seeing him again. I keep thinking about touching him last week and the text message he sent and wondering if he dates a lot of women now that he's single.

"Mommy! I asked if you'd like more tea!" Elizabeth yells at me.

I have to stop daydreaming and be in the moment with my daughter, I'm going to do it. "Sorry Lizzy, Mommy's ready. I would love more tea. This is delicious! Should we see if the bears want to join us?"

"Yes! Let's get them," and with my renewed enthusiasm, she grabs my hand so we can go upstairs and look for teddy bears.

***

It's just like last week, I am back on the train on the way to see Chris and Charlie is in Chicago. I'm pretending that tonight is the most convenient night for me to go out, but a big part of that convenience is that Charlie is in Chicago and I have a babysitter that I don't owe any explanations.

I am dressed a little less casually this week. I'm wearing a turquoise and black print Diane von Furstenberg silk wrap dress and black LK Bennett 4-inch heels. Chris picked a bar right across the street from Grand Central, so I know I don't have very far to walk.

I walk in to the bar and see the back of Chris's head. He is sitting at the bar and there is an open seat next to him, just like last week. But this time he's talking to a woman. Oh my god, that's Jennifer. I feel a burning lump forming in my stomach. I'm so stupid. What am I doing here – I've been thinking about this for a week and changed my outfit six times and I've gotten it all wrong – not to mention, I'm married, so what the fuck am I thinking anyway. Ugh, I feel ridiculous.

Maybe I should just leave, text him from outside the bar and tell him I couldn't make it?

"Liv! We're over here!" Jennifer yells to me, as I am trying to slowly back out of the bar.

"Oh, there you are," I say as I walk over, pretending that I was having trouble finding them.

"What a great surprise!" I say, giving Jennifer a kiss on the cheek.

"Hi Chris," I say, offering my hand for him to shake. He looks confused, but takes my hand and shakes it.

"Good to see you Olivia," he says formally.

I'm just a little over-dressed - this is a business meeting, I can do this, I just need a minute to regroup.

"Jennifer and I were meeting with clients right before this on Park and 46th and then she insisted on joining me for a drink," Chris tells me.

"Sorry to disturb your date," Jennifer says laughing," but I didn't get to see you for very long the other night and then when Chris told me he was going to see you tonight, I had to find out what you two were cooking up!"

Chris shoots me a look that seems to say 'I promise, this wasn't my idea.'

"Well that's great," I feign," I didn't know what Chris and I were going to talk about anyway." And all three of us laugh, but Jennifer is the only one who is genuinely laughing.

Three glasses of wine later, I'm no longer upset about Jennifer being there. The evening didn't turn out how I expected, but it was fun to reconnect with both of them and I wasn't wrong about the initial invitation – Chris did invite me for drinks by myself and then Jennifer crashed the party.

"Excuse me, I'm going to run to the ladies room before I have to catch my train, I'll be back in a minute," I tell them as I excuse myself.

I haven't been to this bar before and have to ask for directions to the ladies' room. I'm not as drunk as last week, but I'm not quite as steady on my feet as I was at the beginning of the evening. The bathrooms are down a long dark hallway separated from the main bar by heavy floor-length velvet curtains. When I come out of the bathroom, someone is standing right next to the door, but my eyes are still adjusting from the bright lights inside.

It takes me a minute to see that it's Chris.

"All yours," I joke.

"I thought I would never get you alone," he bends down and whispers into my ear.

Oh my god. Oh my god. I wasn't wrong. I didn't mis-read everything.

"Olivia, you are so beautiful," he continues to whisper into my ear. He is so close now that I can smell his cologne again and the wool of his suit jacket and feel his breath on my neck. He has pressed me up against the wall and has one hand on the brick wall behind me supporting his weight and his other hand is now on my waist, but moving quickly downward.

I almost laugh because this seems like such a cliché. Older divorced boss and suburban housewife in the dark back hallway of a bar. But it doesn't feel trite, and it doesn't feel funny. It feels real. And all I can think about is right this second. Chris moves his mouth from my ear to my cheek and I move my mouth an inch to the left, but it might as well be a mile for what I've started. I meet his lips with mine and now we are kissing.

It is soft at first, but then our mouths open and I taste him and the beer he has been drinking and it's so different than kissing Charlie. There's a sense of urgency and passion in our kissing that I haven't had since I was in high school. I'm worried someone will come back here and see us, but it doesn't bother me enough to stop kissing him.

He pulls away slightly and is now kissing my neck and whispering in my ear, my whole body is on fire feeling his lips on my neck as he says, "you don't know how long I've thought about kissing you, it's even better than I imagined."

I see someone opening the curtain to the hallway and I pull away. He sees what I see and moves back against the wall next to me as if we're both waiting in line.

"We should probably go back before Jennifer starts wondering," I say to Chris, "I'll go first."

"Makes sense," Chris says, giving me a mischievous smile.

I turn around to look at him before I walk back into the bar and I know that I am already in over my head.

Chapter 17 – Laura

I hear their car pulling into the driveway before I can even see it. I take a few deep cleansing breaths and tell myself that they are only here for three days, well really two and a half days, and it won't be that bad.

I hear the car engine die down, although not before the car makes a few knocks and a hissing sound that I can hear from inside the front door. I offered to buy them a new car last Christmas, but that didn't go over well. They are driving a 15-year old Nissan Altima and every few months they pour more money into it, so I thought they would appreciate the offer, but they were offended and said they didn't need my 'charity'.

I open the door and plaster a smile on my face. "Mom, Dad. You made it!" I exclaim, hoping I sound genuinely excited.

"Loo-loo!" my dad yells as he comes toward me with outstretched arms.

"Dad, you know I hate that name. Please don't call me that." I ask him, through gritted teeth.

"Oh Laura, don't make that face, you're so pretty, but not when you do that," my mom says as she comes around from her side of the car.

Oh my god, we are still in the driveway and I already want to kill both of them; how am I possibly going to make it until Sunday?

"Okay, let's get inside and get you settled. Claudia can help with your stuff," I offer.

"Don't be silly," my dad says, "we can get our own bags, we're not royalty," he laughs at his own joke.

"Okay, suit yourself," I say shaking my head, as I walk back inside wondering what I am going to do with them for the day.

"So where are my grandchildren?" my mom asks as we walk into the kitchen, my dad on his way upstairs with the bags.

"It's Friday morning mom. They're at school," I say, trying to keep my voice even-toned.

"Well, where is Cameron?" she challenges me.

"He's in the upstairs playroom with Robin," I tell her.

"I'm on my way to go squeeze those little cheeks," she says as she marches out of the kitchen and up the back staircase.

I look at my watch – 10:37. They have been here for 8 minutes and it feels like 8 hours. I was so good this morning and didn't take anything because I thought I could make it through the day, but clearly that plan isn't going to work. I put 2 Xanax in my front jeans pocket just in case I needed them sometime today, and I guess 10:37 is the magic time.

I put the pills on my tongue and grab my coffee mug to take a sip and wash them down.

"What are you taking?" My dad asks.

I scream and almost drop my mug, "Dad, you scared me half to death."

"Sorry, didn't mean to startle you. So what are those pills? Something wrong?" he asks again.

"Oh, no, nothing's wrong. A headache. Just taking some Tylenol," I tell him, flashing him my best daughter smile, hoping it still works as well as it did when I was 15.

"Oh, um, okay," he says, "So what's the plan for the day?"

"Well, it depends what you want to do? Are you tired from the trip? You could just relax here and then maybe later…"

My dad cuts me off, "Laura, it's a two and a half hour drive. We don't need to rest after the trip. We're just here to see you and Michael and the kids. It's been a long time since we've seen you, and your mom and I are worried about you."

"Worried about *me*?" I say with disbelief.

"You don't want to see us, you always have a reason why we can't come here or you can't come visit us. You haven't seen either of your brothers in over a year. I know your life here is busy, but it can't be *that* busy, so we figure there must be something wrong. What else could it be?"

The guilt is overwhelming. I don't know why I thought they hadn't noticed I was ignoring them. I can't deal with them in Rye because they're an eyesore here, but every time I go visit them at their house it reminds me of what life used to be like and it all feels small and sullied – and I live in fear of running into someone from high school and having to admit we actually have anything in common.

My dad is sitting at the barstool at the counter looking at me with a worried and loving expression. And he is the same man that was there for me from the day I was born, treated me like a princess, and spent every extra penny on gowns and tiaras and voice lessons; and when I look at him all I see is the battered Mets baseball hat that he always wears and I'm so annoyed I just want to take off the damn hat and throw it at him. What the hell is wrong with me??

My mom comes in to the kitchen and her entrance thankfully breaks the tension. She chirps, "good news! I gave Robin the rest of the day off."

"What?" I practically scream.

"Well, why would she need to be here when your father and I are both here? I want to spend some time with the kids, I don't just want to look at them."

"Mom, you don't get to give Robin the day off, that's not for you to decide," I say tight-lipped.

"Well, it's done now. And she seemed quite happy about it," she adds.

"Well of course she's happy. Never mind. Fine. So what are you going to do with your grandchildren now that you have them?" I ask her.

"Well, Robin is getting Cameron ready before she goes, but first we are all going to go to the park. You too Laura."

I open my mouth to protest, but then look over at my dad and decide that it's not worth it. It's a chilly November day, maybe there won't be too many people at the park.

My mom continues, "and then I thought we would pick Logan and Avery and Emma up after school and take them for ice cream."

"Sounds fun mom, but they're busy after school."

"They're children. How are they too busy to see their grandparents on a Friday afternoon?" she asks, dumbfounded.

"Mom, they have activities after school. It's not like when Danny and Tony used to come home from school and watch TV for 6 hours straight. They have things planned every day. Logan has chess club today and Avery and Emma have horseback riding," I explain.

"Well, the world isn't going to end if they miss it for one day," she says with an air of finality.

***

Amazingly, Friday came and went and now it is Saturday morning. At least Michael is here with me so I don't have to face my parents alone for another day. I don't know how he does it, but Michael doesn't seem to be bothered at all by my parents.

"Good morning love," I say as I reach across our bed to stroke Michael's back.

"Morning darling," he says still half asleep. "What time is it?"
"It's only 7, you can still go back to sleep," I tell him, lightly tickling his back.

"How was yesterday with your parents? Did you have a good time?" He asks, his eyes still closed.

"It was okay. A long day. But they're looking forward to seeing you today," I say.

Michael sits up and rubs his eyes. His beautiful hair is matted on one side of his head and sticking straight up on the other. Secretly I like this part of being together in bed the most, it feels more intimate than anything else that happens in here. First thing in the morning, vulnerable and creased from sleep and I'm the only person who gets to see him like this.

"Please don't be upset, but I do have to go in to the office for a few hours this morning, but I promise I'll be back by noon," he says regretfully.

"Oh. That's fine," I say, even though it's definitely not fine.

"Oh my beautiful girl, please don't look so sad. I promise I'll be back by lunch. Or maybe you could bring your parents and the kids into the city and we could have lunch there? They'd love that!" Michael says, already patting himself on the back for his great idea.

"No, we'll just stay here and you come back when you're done. It's fine, really," I say, this time with more conviction. The idea of being a tour guide to my mom and dad in 'The Big Apple' as my dad says, is too much to bear.

Michael hops out of bed to get in the shower and I lay there, thinking about the next 5 hours without him. I hear the water for the shower start to run and I start counting on my fingers, trying to remember the number of pills I took yesterday. I took 2 Xanax in the morning, then 1 more in the afternoon and then either 1 or 2 more before dinner. No wonder yesterday didn't seem so bad. But I can't do that again today. I'm only going to take 1 or 2 today, at most 3 to get through the time with my parents. And then after tomorrow when my parents leave, I'm not taking anything all week. I already feel better having made this pact with myself.

"You look like you're deep in thought," Michael says. He's wrapped in his towel and has a face full of shaving cream.

"Just thinking about an idea I had for today, that's all. Maybe we *could* come meet you for lunch," I say, giving him a big smile.

"Okay great, you can come straight to the office, your parents would probably like that."

"Yes, we'll do that," I say. I'm already revising my promise to myself in my head about how many pills I can take today – it's going to be a tough day to limit myself, but starting tomorrow, I'll be good.

Chapter 18 – Danielle

I've been standing in front of the bathroom mirror staring at myself naked for over twenty minutes and I am convinced I don't look any different. I'm a little worried, but also relieved that I haven't gained any weight yet; I called the doctor yesterday to check and she said that some women don't gain any weight in the first trimester, and I am still only 9 weeks pregnant.

No matter how many different ways I look at myself, I still don't see any changes. My stomach is as hard as it was a few months ago. From all of my reading it says that women who are extremely athletic or muscular may show later because the abdominal walls are so strong. It's certainly made it easier to keep this to myself, but I have to tell Jim this week, I can't believe I have let it get this far.

I put my running clothes on and make my way downstairs to stretch before I head out to run. I think the doctor must think I'm crazy, because I keep calling to double-check that it's really okay that I exercise this much, but she told me that as long as I'm not starting any new type of exercise it is fine to continue my current regime. She did say that once I get to four months I will probably need to cut back and then each successive month will need to continue to cut back in intensity. However, she said I could continue to exercise up until I go into labor as long as I feel okay and everything looks fine at my check-ups.

I am sitting on a yoga mat in the front hall with my nose bent down to my knee when I hear keys in the front door. I glance up at the grandfather clock to check the time – 9:15am. Who could possibly be here at 9:15 on a Tuesday morning? I should be alarmed, but I'm too busy trying to think about the possibilities: the cleaning ladies, the alarm guy, the landscaper, the decorator? Unfortunately there is a long list of people who seem to have keys to the house and in the few months I have lived here, I have not figured everything out.

When the door opens I am shocked to see Megan walk inside, with a large duffle bag in one hand and her iPhone in the other. I've never seen Megan look anything other than perfectly pulled together, she spends hours doing her hair and make-up and looks closer to 18 than 14 even when she is sitting around the house on the weekend playing Angry Birds in her pajamas.

However, today her eyes look red and her face looks puffy, there is mascara smudged around her eyes, and her hair is matted down on one side of her head and the rest is falling out of a loose ponytail. She looks like hell.

"Megan?" I say tentatively, "Are you okay?"

"Oh," she says, taken aback, "I didn't know anyone was here." Megan tries to wipe her eyes to hide her tears, but it only makes it worse.

"Um, just me, but I am going out for a run, so I'll be gone in a minute, at least for a little while," I say apologetically, but also annoyed with myself for acting like this. Why am I sorry for being here? I live here now. And shouldn't she be in school? I have to stop being scared of this kid.

"Right, I guess I kind of forgot you would be here. Sorry." She says quietly. Wow, that might be the nicest or meanest thing she has ever said to me – she did apologize at the end, and that's definitely a first, but she also forgot that I live here.

"Shouldn't you be in school? And how did you even get here?" I ask Megan, trying to steer the conversation back to her.

"I took a cab. And I should be at school, but I had a huge fight with my mom this morning and I just had to get out of there, so I thought I would come here and hang out and be alone. But I guess I'm not alone. Please don't tell my dad," she says awkwardly. I've never seen Megan look this vulnerable. I'm not happy that she's upset, but it's nice to know that there is a human being inside of the devil I've been seeing for the last 18 months.

This moment feels like a critical opportunity in our relationship – I want to choose my words carefully while her guard is down.

"Is there anything I can do?" I offer. "If you want to talk about it, I'd be happy to listen."

Megan just stares at me for over a minute, not saying anything. I brace myself for whatever nasty remark she is going to throw at me, sure that she has remembered her customary bitchy manner.

But instead she says, "Thanks. I don't really want to talk right now, but could I borrow your phone? Mine is dead and I just want to call Kyle and let him know I'm okay."

"Of course," I reply, stunned by her simple request and her concern for her brother, "follow me, it's in the kitchen." I wince after I say this hoping she doesn't think I am giving her directions in the house she was born in and lived in for 12 years; but she doesn't seem to read anything into my comment as she walks with me into the kitchen.

"It's on the counter, and my charger is right next to it if you want to plug yours in," I tell her as I leaf through some papers on the desk, trying to look engrossed in the task while Megan makes her phone call.

"Are you pregnant?" Megan asks accusingly.

"What?" I almost scream, looking at her in utter confusion. And then I see what she is looking at on my phone and all I can think is 'oh shit, oh shit, oh shit!"

"So are you?" Megan asks again, holding up the screen on my phone that has the open Babycenter app with the title 'Your baby at 9 weeks – what to expect in your pregnancy this week.'

I have heard people describe themselves as speechless before, but I always assumed they were exaggerating – now I know what it means to be speechless because I cannot think of a single word to say. My brain is running through all of the possible truths or lies I can tell her, but the words aren't coming to my mouth.

"Oh my God, you are!" she screams. "So that's my half-brother or half-sister in there," she says and points to my stomach. I'm sure I'm imaging it, but she almost sounds excited when she says it.

"Megan, let me explain," I finally manage to say, although even as I'm speaking I'm not sure yet how I'm going to complete my sentence.

"I can help take care of it. I'll come live back here and help you with the baby," Megan says and flashes me a huge smile.

I am so confused by this sudden change in her demeanor and attitude, I don't know where to begin, I also feel like I must be missing something.

Okay, I'll start with something positive. "Wow, I'm so glad you're excited. I know you'll be a great big sister," I tell her.

"I could probably be a big help even before the baby comes, so I should probably move back in soon so I can be ready," Megan says eagerly.

I'm missing a lot of pieces, but some of this is starting to come together. I don't know why she wants to move back here or probably why she wants to move out of Linda's house, but I think she feels like she just found her ticket home.

"I'm sure you would be a huge help, but I think your mom and dad need to make that decision," I tell her calmly.

The sunny expression fades from her face and is replaced by the sour look I'm used to seeing. Megan says bitterly, "my mom doesn't care what I do, and my dad only listens to you now."

I want to tell her she's wrong, but I know she won't hear anything I say, my window of opportunity has closed for now.

***

Megan has been in her room for hours and she left her uncharged phone on the counter, so I'm not sure what she's doing up there.
I called her school and told them she was sick and I texted Kyle and told him that she was here. Megan might hate me later for both of these things, but it felt like the adult thing to do; I'm actually secretly pleased with myself for handling my first step-mother crisis so well. If I weren't facing a complete catastrophe in six hours when Jim comes home, I would be patting myself on the back.

Two years ago when Jim and I were engaged and I was still working at the firm, I would sit at my desk and daydream about this moment. Well, not this exact moment. When I pictured it I imagined all of the different ways that I would tell Jim he was going to be a father again. In one scenario I wrapped up the positive pregnancy test in a box and gave it to him as a present. In another version, I had a sexy fitted t-shirt customized to say 'mommy to be' or something like that, and I was waiting for Jim on our bed wearing just that shirt when he got home from work. There was never a scenario where I had neglected to tell him about the pregnancy for over four weeks and then his teenage daughter found out by mistake and was in the house hiding in her room waiting to confront him as soon as he walked in because she had no way to know that he didn't even know about the baby yet. Nope, amazingly I didn't waste hours of billable time dreaming up this nightmare.

I think a version of the truth, or as close to the truth as possible is my only option. Jim knew I wanted a baby when he met me, and certainly knew that I've been trying to get pregnant since we got married, so this shouldn't be a surprise. I just got a little scared because he seemed less into it recently, but as soon as he realizes it's a reality, I know he'll be excited. I'm hoping if I repeat this pep-talk a dozen times this afternoon, I will convince myself.

***

"Dani, you home?" Jim calls as he walks through the front door.

"I'm in the kitchen," I call out, hoping my voice doesn't sound as panicked as I feel.

Jim walks into the kitchen and gives me a quick kiss on the lips as he starts to de-robe, taking off his tie and jacket and button down in a matter of seconds, and carefully hanging them on the back of a kitchen chair.

"So much better," Jim says as he stands there in his fitted white undershirt and navy pinstriped suit pants and stretches his toned arms toward the ceiling.

"I cut up some cheese and veggies," I say, stating the obvious as I point toward the plate on the counter. I'm stalling because I don't know how to start the conversation, but I'm on borrowed time with Megan upstairs in her room. I charged her phone and brought it

114

up to her about an hour ago, so that should keep her busy, but honestly I have no idea what's going through her head or what she's going to do next – she's like a ticking bomb.

"That looks great. And I know we've been trying not to drink because of our training, but it's been a long week and I think we deserve it. I'm going to open a bottle of wine too," Jim says happily as he makes his way toward the wine fridge.

"Um, no wine for me," I say hesitantly.

"Dani, one glass of wine won't kill you. And you've been really tense lately, I think it will help you relax."

"Well, actually, I can't have any wine for another 7 months," I say, my voice a little steadier now.

Jim is pulling the cork out of the bottle now, with his back to me, as he says, "but the race is in three months, why can't you drink for seven months?" he asks naively.

I hoped he would figure it out from my subtle hint, but it looks like that didn't work.

"Honey, I'm pregnant." I say matter-of-factly, with only a little quiver in my voice. At least it's out there.

Right before I said it, Jim had just taken a big mouthful of wine and now that red wine has come right back out all over the counter. Well, that can't be the best sign.

"What did you say?" Jim asks, dumbfounded.

"You heard me. I'm pregnant. We're going to have a baby," I say as I walk over and put my arms around him. "Remember all that amazing sex we had without using anything because we were trying to have a baby? Well, it worked." I'm sitting on his lap now and playing with the hair on the back of his neck. I should have thought about delivering the news this way earlier.

"Wow," Jim says.

"Well, what did you think was going to happen silly?" I'm kissing Jim's neck as I'm talking, "and I think your little swimmers were just too powerful." I hate myself for sinking to this level, but the flattery angle seems to be going well; I can't believe I waited this long.

"Well, you're right about that," Jim says, clearly aroused and getting into it. This is probably a good time to tell him that Megan is upstairs before we get any further and Megan walks in.

I pull away from him and say, "This may have to wait until tonight, and Megan is actually upstairs. She's been here for a little while and she was upset when she got here, but she didn't tell me why."

"What? Megan's here?" Jim asks.

"Yes, you should probably go talk to her, and then we can continue this later," I say, trying to regain some of the mood from a few minutes earlier, but it doesn't work.

"Okay, I'll go check on her," Jim says in a deflated tone as he stands up and grabs his wine glass, and then he turns to me and says, "by the way, why only seven months? I know it's been a while since I've had kids, but doesn't it take longer than that?"

"I'm actually already 9 weeks pregnant, but I just found out," I tell him with a goofy grin. One little white lie won't hurt.

"Nine weeks? Huh. That's great – you can't tell at all. I think when Linda was 9 weeks pregnant she had already gained 10 pounds, she ate everything that wasn't nailed down. Maybe this won't be so bad after all," Jim says as he turns to go upstairs and find Megan.

Chapter 19 - Gretchen

"She did what?" Olivia screams, as I re-hash the story of Alice and her friends' subterfuge.

Olivia is sitting in my kitchen nursing a cup of coffee as I slice apples for apple pie, boil cranberries for cranberry sauce and cut bread for stuffing. She has asked several times if she can help, but just having her here to keep me company for a couple hours makes the Thanksgiving preparation seem more manageable.

"I know! It's crazy, right?" I say, as I move back and forth between the stove and the cutting boards on the counter.

"What did you do? Did the girl find out? I'm just in shock; I can't believe Alice would do that! Maybe I should home-school Julie and Elizabeth so they are never exposed to the outside world," Olivia groans.

"I'm not sure it would help, there's still the online world," I joke and then see the look on her face. "No honey, I was just kidding. Your girls will be fine. And Alice will be fine too; she just made a bad decision. I mean a really bad decision, but it's going to be okay."

"How did Alan handle it?" Liv asks.

"Actually, Alan was great. I had no idea how he would take it, but he was the one who found the person at match.com who helped shut down Kelly's page and contact the guy. He called someone in the digital section at the paper that he works with and they figured it out pretty quickly."

"Did you talk to the sketchy guy?" she asks.

"I did talk to him. It was so awkward! Alice was dying of embarrassment, but she had to sit right next to Alan and me while we called him. We explained most of the situation and that the girl was under-age by a lot. At that point he had done nothing wrong, because he had been deceived, but if he did anything going forward it would be solicitation of a minor and then I'm not sure that I was right but I told him that it would be statutory rape and he would go to jail if he even touched her. Regardless, once he knew she was 13 he just sounded annoyed. I don't think he was that sketchy of a guy, I think he was just mad that some kids had wasted his time. I'm hoping that it all goes away."

"What about the girl who they used for the site, does she know?" Olivia asks.

"So, that is where it gets tricky. Right now she doesn't know. We called the two other girls' parents who did the profile with Alice, and of course Alice was really mad about that, because they both got in trouble and now they are mad at her. But one of them knew something was wrong anyway because she was dumb enough to use her mom's credit card for the match.com subscription! Alice begged and pleaded with us not to tell Kelly's mom though – the girl in the page – so for now we didn't. I was going to call the police, but once Alan was able to shut it all down and we got in touch with the guy, I didn't think we needed to do that."

"So what's her punishment?"

"She is grounded for 2 weeks. She can go to school and to field hockey, but that's it. She can have her phone for emergency purposes, but when she gets home from school she has to give it to me. I still can't believe she did it, but at least she told me before anything really bad happened, those other two girls were just going to sit back and let this man come over to Kelly's house and who knows what would have happened – I'm still proud of her for that," I say and glance up at the clock to see how much of the morning has already gotten away from me.

"You couldn't pay me enough money to be 13 again," Liv says as she looks down at her phone for the fifteenth time since she's been here.

"Are you waiting for a message?" I ask her.

"No, no. Just out of habit," she says and pushes the phone away, but it definitely looks like she is expecting to hear from someone.
"So when do you leave for Westport? Are you just going for the day or will you be staying over?" I ask, while starting to level cups of flour into a bowl to start making my pie crusts.

"Oh, we had a change of plans last week. We aren't going to Charlie's brother's house for Thanksgiving. Charlie had a client who wasn't using his house in Stowe, so we are all going there instead," Olivia says.

"Wow. All of you? How big is the house?"

"I guess it's pretty big. There will be…" Liv pauses to count on her fingers, "8 adults and 7 children and this guy swears there will be plenty of room. It's Charlie's brother and sister and their families and then his parents. It should be fun," Liv sighs.

"You don't sound very excited. Maybe I should go instead of you and you can stay here and cook for 25 people that don't fit in your house," I tell her, although I am only half joking. I love Thanksgiving, but each year it feels like more and more work and the guest list grows by one or two, but our house doesn't get any bigger.

"No, I am excited. Maybe it will be good to get away for a few days."

"Is everything okay? Are you and Charlie fine now?" I ask, trying to pay attention to what she says.

"Yeah, everything's good," Liv says brushing over the topic, "So how many bottles of wine, or cases probably, do you think I need to bring? That is the only thing I was assigned for the weekend. This may be the easiest holiday ever. Oh sorry, not trying to gloat. There will be payback at Christmas, I'm sure."

"It's better to have too much, right? So 8 adults and what, 4 days? I think that's at least a couple of cases of wine. Which reminds me, I think I probably need more wine too. Oh and kind of related to that. Did you think Laura seemed kind of 'off' on Monday?" I ask.

"What do you mean, 'off'?" Liv questions, and I notice that she has pulled her phone out of her bag again and has put it on her lap.

"You were at that meeting for the winter carnival, right?" I ask.

"Yes."

"Well, didn't she seem funny to you?" I prod.

"Funny, how?"

I was hoping that Olivia noticed it too, so it would seem less gossipy if I said anything, but this doesn't seem to be going anywhere. "I don't know, she seemed pretty out of it to me. Like almost drunk. And it was 10 o'clock in the morning. But maybe it was just me, or maybe she was really tired," I'm back-pedaling a little bit since Liv is looking at me like I'm crazy.

"You know I love Laura, but I've never been as close to her as you have. I always think she acts a little funny," she says, trying to make a joke.

"Okay, maybe it was nothing. Maybe she's coming down with something or she's just really stressed about the holidays. We all have our bad days. If you didn't notice anything, then it was probably nothing. I'm glad I asked you," I say, somewhat relieved that this is not another problem I need to manage.

"What were you going to do anyway? Confront her? Have an intervention? I would love to be a fly on the wall for that!" Liv is giggling so much now she looks like she might fall off her chair.

"I honestly didn't know what I was going to do, so now I don't have to worry about it. I can just worry about my own problems, like how I'm going to get all of this done by tomorrow," I sigh.

Chapter 20 – Olivia

I'm officially a wreck.

It has been two weeks since the night I kissed Chris, and it is all I think about. I do have moments where I go about my normal day and don't think about him, but then 'boom' there it is. I'm driving the girls to ballet and out of nowhere I flashback to his hand on the small of my back and I'll think about what it would feel like if it slipped down a little lower. Or I'll be folding laundry and suddenly remember how his breath felt on my neck and how it felt to be pressed up against him, with the full weight of his body pushing me against the wall.

But, by far the worst is that every time Charlie and I have sex all I can picture is having sex with Chris. I feel so guilty about kissing Chris that Charlie and I have had sex almost every other day for the past two weeks, but then I feel even guiltier afterword because I imagine Chris the entire time and that makes the sex even better. And of course Charlie has no idea what's going on, so he just thinks our sex life has taken a miraculous uphill turn.

I wanted to tell Gretchen about it this morning, but I don't want her to judge me. Although, I think the real reason I didn't tell her is that I'm not done with whatever this is yet. I haven't seen him again since that night because he has been in Los Angeles for work and then he has had his kids with him this past week while his ex-wife is away somewhere.

I didn't know what to expect after that night – if I would hear from Chris again, if I should call him, or text him, or

pretend it didn't happen? But the next morning I got a text from him in the morning that said:
"can't stop thinking about you. Impossible to get work done." And since then we have been texting like teenagers. We have only talked twice on the phone, but I text him throughout the day. I've had to start keeping my phone in my pocket even when I'm at home because I don't want to risk Charlie seeing one of the messages pop up.

Chris understands me so much better than anyone else in my life right now. He gets how much I miss working, but that I need to be home right now. I don't think Charlie even remembers that I used to be a valuable member of society.

I don't know how I'm going to make it through the next three and a half days. Charlie told me last night that he doesn't think there is any cell service at the house, since it is so far up in the mountains.

I finished packing when I got home from Gretchen's and now Charlie will be home soon from work so we can leave to drive up to Stowe. I argued that traffic on the Wednesday night before Thanksgiving would be bad, but he pointed out that if we didn't leave until tomorrow morning we would miss half of the actual holiday and that his brother and sister both arrived this morning, even though it is *his* client that got us the house.

Even to my ears the protest sounded feeble, so I had to give in. He looked so excited last night at the prospect of spending three days with his family and taking a break from work. God, I'm such a bitch! Maybe it will be good to go away and have no cell service. Maybe if I don't talk to or text Chris for a few days it will be good for me and I'll stop thinking about him.

***

I should win an Oscar for my best actress performance.
I don't know how I made it through the last three and a half days, but I did, and I did it with flair.
I was the perfect wife, mother, aunt, sister-in-law, and daughter-in-law. Not that I'm normally a difficult person, but guilt is a powerful motivator.
But now it's Sunday night and Charlie has gone to bed early, tired from the long weekend, and I am finally alone with my phone.

I sneak down to the basement, ostensibly so I don't wake anyone, and sit on a beanbag with my back against the wall, facing the stairs so I can see if anyone is coming, and I dial.

"Hey sexy," Chris answers on the first ring.

I exhale when I hear his voice and I sink deeper into the chair. "Hey there," I say, unable to think of anything better.

"So, how was your trip? Did you have a good time?" he asks.

I hesitate before I answer knowing that I can go for conversational or flirty, I opt for the latter, "it was good, but I couldn't stop thinking about you."

"Oh really. Well, I too have been spending a lot of time thinking about you. Do you think you can get away in the next few days? I'm in town all week."

I'm mentally going through my schedule for the week, "I think so. I could probably do Thursday night, is that okay?" I ask Chris.

"Sure, I can make Thursday work. There's this great Jazz club in the village that we could go to, how does that sound?"

"That sounds like fun," I say. Thinking how much cooler it sounds than any of the things I would normally do with Charlie or my girlfriends. I don't usually like Jazz music, but I bet it's because I haven't had the right experience.

We talk for a few more minutes about what's going on at the firm and I tell him some funny stories from the weekend about my nieces and nephews and my in-laws. I manage not to mention Charlie in any of my anecdotes, which takes a bit of editing; this should be a huge sign that what I'm doing is wrong, as if I needed another sign, but I'm not listening to reason right now.

"Okay, it's getting late, I should probably go to bed," I say.

"If you must," Chris says.

"Remember, I have to get ready for an exciting day of running all over the place, but never really *doing* anything," I joke.

Chris's tone gets very serious, "hey, don't say that. What you do is incredibly important. You are shaping lives every day. You are building people. I'm just trying to help companies twist their words around to confuse consumers and make a few extra dollars, that's nowhere near as important and it's definitely not as difficult."

"Thank you," I whisper.

"You're welcome," he says, and I can tell he has a big smile on his face. "Now go get some sleep, you have a big day tomorrow."

"Good night," I say.

"Good night," Chris says.

I walk back up to bed as if I am floating. I know it isn't quite the same as talking to Gretchen or one of my other girlfriends, but Chris is just a friend, he makes me feel good, and that is what I need right now. Maybe the kiss was just a one-time thing and the talking and texting is more important and that's really just a friendship, which isn't such a big deal, right?

Chapter 21 – Laura

"Mommy, get up. Mommy, get up. It's time to get up. That beeping has been going off forever, come one, get up!" Logan is yelling at me and shaking my shoulder and I am trying to open my eyes, but they feel like they are glued shut. I am trying to answer him so he'll stop shaking me, but I can't make my lips move.

Finally, I am able to raise my eyelids and when he sees my eyes he stops shaking me, but he doesn't stop yelling.

"Mommy, get up! You have to make that beeping stop! And remember you have to take me to the dentist this morning. Remember!"

How can someone be this excited about the dentist?

I find the ability to speak, but my voice comes out thick and gravelly. "What time is it?"

"It's 8:15."

Oh shit. "Where is Jody? Where are your sisters? Where is Cameron?"

"Jody is getting everyone in the car for school. It's just you and me," Logan says happily.

I try sitting up and feel a little bit better. I set my alarm for 7, I can't believe it has been going off for over an hour and I slept through it. I had trouble falling asleep, so I took an Ambien in the middle of the night, but it doesn't normally effect me like this. Oh well, maybe I'm just more sensitive than I used to be to medication.

"Okay love, give mommy a couple of minutes to get ready and then we'll leave, okay?"

"Okay. Can I watch TV while I wait?" he asks.

Usually I would not let him watch TV, especially not on a school morning, but I'm too tired to argue or find something else more constructive for him to do.
"You can watch TV, but just until I'm ready and then it goes off," I say.

Logan looks at me with shock. Clearly he wasn't expecting me to say yes. "Wow, thanks mom!" he yells as he runs over and gives me a huge hug.

I examine myself in the bathroom mirror and see that luckily I don't look anything like I feel, even my hair looks relatively good. I do take excellent care of myself and there are some areas where I get assistance from my dermatologist, but the rest is just luck. I look at some of the other moms from school that try so hard and spend hundreds of dollars each week on blowouts and gym memberships and makeup and they are 'put-together', but they will never be beautiful – that must suck.

I spray in some dry shampoo and run my fingers through my long buttery blonde hair and then sweep it into a ponytail. I put on tinted moisturizer, lip gloss and mascara to highlight my bright green eyes and in three minutes I look better than most 35-year old women look after a 2-hour makeover.

I throw on a pair of Lululemon running tights and a matching top so I can go to the gym after Logan's appointment and yell to Logan that I am ready to go. He looks a little disappointed that I am ready so quickly, but he's also excited for the dentist, so he hops off my bed and runs downstairs. I still marvel at children's ability to take pleasure in such little things; I wish that didn't have to end once you got older.

***

Logan is sitting in the dentist's chair and I pull out the folder with the papers from the winter carnival meeting so I can look over them while I wait.

What is this? This is my handwriting, but I can't even read what it says. It starts out okay, but then it's just gibberish:

Winter Carnival Mtg

- Sharon to call company
- Games coming
- Kids 2300000
- Peter is what on the Friday
- Drive the list to table
- Ask Sam many walk too pick up
- Many up paper horse

And it just continues on like that, by the end of the page, I can't even read the words.

I'm trying to think back to that meeting. It was the Monday before Thanksgiving, I remember that much. I was really stressed that Morning because I was trying to plan for the trip to Boston and then I got an email from Michael's secretary that the flight times had changed for the Turks and Caicos flights, but I don't know why that would matter. Unless... I did take a couple pills as I was leaving the house before the meeting, just to help me relax, so I wouldn't be so wound up, but I don't think I took any more than usual. But looking at this, something must have been wrong, since I couldn't even take notes.

Maybe I was just really tired and nodded off during the meeting, which used to happen sometimes in college when I had been up really late the night before. I hope no one else noticed, that would be really embarrassing. I bet no one saw anything. Everyone is always so wrapped up in their own business anyway. I'll just have to call Sharon and see if she can tell me what I'm supposed to do – she'll feel even more important than usual.

Chapter 22 – Danielle

"Danielle, is that you?" I hear, as I am lying on a mat at the gym with my knees pressed to my chest and my butt in the air.

I unfold myself and sit up so I can see who is speaking. I look over and see Laura a few mats away doing reverse crunches. She is wearing a sports bra and running tights and covered with sweat and looks like she should be one of the models on the Equinox posters they have outside; I should take a closer look when I leave, maybe she *is* one of the models. I have always been very proud of my body, but I hope I still look as good as Laura after I have one baby, let alone four!

"Hi Laura," I say, "I didn't know you came here."

"I don't usually come here, we have a gym at the house, but sometimes I like to take classes or just have a change of scenery. "

"I actually just joined. I usually run and bike outside, but Jim has signed us up for this triathlon, so I need somewhere to bike and swim, especially now that it's getter colder." I'm still not sure what I'm going to do about the race. I told Jim I could do it, I would just have to go a little slower, but I haven't asked my doctor yet.

"Jim must love that you are into all of this, quite the change for him," Laura says.

"Yeah, it's fun to do it together, but he's always been into it, I don't think that's a big change," I say, a little confused.

"No, I just meant...never mind."

"Tell me, what did you mean?" I prod.

"I just meant that Linda wasn't really into it. Anyway, do you want to go get a smoothie or something? Now that we're just sitting here talking, we might as well go over to the juice bar," she laughs.

"Sure, that would be great!" I say, as I do one final stretch and then get up to walk with Laura over to the juice and food area.

I feel healthy just being in this gym; the sound of the whirring machines, the high-energy music, and the indescribable smell of cleaning spray mixed with sweat. The juice bar is light wood, combined with chrome and glass – I think it looks like a high-end Ikea, but I know that Laura could tell me the fancy designer who designed it, and it definitely isn't Ikea.

Laura and I each order a green smoothie from the ridiculously hot guy at the bar, who was probably hired to lure middle-age women into buying over-priced and over-hyped juice drinks and I'm sure he does a great job of it.

Hot guy looks at Laura for a few seconds longer than necessary while she is paying for her drink and I wonder what it must be like to be her, gorgeous and lusted after with a fairy-tale life.

"So did you know Linda well?" I ask Laura, as we sit down at a table, hoping I'm not being too forward.

"I didn't really. Her kids are a lot older than mine. Michael and Jim had some mutual work friends, and they play golf together, so I saw her at dinners and other social events over the years, but really I never knew her that well."

"Oh, okay. Sorry if it's weird that I asked," I say.

"No, not at all. I think it is natural to be curious. But Jim seems so much happier with you, so I don't think you need to spend much time thinking about her," Laura says cheerfully.

I give her a big smile, and take a drink of my less-than-delicious smoothie, not really sure how to respond.

We sit quietly for a moment and then I say, "can I ask you a question about Gretchen?"
She looks at me quizzically, clearly not expecting that question, and answers tentatively, "sure, what is it?"

"Well, it isn't really a question about Gretchen, as much as a question about her daughter, I think her name is Alice."

"Okay," Laura says, but I can tell she isn't very comfortable and I'm almost regretting bringing it up, but I don't know who else to ask.

"So Megan moved in with us, or I guess I should say she moved home, I don't really know what to say, but she's been living with us for about a week now."

"Wow, that must be…" and she pauses, not sure how to complete her thought, "um, that must be different than how you imagined it would be," she finishes.

"Honestly, I still don't know what to think. It's definitely not what I expected when Jim and I got engaged or when we got married and I moved here; but Megan has really hated me since she met me and now she is having a horrible time with her mother and with some of the girls at her new school. So she begged Jim to let her move back here, and now she is so happy to be here, I mean home, that she is being really nice to me and just nice in general, so again I'm not really sure what to think," I stop and take a big sip of my drink to stop myself from talking because I can hear the babbling in my head, but I can't shut up.

"So what does that have to do with Gretchen or Alice?" Laura asks, trying to rein me in, probably bored with our conversation already.

"Well, Megan and Alice are in school together. Megan is in 9th grade and Alice is in 8th grade. I think they are in separate buildings or something, but it's all part of the same school. Anyway, Megan has never really confided in me before, but she came home a few days ago from school and told me something disturbing about Alice. I'm not a mom and I don't really have a relationship with Megan yet, so I don't know what to do, but that's why I'm asking you," I'm almost out of breath by the time I finish rambling.

"Okay, so what did Megan say about her?" Laura asks.

"This is going to sound crazy, but Megan said she heard that Alice and her friends are using some online dating site to meet older men, and then they are planning to meet them in person. I don't know much about it, but it can't be good, right?"

"Okay, slow down. That sounds a little ridiculous, doesn't it? I've known Alice since she was in kindergarten and I can't believe she would do anything like that. Also, the whole thing just sounds absurd. Those girls are in 8th grade, there's no way they are actually parading themselves online to gross old men – these girls might be interested in cute older boys, but that would be like 15-year old boys, not the kind of pedophiles who would be looking at them on there, the whole thing doesn't make any sense. I think Megan either heard the story wrong or maybe she even made it up."

Laura sounds so adamant and confident, that I wish I had never brought it up. This is actually the most energized I've ever seen her, usually she looks like she's in a bit of a daze, but today she seems like she's on fast-forward. I thought she would slow down once we stopped working out, but she's moving just as fast, if not faster.

"You're right, now that I say it out loud, it does sound extreme. I'm glad I checked with you before saying anything to Gretchen. I don't think Megan would make it up, but maybe she got the story wrong or it was just a rumor – you know how bad gossip can be at that age," I say.

"Yes, I definitely wouldn't bother Gretchen with it. You'll understand when you're a mom," Laura says, and flashes me a magnificent, yet condescending, smile.

I almost tell her that I am going to be a mom soon, because the secret is killing me, especially now that Jim and my parents and Megan know, but I'm still only 11 weeks and I'm not even showing a little bit yet.

"I'm curious, if Megan moved back in, did Kyle move home, or is he still with Linda?" Laura asks.

"Oh. We're still figuring that out. It all happened so quickly with Megan. Kyle isn't very happy with his mom; I think a lot of it has to do with her new boyfriend. The kids liked him at first, but now they say he's become judgmental and overbearing. Also, Linda and this guy have been traveling a lot recently and leaving the boyfriend's mom to watch over them – and neither of the kids like her. But, Kyle loves the school in Greenwich; he loves his friends there and I guess he just made the football team and has already made the basketball team for winter. So, he doesn't know what to do. He is still in Greenwich, but I'm guessing he will be back here soon. Definitely not what I thought was going to happen; but for better or worse, right?" I say and try to laugh.

"Well, trial by fire, right?" Laura says and looks at her watch, "oh, I have to go. It was good to get a chance to talk to you. Hopefully I'll see you soon!" And with that, she jumps up from the table and is gone, leaving me alone with two-thirds of uninviting green smoothie left in my cup.

Chapter 23 – Gretchen

I don't really have time for wine club tonight. I should be home making another batch of cookies or wrapping presents, or shopping for more presents, or decorating the house for the party on Saturday night; but, this is the last club of the year and I really need to get out of the house for a few hours.

I have to check the address on my phone before I start the car because I only go to Stephanie's house a couple of times a year and I can never remember if she lives on Pine or Wilton. I enter the address in my GPS and back out of my driveway.

Alan got home just as I was leaving tonight, but there shouldn't be much for him to worry about. Ethan and Natalie are both in pajamas and ready for stories. I'm sure he will get them all riled up before he actually puts them to bed, but as long as they are asleep before I get home, I don't really care what he does. And Alice was in her room with her door closed, busy on her computer; but she showed me her homework and everything was done, so I guess I can't complain. I knocked on her door before I left to tell her I was leaving, but all I got was a "bye Mom." It sounded like she was on the phone, and now that she is no longer grounded; she is allowed to be on the phone until 9. It seems that she is back to being on good terms with all of her friends, but I'm not sure if she would tell me if she wasn't.

I pull into Stephanie's driveway and take a moment to admire how beautiful the house looks with the classic white Christmas lights outlining the frame of the magnificent house and wrapped around all of the bushes on the vast property.   Stephanie's house is not as large or intimidating as Laura's, but it has always been one of my favorite homes in Rye. It is a Georgian Colonial that she restored a few years ago when she and her husband bought the house. I think it is about 7,000 square feet, which is more than twice the size of my house, but I don't feel overwhelmed when I come here the way I do at Laura's house, or even at Danielle's.

I ring the doorbell and Stephanie answers the door, wearing a long black velvet skirt and a black silk blouse, both of them in beautiful fabrics, and tastefully covering her ample body. That is one of the other things I love about Stephanie, she is one of the few women in Rye who wears anything bigger than a size 6, and seems very comfortable with that fact.

"Hi Gretchen! Happy Holidays! Come in!" Stephanie says, pulling me into a big hug as I walk into the foyer.

"Everything looks beautiful," I say, looking around at the decorations in her house that look as if they have been pulled straight from a catalog. I'm a little jealous, but Stephanie's house always looks like this, and it always takes me a few minutes to get over it and accept that my house will forever have that 'lived-in' look.

"There are only a few people here so far, I think everyone is on holiday time," she laughs, "but they're in the living room, if you want to go get a drink."

I walk in to the living room looking for Laura or Olivia as I always do, but don't see either of them yet. I pour myself a glass of pink fizzy punch from the beautiful crystal punch bowl and take a seat on the couch; I like that Stephanie took some liberties with the drinks tonight and added a holiday punch to our normal wine selection.

I should probably be more social and go talk to one of the other women that is here instead of waiting for my close friends to show up. It's silly that I come here once a month and then talk to the same people I see almost every day. Just as I am about to get up and make my way over to the group by the fireplace, someone sits down on the couch next to me.

"Hi Gretchen! Happy holidays! It's been a while," says Kristen.

"Hi Kristen! Good to see you!" I say, and I mean it. I actually can't remember the last time I saw her, but we always enjoy talking to each other. The problem is that it's so long between conversations that usually I can't remember much about her - like how many kids she has, where she works, or her husband's name – let's see how this goes.

"So how's life?" Kristen asks. She's being vague too, it seems she may not remember much either, so now I don't feel quite as bad.

"Everything is okay. This time of year is so busy. I love the holidays, but it never seems like there's enough time to get it all done. And the kids are done with school tomorrow until after the New Year! I'm not sure what I'm going to do with them for the next two weeks. What about you? How's work?" I take a gamble asking this question. I'm fairly certain Kristen was returning to work after maternity leave the last time I saw her, but there's a chance I'm not remembering correctly.

"It's going well, but you know how it is. I don't feel like I see the boys or Jon enough, but when I am with them I feel like I should be getting something done for work." Kristen raises her glass to mine in a toast, "to working mothers everywhere!"

Now I remember why I enjoy talking to Kristen! I love Laura and Olivia, but they don't understand what it's like to "need" to work. Sometimes I believe Laura thinks money actually does grow on trees; I wonder what it would be like to look at your bank account and see that many zero's, or more likely to never have to even *look* at your bank account.

"What are you ladies talking about?" Laura sighs, as she practically sinks into the cushion next to Kristen. Laura is wearing black leather pants and 4-inch black heels with telltale red soles and a fitted red cashmere tank top that is probably made by some designer so exclusive I have never even heard of it. On anyone else the ensemble might look trashy, but on her it looks incredible; if I didn't know that underneath it all she is a great person, I would likely hate her.

"We were talking about the plight of the working mother," Kristen jokes.

"Ah, yes. It must be soo hard for you," Laura says. But there is something about her tone that sounds condescending and off kilter.

I try to ignore Laura's remark and address my comment to Kristen, "What time do you usually get home at night?" I ask.

"It depends on the night, it can be a real challenge..." Kristen starts to say and then Laura cuts her off.

"Wah, wah. Stop complaining," Laura says.
I look at her, shocked. I thought she was being funny, but now I see that she's serious.

Laura continues, "It's always something. Too much work to do, or your husband doesn't do enough, or your kids are driving you crazy," Laura is starting to slur her words now and I can't believe I didn't notice before how drunk she is.

"Laura I think that's enough," I say, seething with anger.

"I know where I'm not wanted," Laura says, as she gets up, she trips and falls flat on her face, she doesn't even have the capacity to put her hands out in front of her to break her fall.

"Laura! Laura, are you okay?" I call to her.

Kristen bends down and grabs her shoulder and says, "Laura? Laura?" To me she says, "Gretchen, she's not answering, I think she passed out."

Within a minute, all twelve of us are gathered around Laura, who is still passed out on the floor. I can hear the following comments in whispers around me:
"Should we call someone?"
"Was she that drunk?"

"What happened?"
"What are we supposed to do?"
"Did she hit her head?"

Laura makes a little moan and moves her head, and I exhale a breath I didn't realize I had been holding. I'm still furious at the comments she made earlier, but I couldn't imagine if something happened to her.

"Can someone help me get her in my car? I'll call Michael and tell him I'm bringing her home," I say to the group.

"I'll help," Stephanie says.

I can't tell if Laura has passed out again on the ride home, or if she is just staring out the window, but we don't exchange any words the whole ride home. I hope there is a simple explanation for what happened tonight, but I'm not optimistic.

"How are you feeling?" Michael says.

"Ugh," I groan.

"That good, huh?" he says.

I haven't opened my eyes, but I can tell from how he smells that he is showered and shaved, and I can smell the faint smell of lavender that his shirts have from the cleaners and the wool of his suit jacket, God he looks so good in a suit.

I roll over and wrap my arms around his waist and bury my head in his lap, so I don't have to look at him.

He combs his fingers through my hair, and says quietly, "so what happened last night?"

"I'm not sure," this isn't really a lie, since I honestly can't remember much of what happened last night.

"Gretchen says you passed out at wine club, about half an hour after you got there."

Michael didn't ask a question, but I can tell there were twenty questions embedded in that one statement.

"I had a glass of wine here while I was getting ready and then I had a couple drinks right when I got there, but I hadn't eaten all day. I was running around doing last minute shopping and just didn't have time. I was so busy I didn't even feel hungry and I thought I would eat at wine club, but I guess I never got that far," I give him my best pout and hope that it works.

"Well, you really had me worried; and all of your friends. I think one of your friends dropped your car off last night so you don't have to worry about that. You should get some rest today, and you need to eat something," he lightly pats my bottom as he gets up from the bed and continues to tie his tie.

"I promise I will. I know it was stupid," I say, and I mean it.

I roll over and close my eyes. Already looking forward to going back to sleep for the next few hours, hoping this pounding headache will go away.

As I start to drift off to sleep, an image from last night pops into my head, but I can't quite grasp it. I have a pit in my stomach as I float off into a dreamless sleep.

Chapter 25 – Olivia

I am sitting on the metro-north train once again, heading into Manhattan to meet Chris. I am trying to get Charlie out of my head, but he won't budge. I actually try rubbing my eyes to see if that will erase the image of him waving to me from our front door as I left tonight, but he's stuck there.

I told him I was meeting Chris for a drink tonight. Because Charlie was out of town the last couple of times I saw Chris, he didn't think there was anything unusual about it – and of course he doesn't know that we have been talking and texting for the last month or so. Charlie seemed exceptionally happy that I was going out for the night. When I was leaving, he said, "I'm so glad you're getting a chance to meet up with Chris. You can see what's happening at the office, not think about the girls for the night, and just relax. You deserve a night out!" He either knows what is going on and is playing mind games with me, or he doesn't have a clue – I'm guessing the latter.

As the train speeds along through the privileged suburbs of New York City, lit up with twinkling Christmas lights, I reflect more on Charlie's comment and it doesn't seem quite as thoughtful. Why should I only enjoy one night out without the children? What does he mean, 'I deserve it'? I used to have a life full of grown up conversations that did not involve debates about which gymnastics classes had the best teacher to student ratio or which sippy cups didn't leak, or the best way to potty train. And now I am supposed to be happy with a couple of drinks and a few hours talking about marketing?

As my train pulls in to Grand Central, I am like a bull being held behind that gate waiting for the fight. I am sitting on the edge of my seat, clutching my bag on my lap, ready to pounce when the doors open. I keep playing Charlie's words over and over in my head and each time I ascribe new meaning to them. I don't usually feel the 'need' for alcohol that people describe, but right now I think I understand what people mean when they say they 'need a drink.'

The train finally makes its last thrust, jostling the standing passengers, and then it comes to a stop. I practically fly out of my seat and down the platform into the cold night air of 42nd St. to hail a cab to the lower east side. I looked at the address and there might be a subway that gets me there faster, especially in Manhattan holiday traffic a few days before Christmas; but, the last time I was near this part of town was in business school going to dive bars, and I'm sure I'll get lost if I try to navigate the ultra-hip neighborhood now.

The taxi pulls up right in front of the jazz club where I am supposed to meet Chris. I open the door and pull back the purple velvet curtain and it takes my eyes a minute to adjust to the dimly lit, smoke-filled room. It seems the city-wide smoking ban, passed many years ago, does not apply to this establishment. I see Chris sitting at a table in the corner near the back and I make my way through the club, whispering apologies as I bump into people along the way.

"Is this seat taken?" I bend down and whisper into Chris's ear, and then immediately regret saying such a cheesy line.

He looks up at me and smiles, "it is now." Well, one cheesy line for another, maybe he was trying to make me feel better.

I sit down and notice that there are two drinks on the table. "Did you order for me?"

"I did, I hope you don't mind. The waitress took forever, so I figured when she finally got here I would get you one too. Dirty martini, right?" He says and winks.

"That's perfect, thanks! It's exactly what I need tonight, but I do need to remember to order something to eat this time," I say.

"I'll flag her down the next time I see her," Chris whispers.

I take a long sip of my drink and try to relax as I turn to face the jazz band. It looks like it will be a lot of whispering tonight or maybe we won't talk much at all and we'll just listen to the music, that would definitely be a nice change of pace from my normal evenings.

Chris leans over and whispers, "Do you like Jazz? I guess I should have asked you that before."

I lean back and whisper, "I don't listen to much, but I do like it. This is good," and he gives me a look that says he doesn't believe me, "no really, I mean it," I say and lightly touch his arm to show him I'm serious.

"Well, even If you're lying, I'm glad you came," he whispers, but as he leans back toward his side of the table he leaves his hand resting on my leg.

Chris is facing the stage, but his hand is resting halfway up my thigh and he is lightly moving his thumb in circles. From the look on his face, he is intently focused on the jazz band; but from the way he is making me feel, his hand might as well be directly in between my legs. I have to cross and re-cross my legs to try and deal with how aroused I am, but neither one of us can look at the other. Chris also maintains a firm grasp on my leg, so I couldn't move away without making a scene – although I would only want to move if it were to result in his fingers moving further up my thigh.

His hand is still 4 inches from being completely inappropriate, and no one at the tables around us has noticed anything going on, but both Chris and I know that isn't true.

The band finishes their first set and the lights in the club get a little brighter. Nothing *actually* happened, but I look down into my drink when Chris tries to make eye contact.

"So did you like it?" Chris asks.

It takes me a second, but I realize that of course he is talking about the music and not the other thing that just happened, maybe it wasn't even a thing one could ask about. "Oh, yes. It was great. I think I should listen to more jazz at home."

"Do you want to stay for the next set?" he asks.

"Actually, I don't think I do, if that's okay." Suddenly I'm ready to go home.

We get our coats and make our way onto the sidewalk. It's only 10pm and for most of the city, the night is just starting, especially in this part of town.

"Do you want to get something to eat?" Chris asks.

"No, I don't think so. I have so much to do tomorrow, with only three days until Christmas, it just gets so crazy," I know that I am making excuses, but I can't help it, I'm so confused and nervous that I need to get away from here.

"Sure," Chris says, "but next time, let's plan something where we have more time." And then he bends down and kisses me firmly on the mouth.

"Okay, next time," I say anxiously. I'm not sure what I have just promised, but I know there will be a next time.

Chapter 26 – Danielle

"So, was that my present?" Jim murmurs, as he rolls off of me and back to his side of the bed. "That's definitely the best way I've ever started Christmas morning. So much better than getting up early and the madness of stockings and Santa, I'm so glad the kids are past that now."

It's only a second before he realizes what he has said, but it's too late now.

"Sweetie, that's not what I meant," Jim says and he tries to reach over and grab my arm, but I am already sitting up on the side of the bed, reaching for my robe.

"I'm going to take a shower," I say stiffly, "Linda is dropping off Megan and Kyle around 10 and I want everything to be ready before then."

I think Jim is saying something else, but I can't hear him as I firmly close the bathroom door and turn on the shower. I know he didn't 'mean' what he said, but it further illustrates our divergent attitudes - I think about this baby 24 hours a day and I think he's forgotten there is even going to *be* a baby.

While the water heats up, I conduct my new daily ritual of staring at my naked body in the mirror and trying to assess if I look any different from the day before, and more importantly if I actually look pregnant. Today I am officially 13-weeks pregnant. All of the books and websites say this is a huge milestone – the end of the first trimester, the time when I can officially start telling people. I had my big ultrasound last week and the doctor said everything looked great; she also said it was fine that I *still* had not gained any weight, but from this point on I needed to start gaining about one pound per week or she would be concerned.

I look at myself again in the mirror from the side and my breasts definitely look bigger – Jim is quite pleased with this pregnancy side effect. I think right under my belly button might look a little bit rounder, but I can't tell. The mirror starts to fog up from the steam and I step into the shower thinking of the irony that in a few months I will look into that same mirror and desperately wish I looked like I did right now instead of having a huge pregnant belly.

***

Linda drops off Megan and Kyle as planned and they run into the house screaming "Merry Christmas!" carrying shopping bags full of presents. They each have to go back outside twice to bring in the rest of their luggage and the presents that they apparently already opened at Linda's house.

From the noise and excitement in the living room, you wouldn't know that the children were 14 and 12, you'd think they were 5 and 3 discovering Santa's half-eaten cookies and leftover milk.

Surprisingly, Jim seems to love all of the commotion with his children. I'm watching the three of them open their stockings on the floor next to the Christmas tree and feeling hopeful that Jim really will want to do this all over again.

We haven't told Kyle about the baby yet, and amazingly Megan has kept it to herself. Even though today is the sanctioned day according to the pregnancy gurus, I can't make Christmas about me or the baby, and I haven't thought about what might happen when Linda finds out, so once again, we will keep this secret a little while longer.

Halfway through our Christmas brunch, Kyle and Megan declare that they have an announcement. Over the past few weeks, Kyle has warmed up considerably, but I've never seen him this affable – I almost wonder if Jim poured champagne in everyone's orange juice except for mine, it would explain a lot.

"You can tell them," Kyle says to Megan.

"Okay, if you're sure," she says to Kyle. And then to Jim and me she says, "so Mom and Bill are getting married."

"That's great," Jim says in a voice I've heard him use at work a thousand times; it conveys zero emotion.

"Bill proposed last night. In front of us. It was gross," Megan says.
I'm trying not to laugh, but I can't tell if I think it's sweet that he was trying to include them, even though I know the kids don't like him, or if it's just creepy.

"But that's not all," Megan continues, "they're moving!"

This get's Jim's attention. "What do you mean they're moving? Where are they moving?"

"To Wyoming!" Megan shouts.

"What the Hell? She can't move to Wyoming! We have agreements! This is ridiculous! Guys, don't worry about it, no one's going anywhere, I'll figure this all out tomorrow and nothing will have to change." Jim puts a piece of turkey bacon in his mouth and chews, the wheels spinning in his head as he tries to determine exactly how he is going to use the law to put Linda in her place.

"But Dad, it's not a problem," Kyle offers. "We all talked about it last night and Megan and I both want to live here full time and Mom and Bill can move off to Bill's ranch in Wyoming. We'll go see them for vacations or a couple weeks in the summer, but we want to be here!" Kyle is beaming with his announcement as I feel a knot form in my stomach.

"Well, your mom and I will still need to talk about it. This isn't what our original agreement was – but I would love to have you here. Especially now that Danielle's here, we won't have to worry about someone being home when I'm at work all the time like we did when mom and I first split up – because Dani's always here." Jim gives me a big smile and I smile back, but quickly excuse myself to go to the bathroom.

I'm in the powder room in the front hall, so I can still hear the three of them chatting happily about their plans which will impact the rest of my life. What happened to the happily divorced man I met who only saw his kids every other weekend? It's nice that everyone's getting along better than they did a few months ago, and no one seems to hate me anymore, but I think I would trade that for my new role as permanent step-mother to two teenagers, um forever! This is supposed to be a long drawn-out discussion, that we have over several weeks and we go back and forth about what it means for each of us and for the kids, this is not supposed to happen instantaneously over Christmas brunch before I can even swallow my mouthful of raspberries. And to top it all off, Kyle doesn't even know I'm pregnant! He's moving back home, and surprise in six months, there's going to be a baby!

I can still hear all of them laughing and talking in the dining room. I carefully pat cold water under my eyes, so it doesn't look like I've been crying, and I take a few deep breaths before going back to the festivities.

As I take my seat, Jim clears his throat and raises his mimosa, "To add to the good news of the day, Dani and I have something we want to share with you too."

"Is this about the baby?" Megan says.

"What baby?" Kyle asks, "who's having a baby?"

"Wait, how do you know about the baby?" Jim says, looking at Megan and then at me.

"What baby?" Kyle asks again.

"I saw something on Danielle's phone, like weeks ago," Megan says.

I want to slide under the table and disappear.

"So you've known and didn't say anything?" Jim asks her.

"Danielle didn't want me to say anything. I found out the morning I moved back home – she didn't tell me, I saw it on her phone."

"I remember that day," is all Jim says, but looks meaningfully at me. I'm not sure what to make of Jim's stare, but he doesn't seem thrilled with this development. But that's fair, since I'm not exactly thrilled with anything that's going on right now.

I ignored almost all of the advice I got from my friends when I met Jim and then when we got engaged and later married – I'm trying to ignore those words of wisdom now as they float through my brain, since it seems a little too late to start listening.

"What baby?" Kyle asks again, still not following the conversation around the table.

"Danielle's pregnant!" Jim yells in exasperation, "you're going to be a big brother," but his tone is anything but congratulatory. And with that our lovely family Christmas brunch is over.

Chapter 27 – Gretchen

The sound of silence echoes throughout the house. I had to practically dress and feed Alice, Natalie and Ethan this morning and push them into the car – our entire routine forgotten after ten days at home over the school break. Even Alan was running late and missed his normal train.

Notwithstanding the gray skies and 23 degree temperature with a forecast for snow, I almost leapt out of bed this morning, anticipating the return to normalcy and 6 hours of uninterrupted silence in my own home – something I never knew I would come to treasure.

I have a lot of work to catch up on today, but hopefully I can do some chores around the house while I'm working – one of the benefits of working from home. I've gotten the laundry from Natalie and Ethan's rooms, but I'm scared to open Alice's room for fear of the disaster I will find. She has made it clear that she doesn't want Alan or me in her room, but until she starts doing her own laundry, or more importantly, paying rent, we've told her that she doesn't get to make those kinds of rules.

As I grab her laundry basket I notice that her phone and her laptop are on her desk. Alice never goes anywhere without her phone, it's an extension of her hand. She also usually brings her laptop to school with her; even in middle school so much of her homework and classwork require the computer, that she's started bringing it every day. She must have been in such a rush this morning that she forgot them. My first thought is to get in the car and bring them over to the school so she'll have them, but then I chastise myself for this thought and realize that she should suck it up for one day and live with the consequences of her actions. I smile as I think how crazy she must be going without her phone, it will be good for her to have a day without technology.

I put in some of the laundry and clean up the kitchen and then get settled at my desk around 10 o'clock, still plenty of time to do several hours of work before anyone needs me.
I look at the 'to-do' list I made last night, I'm probably one of the only people who still uses a pen and paper to make lists, but I haven't been able to let technology take over my life completely.

The first several items on my list are emails that need to be composed or returned regarding the small family businesses for which I do bookkeeping. Then I need to create a budget for a new company I just started working with in December. And then on my list I have written 'Call Laura'. She has called 5 times in the last week and I know I need to talk to her, but I don't have the energy to call her back yet. Now that the glory of December is over, with its parties and energy and gluttony and January is settling in with its sense of renewal, I won't have an excuse to ignore her anymore. But I still move that particular item from my list for today into tomorrow and feel a sense of relief.

***

I'm churning through my work, but I can't stop thinking about Alice's laptop and phone sitting in her room, finally unattended for a few short hours. I know that a lot of other parents insist on looking through their children's phones every night, or doing 'spot-checks' at random, but

Alan and I felt this would be an invasion of her privacy and until recently, we never had a reason to worry.

My work progress continues to slow, as all of my concentration is on the two devices in Alice's room. I know this is rationalization, but if I take a quick look, it will likely show me that there is nothing to worry about and then I can relax. It's already one o'clock and I need to leave by two thirty to pick up the kids, so if I'm going to do it, I have to do it now.

I feel like a burglar when I go into her room this time. I pay close attention to how her phone and computer are placed on her desk, so that I can put them back in exactly the same position. I sneak back into my bedroom, realizing that I would look ridiculous if someone were actually here to see me tiptoeing in the middle of the day in my own home. I sit down on the bed and open up her computer, hoping she hasn't been clever enough to change the password since we gave it to her.

I'm not sure where to start my trespassing, but I think on every episode of Law & Order I've ever seen, they look at the internet browser history, so that seems like the place to start. Luckily she isn't smart enough to have cleared this either. The first site is a math site that they have to use for school, which is very reassuring. The next few sites are all for clothing stores that she likes, which is equally good news. But as I look down to the rest of the pages, my stomach starts to tighten. The next several pages are all for match.com, and the date says that these are from yesterday so I know this isn't from the incident with Kelly from a couple of months ago. There are also several Google searches, so I click on those to see what she was searching for. I instantly regret my decision to do so when I see that her Google searches were all for 'how to give a blow job?' or 'how to give the best blow job?'

I want to close the computer and pretend none of this ever happened, but I'm well beyond that now. I open the match.com site and again see that she was naïve enough to keep herself signed in.

Holy Shit.

That is my little girl advertising herself on a dating site. This isn't a picture of Kelly anymore; this is now Alice's profile with her own slutty picture and an entire page dedicated to Alice. How is this possible?!
I am mesmerized as I scroll through her dating page and then see all of the men who have 'winked' at her. Ugh, this is disgusting. These men are all pedophiles and should be put in jail. Even if they think she is 18, half of them are way too old to be looking at an 18-year old, what is wrong with them?!

Once I figure out how to navigate the site, I see that there is really only one guy she is 'talking' to - Derek. I look up his profile and he is actually pretty cute, oh god did I just think that, what is wrong with me? It says he is only 21 – still a disaster, but not as bad as it could be. I'm able to read their initial conversations – it seems that they have since gone to texting, but their initial conversations seem pretty harmless. I can't believe he can't tell that she isn't 18 from how she writes, but maybe he doesn't care.

I pick up her phone and open up her messages. There is one new message and all it says for the sender's name is "D". Maybe she has gotten a little smarter. The message just says. "u there?" It came about 20 minutes ago. It could be one of her friends from school, but I just have a feeling that it's this guy.

Before I can think any more about it, I write back as Alice:

Alice: I'm here

D: cool

I can see that he is quite the conversationalist.

Alice: where r u?

D: in class. boring.

Alice: me 2

I'm literally sweating as I type back to him. I have no idea how to impersonate my daughter, especially how to impersonate my daughter pretending to be an 18-year old flirting with this guy. And I'm not sure what I'm possibly going to learn from this illiterate text session.

D: talk l8r

Alice: K

I erase the chat session from Alice's phone and notice that it is 2:35. I hurry to put everything back in her room and scramble to get my things together and get to school for pick-up.

On the drive to school I think about how I am going to handle this with Alice, but I have no idea where to start. I know I need to talk to Alan, but I can't imagine what he's going to do when he finds out what's been going on.

Alice gets in the car from school and the first thing she says is, "did you see my phone? I think I left it at home today! I can't find it anywhere!"

I can barely look at her, but I stare at my beautiful first-born baby girl and say calmly, "I don't know Alice, I haven't seen it. You really need to keep track of your own things."

Chapter 28 – Laura

"Do you really have to go to work?" I ask Michael. Of course I know that he has to go to work today, but once he leaves and the kids go back to school then I have to admit that our vacation is really over and we are back to reality.

"I wish I didn't have to go, but I don't think I can be away any longer. This is the longest I have been away from the office since our honeymoon. They may have forgotten me," he jokes.

"It's your company, I'm pretty sure they can't forget you. I think we should move to Turks and Caicos, you could work from there."

"Maybe someday, but I don't think you'd really like it after the novelty wore off," Michael says as he comes over and kisses me on the forehead and then starts to walk out the door, "have a good day beautiful, I'm out with clients tonight so I'm going to be really late." And just like that, he's gone.

I miss him already. I miss the warm weather and the days on the beach and our cozy beach house. The house was beautiful and I know it was expensive, but it was a fraction the size of this house and the kids shared rooms and we were fine without the extra space; it was actually nice to be so close together all of the time. Michael has taken vacations over the years, but never ten days and never a vacation where he only spent a couple of hours on the phone or doing work.

I can close my eyes right here and see Logan and the twins playing in the undulating turquoise waters of the Caribbean, their brown little bodies glowing in the sun and their little legs caked with sand. They played together for hours without a single fight or harsh word, we were all under a magical vacation spell and nothing could break it. The first few days I could tell that the kids kept waiting for us to tell them that it was time to come inside or that we had to stop and go do a planned activity – all of us scarred by the structured lives we lead at home, planned down to the minute. But by the third day we all adjusted to island time and developed a new schedule where time didn't matter – we ate when we wanted, we went into the pool then to the beach, then back to the pool, then took a nap or read or played ping pong. We hired a local nanny for Cameron and to watch the other kids for a couple of hours here and there, but it all felt so effortless.

I felt nauseous getting on the plane yesterday to come home. Michael and the kids were sad to leave the warm weather, but I know they wanted to get back to work and friends and school – I know Michael thinks I'm kidding, but I could have stayed there forever.

After the disaster at the holiday party, I promised myself I would stay away from the pills. And to my great relief, I found that I took very few – only one here or there to help me sleep, but overall I drank when Michael drank and I felt a natural sense of tranquility that I haven't felt since before Logan was born.

But now real life comes flooding back to me and it's like a weight on my chest – the day stretches out in front of me and seems endless. I want to lie in that lounge chair and feel the warm ocean breeze blow across my bare skin and listen to the laughter and screams of Michael and the children as they run through the sand, each of them hoping to be the first one caught and thrown in the ocean.

I force myself out of bed and into the bathroom to start getting ready. I congratulate myself on having the foresight to have Robin, Jody and Claudia all working this morning. Maybe I knew I would feel like this today, or maybe they've all had ten days off so they had to be here, but either way, I'm glad that no one has to see me like this.

I hate what I am about to do, but the only other option I see is crawling back under the covers and that seems even worse. I take both bottles out of my yet-to-be-unpacked Gucci cosmetics case and hold one in each hand. I debate which one to take and feel a little bit like Alice in Wonderland – one will make me bigger, one will make me smaller. I know there isn't anything funny about it, but it's the first thing that makes me smile and I take that as a good sign. I decide on a couple of Ritalin for a burst of energy; I hope I won't need a Xanax later, but if I'm being honest with myself I probably will – but only one…

***

The magic of the chemicals blissfully sets in shortly after my shower and I feel like myself again. Or at least enough like myself to go to the gym and the grocery store. I could send Claudia to the store, especially since there is so much to buy, but today I'd rather do it myself.

I'm almost enjoying the soothing task of replenishing the staples for our kitchen, and shopping at Whole Foods makes the experience more enjoyable than at any other store, with the flawless pyramids of organic fruits and vegetables. I remember my mother picking through every fruit and vegetable she ever bought at the grocery store to get the least blemished pieces, but someone's already done that here – I can pick a $4 apple of the top of the pile and know that it is just as perfect as every other apple, the ladies of Rye wouldn't have it any other way.

I wander over to the butcher's counter and take a number, not paying attention to anyone or anything around me, when I hear a familiar voice and the enormous weight from this morning is back, my legs too heavy to move.

"Hi Laura," Gretchen says in a level tone, as she grabs her own ticket from the counter.

"Hi Gretchen," I reply, unsure what I'm going to say next. I tried to call her a few times from vacation when I felt relaxed and that I could properly handle the much-needed apology. But now she's caught me off guard and I'm not sure how I can explain my behavior to one of my oldest friends when I can't even explain it to myself.

"I tried to call you," I say, but she cuts me off.

"I know, I wasn't ready to talk to you," she says curtly.

Oh God, she's still really mad at me. I actually don't even know what happened that night, but I know that my behavior was 'offensive.' That's all Stephanie could tell me when I called her the next day to apologize for passing out, which is all I thought had happened. She informed me that I might also want to apologize to Kristen and Gretchen for my "offensive behavior". I sent Kristen an email, since she is only a casual acquaintance, but I haven't figured out how to reconcile with Gretchen, and it feels like it is going to be a lot harder than I thought, especially since I can't admit that I don't know what I did wrong.

"I don't think this is the right place to get into it," I gesture to our surroundings and hope this added convenience also buys me the luxury of ambiguity, "but I'm sorry about everything."

I can see Gretchen soften a little with my last comment as she replies, "I'm not going to say it's all okay yet, but I *will* get over it."

Just as I let myself exhale, Gretchen hits me with a jab that I should have been expecting, but it still takes me by surprise. "I'm really worried about you Laura. I'm still upset about what you said, but I think there is something else going on. You haven't been yourself lately. You're either full of energy or totally out of it." She lowers her voice to a whisper so all of the other shoppers don't hear her, but continues, "I wasn't going to say anything, because I was sure I was wrong, but I'm worried that you have a drinking problem."

I almost feel relieved that someone knows there is a problem, particularly since that someone is one of my closest friends. It might be so easy to collapse into Gretchen's arms right here in the middle of Whole Foods for everyone to see and tell her that I am miserable. That there is not a single hair out of place in my perfect fairy-tale life and yet I am miserable – even with the comfort of all of my little pills, I'm still not happy, and I don't understand why not.

But I haven't fallen that far. I am not going to be the subject of gossip at school pick-up and morning coffees across town. It would be the best piece of gossip in a long time, but I can't let them have it; I have worked for too long to build this life and I will fix it by myself.

So I collect my free-range organic chicken from the butcher and flash him a dazzling smile and then turn to Gretchen and say, "I drank a little bit too much one night, and I didn't have enough to eat that day – that's all that happened, it's happened to everyone. I really appreciate your concern, but I promise there is nothing wrong." I don't know if we're ready for a hug yet, but I open my arms anyway with the invitation and leave the decision up to Gretchen – we'll both look ridiculous if she refuses, but I'll look like the bigger person. She gives me a hug and as I hug my friend I think again about telling her everything, but know that I can't take the risk.

Chapter 29 – Olivia

I begin writing the text message three times and then erase everything and start over. Chris was in Mexico with his kids for Christmas and my parents were here for almost the entire break, so we haven't been able to talk or text since I saw him that night at the jazz club.

I was so busy over the holidays that I didn't have too much time to miss our 'relationship', although I hesitate to call it that and I'm sure I give it more importance than it deserves. I don't know what it is, or what to call it, but I know that I have an intense desire to know what it would feel like to be with him; it's like a scab that I have started to pick and I can leave it alone for days at a time, but then I start to go after it again and I can't stop until it's bleeding. That's probably not the metaphor Chris would want me to use for him, but it fits perfectly.

I should just text Gretchen instead to confirm the timing for lunch, but instead I go back to my text for Chris and type:

Olivia: hope xmas and mexico were good – all well here – free next week?

I press send before I can change my mind again. Now I text Gretchen and confirm that we are on for lunch.

***

I get to Lucy's first and grab a table. It's busier at lunch then when we normally come in the morning, but Gretchen had to work this morning, and I haven't seen her since that bizarre wine club in December, so I dropped Elizabeth off at a friend's house and here I am.

Gretchen comes in and sits down across from me without our usual hellos or hugs and kisses.

Almost out of breath she says, "You're not going to believe what just happened at Whole Foods!"

"You over-paid for everything you bought?" I say with a big smile.
Gretchen gives a little laugh, but clearly has more important things to focus on than my bad jokes. "I just ran into Laura and had the weirdest conversation."

Now she has my attention. "What did you say? What did she say?"

"She apologized for the party. We didn't get into the details, but she seemed sorry. But then I actually told her I thought she had a drinking problem."

"Oh my god! You did not actually say that, did you?" I ask in disbelief.

"I did. I wasn't planning on it, but I felt like we were having a moment. And then it was really weird, because she took a long time answering me and she looked like she was going to cry, and then poof, she snapped back into the Laura we know and she very politely told me that I was wrong and gave me a hug and then walked away. I swear, when she left I almost forgot I was still mad at her. She looked so small and fragile and then totally pulled together the next minute, back to her old self." Gretchen shakes her head as she finishes her short story, clearly upset by the situation.

"I don't know what to tell you. This certainly doesn't help me understand Laura anymore than I did before! I have trouble believing she's really having any problems. Whenever I see her I can't help thinking about a Barbie doll – bad things don't happen to Barbie, right?"

"Since when did you get so catty?" Gretchen says. "I'm still mad at her, but she is one of my closest friends, and she isn't dumb."

"I know, I know. I'm sorry, I don't know why I said that," I say regretting my Barbie comment as I feel my face grow hot with embarrassment. I'm not sure why I even said that, I like Laura – and although I don't think she's brilliant, she has never struck me as dumb.

I try to recover, "I just meant that I think of Laura's life as being perfect, so I can't imagine her having a drinking problem, or other big issues, but I guess we never really know what's going on in someone else's life." The enormity of that statement hits me and I hope Gretchen doesn't want to continue on the topic.
"Well I think the same could be said for you, I don't think anyone could imagine that you have any problems..." Gretchen catches herself, and looks like her foot is stuck in her mouth.

I rescue her before this conversation can get any worse, "Fair enough, those who live in glass houses shouldn't throw stones." I try to lighten the mood. "How did lunch get so serious? Shouldn't I be telling you stories about how my mom annoyed me over Christmas and you can tell me something Alice did that will make me want to lock Julie in her room until she's 20?"

I laugh and take a sip of my water, but notice that Gretchen isn't laughing; she actually looks more somber than she did before.

"What did I say?"

Gretchen sighs as she says, "it's Alice, isn't it always Alice?"

"Oh no, what is it? You know I was kidding, right? I was just trying to be funny. I really do have a lot of annoying stories about my mom from Christmas," I say with a half-hearted smile, but Gretchen doesn't return the gesture.

"Do you remember the online dating thing I told you about at Thanksgiving?"

"Of course," I nod.

"So it seems Alice is back on the dating site, but this time it's much worse."

"Ugh, that poor girl. Why are they being so mean to her? That's so unlike Alice," I say.

"No, no. It has nothing to do with the other girl now. Alice has set up her own dating page and she is meeting men online," Gretchen confesses.

"What!?!" I scream so loudly that the people at the table next to us turn to stare.

"Sorry," I say quietly, "I wasn't expecting that."

"Me neither," says Gretchen.

"So what did you do? Has she met someone? How do you stop her? Why would she do this?"

"Liv, this isn't Twenty Questions. And I don't have any of the answers. I found out right before Christmas and I'm not sure what to do. You're the only person I've told – it feels so good to tell someone."

I wince as she reveals her secret, knowing that I am keeping quite a big one from her.

"You haven't even told Alan? I thought he was great when there was the problem before?"

"He was, but that was different. That wasn't about his daughter prostituting herself on the internet, I'm pretty sure he won't be so level-headed now."

"Oh Gretchen, I'm so sorry. And now you have Laura to worry about too. That sucks – sorry I can't be more eloquent, but I think it's accurate."

"Thanks, Liv. It isn't like I'm not doing anything about it. I've become the stalker mom I always said I wouldn't be. I look on her computer every chance I get and, ugh, I can't believe I'm admitting this, but I synced her text messages to my computer and now I can read all of her texts, so at least I know what she's saying to this boy, I mean this man that she is talking to. I have to end the whole thing, but I'm not sure how to do it yet, so I feel like this gives me some control while I figure it out."

"Wow. I'm impressed! I'm also a little scared – I'll know never to get on your bad side, you could work for the NSA," I joke.

"Thanks, I think. I've learned that she isn't the only one doing it. It looks like a few of her friends have also put themselves up on the site, and that girl Kelly is back up there too! Which is crazy. I'm having trouble imagining where they think this is all going to lead, but that's probably part of the problem, they haven't thought about that at all."

"I'm so glad you told me," I tell her, "I don't know if I can help, but I'll do anything you need me to do."

"Thanks. I know I need to tell Alan, and I need to put this all to an end soon. And then ground Alice for the rest of her life. I just want to make sure I do it the right way," Gretchen says.

I tell her that I'm sure it will be okay, because that's what everyone always says, although I can't begin to imagine what I would do if I were in her shoes. The hardest parenting issue I've had to face so far is advising Julie on choosing between two of her friends on the playground.

Gretchen and I eat our salads, and try to recover from the gluttony of holiday eating. We talk some more about Alice and teenagers and how everything has changed since we were younger, until we notice that the time as always has passed too quickly and she has to get back to work and I have to go pick up Elizabeth and get on with my day.

"I'm so sorry we talked about my problems the whole time!" Gretchen apologizes, "we didn't talk about you at all."

"Oh don't worry. I'm boring, nothing new to report on my end," I say cheerfully, feeling both guilty and relieved that I'm still keeping everything about Chris to myself.

We pay our bill and make our way out the door, both of us bracing as the cold air hits our faces, a sharp contrast from the warmth inside Lucy's. It's only the beginning of January and already I'm tired of cold weather and ready for spring.

Gretchen and I hug and say our good-byes, each heading to our own cars and our own separate agendas. By the time I pull out onto the road, thoughts of Alice have moved to the back of my mind and I am already worried about the overdue library books I just remembered and getting a bigger ballet leotard for Julie before tomorrow and planning three nights of dinners that everyone will eat, and then Chris and Charlie, and really what the hell am I doing – that's the question that keeps coming back over and over again.

Chapter 30 – Danielle

"Bye Megan, bye Kyle," I call out as they head out the door.

"Bye Danielle!" Megan shouts. "Remember you have to be there to pick us up at 3 o'clock. And you can just pull into the line in the front of the school."

"I know, I've got it. I have everything written down. Have a good day!"

The door finally slams and I wait a full minute to make sure that one of them isn't going to come back inside to retrieve a forgotten bag or hat or pair of shoes; but I hear the car engine in the distance and it seems they are actually on their way to school.

I don't know what would have prepared me for this, but I definitely was not prepared to go from step-mother every other weekend to full time mom of two teenagers.

The last ten days have been a whirlwind of activity, moving Kyle and Megan back into the house permanently. The day after Christmas, Linda and Bill came over so we could all discuss the new living arrangements; but everything had already been decided, our get-together was just a formality, and not once did anyone ask my opinion or feelings on the new arrangements.

Linda and I exchanged an awkward side-hug and exaggerated congratulations on her engagement and my pregnancy, but after that I just sat on the couch and watched the conversation; I felt more like the stepchild than the stepmother.

And now the last few days have been spent cramming to learn how to be a full-time parent in Rye. Having only parented on the weekends and for a short period in early December for Megan, which frankly I assumed was temporary, I knew almost nothing about school schdules and carpools and extra-curricular activities. I do know that my life would be a lot easier if there was a school bus, but the fancy day school Megan and Kyle attend, and most of my new friends' children as well, does not believe in busing, it believes in mothers and nannies driving their children around like chauffeurs. Since I was always walked to school on our ever-changing Army bases (and no one cared what we did after school as long as we stayed on the base and were home in time for dinner), this whole world is bizarre.

I decide to delay my run or any of the items on my to-do list and reward myself with a quick catch-up on Facebook. I haven't had time to look at anything for a couple of weeks and with the house finally quiet, I am going to enjoy my one permitted cup of daily coffee and see what my friends have been doing.

An hour later I am still scrolling through the Facebook feed on my phone. I had almost forgotten that New Years Eve was two nights ago- how is that possible?! Last year, Jim and I were in Vail over New Year's, we skied on the 31st and then went to an amazing party at one of his friend's houses that night. We slept late New Year's Day and then had champagne brunch on top of the mountain and finished the day in the outdoor hot tub.

This year Megan was supposed to go to a party and then changed her mind at the last minute, and Kyle didn't have plans because 12-year old boys don't have plans on New Year's Eve, so we all stayed home and had a 'family cooking night.' It was a fine night, and Jim seemed to enjoy it, but I fell asleep on the couch at 10:30, and I forgot it was even New Year's Eve!!

I'm looking at the posts from my friends' nights out in the city, or Miami or Vegas and the crazy pictures they posted all night long doing shots, hanging on random guys, shedding layers of clothing – and it looks like so much fun.

Maybe all pregnant women feel this way – a longing to drink because it's forbidden – but I think it's more than that. I feel like the oldest 29-year old in the world right now looking at my friends' lives devoid of all responsibility, when I just seem to take on more obligations by the day, and I haven't even had the baby yet.

I have a sudden longing to talk to Molly. According to the omniscient Facebook, she should be at her desk right now, still nursing a hangover from four amazing days in Vegas, but able to function thanks to her Starbucks Venti Mocha. I can't remember if I used to post quite this much up to the minute information about my life, but once Jim and I got together, I became a much less frequent poster and more of a voyeur. Jim thinks Facebook is too juvenile and a waste of time, although he might be right on the latter point seeing as how it has sucked up most of my morning. He didn't want me posting anything about him or about us on the site, and since we got together I haven't had much else to report.

I call Molly and hope that she is still at her desk drinking her mocha. She picks up on the first ring.

"Danielle? Is that really you?" she yells into the phone.

"It's me. How are you? How was Vegas? I was just looking at your pics online, it looks like it was pretty crazy."

"Oh Vegas was fun, but really I can't believe you're calling. It has been so long! I haven't even talked to you since the wedding. How is everything now that you're married to the big boss? I can see your husband in his office now if I stand up at my desk, he's in a meeting of course," Molly laughs.

Molly and I joined the firm at the same time. We were summer interns together between our second and third years of law school and then we both came back to start as first year associates 3 years ago; however, my experience at the firm was a little different then hers once I met Jim.

"I can't believe it's been that long," I say, but I know that it probably has been that long since I've talked to anyone from work, or my 'city friends'.

"So how is married life? What do you do all day if you aren't working? Are you bored? You probably spend all day at the gym and then you go shopping with your piles of money, I bet you look even better than you did before. I really hate you now!" Molly laughs as she is talking.

Molly talks a good game, but she loves her job and she loves to party, I know she would never want to trade places with me – even without knowing about my new step-child and baby situation.

 "It's great," I lie, not wanting to disappoint Molly's vision of me laden down with shopping bags. "You'll have to come up to the house soon for dinner! Maybe you could bring your man-of-the-week with you."

"That sounds great. We'll have to make a date," Molly says, but we both know that this dinner will never happen.

"I'll let you get back to work, I wouldn't want Jim to get mad at you," I joke.

"Ha-ha. Thanks for calling! So good to talk to you! Let's catch up again soon, okay?"

"Okay. Bye," I say in an equally cheerful voice. I hang up and go back to scrolling through the endless posts of my former colleagues and friends living their amazing, carefree lives - I feel far worse than before I called.

Chapter 31 – Olivia

"I have to go to Houston for a couple days this week, sorry for the last minute notice," Charlie says as we are on our way downstairs after putting the kids to bed.

"Oh that's fine, not a big deal. When do you leave?" I ask him, my mind already spinning and wondering if I can sneak into the city to meet Chris while he is gone. I tried to go last week, but Charlie was home early every night.

"Are you happy to get rid of me?" Charlie says as he comes over and smothers me in a hug.

"Of course not. I just meant you shouldn't feel bad if you have to go away for a few days. It's been so nice that you've been home early these last few nights." I hope that my reply sounds normal. I know this problem is all my own doing, but I can't help myself – there's something about Chris that I can't explain, but I also can't stay away from. Being with Chris makes me feel like a teenager. No, not a teenager, he makes me feel like a fun and sexy woman, not a mom, or a boring wife; which is how I feel all the time at home.

"Will you miss me?" Charlie asks, giving me his best attempt at a pout, although it's hard for someone his size to pull off the look.

"Of course I'll miss you. Now when do you leave? You didn't say?" I ask, hoping I don't sound too eager.

"Oh right. I leave Wednesday morning and I'll be back Friday afternoon. It's just a quick trip. We should get a sitter for Friday night and go out. Or maybe I'll see if my parents could come and stay over on Friday night and we could get a hotel in the city. It was so busy over the holidays, we barely got to see each other. What do you think?"

"Um, sure. That would be great. If it's not too much trouble. Whatever you want to do," I can't believe that I'm feeling weird about spending the night in a hotel with my husband, because I am planning to see Chris on Thursday night – I am not a good person.

"No, I'm sure they would love to do it. It's only a 45-minute drive and they haven't seen the kids since Thanksgiving. I'm going to go call them, and then I'm going to make a hotel reservation. I'm not telling you which hotel, it will be a surprise!" Charlie wanders off into his office looking very pleased with himself.

***

Thursday night comes as planned; Charlie is securely stowed away in Houston and I am on my way to The Four Seasons Hotel bar to meet Chris.

As I exit Grand Central, Chris texts me the following:

Chris: running late, was on a call. can u meet me at my place?

I literally stop in place while reading the text and two people behind me run right into me. I apologize and move to the side, out of the constant stream of traffic. I don't know if he means this just as convenience, and I am reading too much into it, but this changes everything. So far, we've only met in public, and although I know what

I'm doing is wrong, it still feels like I'm staying on one side of a line.

I text him back:

Olivia: sure. address?

Chris: 129 E. 21st St.

I walk outside and hop in a cab, remembering that he told me he had bought a place right on Gramercy Square Park. For a minute I am more excited to see the apartment, always curious to see a great space in the city, but then I remember exactly what is about to happen, or at least what *could* happen, and the butterflies swarm my stomach.

Of course there is no traffic on the way there – this would never happen when I'm running late, but tonight when I could use a few minutes to analyze the situation or at least calm my nerves, we sail through the city hitting every green light.

Chris's townhouse is impressive based on the address alone, directly across from the park, where only a handful of privileged New Yorkers are fortunate enough to have a key to the private sanctuary of green space. However, standing outside of his house, I am further impressed by the beauty of the building itself. It looks like it was completely restored within the last few years; a four-story home in this location probably costs at least $15 million. I know that the firm is doing well, but I had no idea Chris could afford anything like this. I am annoyed with myself for being impressed, but can't help a tiny bit of envy. Charlie and I used to walk by these houses when we lived in the city and we would joke that someday we would live here and have our own key to the park, but we both knew that would never happen. Now here I am about to go into one of these 'storybook' homes, but not the way I imagined it happening.

I ring the bell and Chris comes to the door wearing faded jeans and a fitted gray t-shirt with bare feet – he looks sexier than he's ever looked in a suit.

"Come in," he says, and moves aside so I can walk past him into the foyer.

"I love your place," I say looking around into the rooms on either side of the hall. The house is decorated in a sleek, modern style. All of the furniture is low and at weird angles, and there isn't a piece of clutter anywhere.

"I can't take much credit. The previous owner gutted the house and re-did everything, and then I hired a decorator. I just moved my stuff in here, and I don't really have much stuff as you can see."

Chris continues, "I'm sorry to change plans at the last minute. I came home to change and then got stuck on a call. I knew I would never meet you there in time, so I figured this would be easier. We can still go out if you want, or we could just stay here," Chris winks at me as he says the last part.

I walk into the kitchen, finding another ultra-modern room that could be featured in a design magazine.

"I love your kitchen. Do you use it?" I tease him.

"I have used the kitchen. But unfortunately you are correct, the microwave is definitely the most used appliance in the room. Although maybe the wine fridge gets more use – does that count as an appliance?"

"What a waste of a fantastic kitchen!" I laugh, feeling slightly more relaxed with our banter. "Does that wine fridge have any Sauvignon Blanc in it?"

"Coming right up," Chris says.

I take a seat on the black leather sofa in the open plan family room section of the kitchen. It is surprisingly more comfortable than it looks.

Chris brings over two glasses of wine and sits down next to me. He raises his glass for a toast and we clink glasses, but are both at a loss for the subject of our toast, somehow saying, "to us" seems wrong. We settle on "cheers" and I take a hefty drink from my glass, almost emptying half of it in one swallow.

Chris takes the glass out of my hand and puts it down gently on the glass table and then leans over to kiss me. It is a gentle kiss at first, but quickly becomes more passionate. We are both aware that there is no one watching us this time and no fear of being caught. I swing my leg over so I am facing Chris and sitting on his lap; he lets out a small groan as I settle myself on top of him.

We continue kissing, but Chris is not taking anything slowly; he reaches down to un-tuck my shirt and then pulls it over my head – I'm glad I wore a pretty lace bra tonight and not one of my usual seamless cotton ones.

I lean down to kiss Chris's neck and start to move my hips back and forth, since I can feel that Chris is just as excited as I am. Chris moves my hair back to whisper in my ear. "You're so hot. I've thought about doing this to you since the day I met you." And then he slaps me on my ass, not a painful slap, but definitely not what I was expecting.

I make a small noise, which he must take as encouragement, because he continues his dialogue.

"You like it rough? I knew you would. You're so dirty. You're such a dirty little slut."

What did he just say? I've heard that there are men who talk dirty during sex, I just haven't experienced it – it sounds so strange coming out of his mouth, and not at all sexy. I try to kiss him to make him stop talking, but I'm having trouble forgetting what he said.

He kisses me for a minute, but then he obviously has more to say and goes back to rubbing my breasts a little too hard and whispering in my ear.

"I knew if I waited long enough, I'd get my turn with you. You're such a bad, dirty whore, but I knew you'd finally be ready for me."

I sit back and look at Chris, trying to reconcile what he's just said to me with the man I've known for the past ten years.

"What's the matter?" Chris says, and then grabs for my left breast, "come over here so I can give you what you want, you little bitch."

Suddenly, I feel nothing between my legs – the urgent desire that was there a few minutes ago has vanished completely and now I feel naked and exposed sitting on his lap. I maneuver myself so I can stand up and grab my shirt off the floor so I can cover up.

"What are you doing?" Chris asks, with a slight edge to his voice.

"I shouldn't be here. I'm sorry about tonight, I'm sorry about everything, this has been a mistake," I mumble as I try to button my shirt facing away from him.

"Are you kidding me?" Chris says. "You've strung me along this whole time and now you're just a big cock tease? Your conscience is bothering you *now*? After all those other guys?" Chris shouts.

"What other guys? What are you talking about? I've never cheated on Charlie!" I say as I am bending over trying to put my boot on, not my strongest position.

"Ha! So you're telling me that this is the first time you've done this? No way Liv, I'm not buying it. The good girl thing is all an act, it always has been. You've strung me along for years, and now you play this game with me? You're too much. Just a big tease. Or maybe a whore and a tease, who knows," Chris says with malice.

I'm stung by his words, I can't believe this is what he thinks of me; but it's not much better than I think of myself right now.

I grab my coat and purse and then turn around to say good-bye, although it probably isn't necessary at this point.

Chris is still sitting on the couch, although when I turn around, he unzips his pants and says, "I think you owe it to me to finish what you started," he starts to laugh when he sees my horror as he starts to finish it by himself and I run out the door.

***

Fortunately, my taxi luck is still with me tonight and a cab shows up almost immediately. I don't even bother with the train and I ask the driver to take me all the way back to Rye – I don't care what it costs; I just have to get home as quickly as possible.

I want to be in my flannel pajamas on my couch, in my family room, with my huge sectional sofa and Oriental rug and toys everywhere – the antithesis of Chris's house. I need to take a shower first, or maybe two or three showers, to try and wash the evening away and maybe I can forget it ever happened.

I don't know how I could have thought Chris was attractive or sexy or more importantly – worth throwing away my marriage. What the hell was I thinking?

I have a wonderful husband and two amazing children. Sure, things aren't perfect all the time, but they are pretty close to perfect, how come I didn't see that until just now? I am going to be the perfect wife from now on. I will never take Charlie or the girls for granted. If I can just get home and put this all behind me, I will start over.

To prove it to myself I go into my phone and delete Chris from my contacts, it will be too soon if I ever have to see or talk to him again.

Chapter 32 – Gretchen

It is disturbing how good I have become at stalking my daughter online. Over the last couple of weeks I have created a system to track her daily updates on match.com and all of her texts. I took a guess at her password for the site and was disappointed in Alice's lack of creativity when I was able to guess it on the second try – 'puddles' – her favorite stuffed animal from when she was little; an additional reminder of how young she actually is.

I know that it is a complete betrayal of her trust when I read through her text messages and her online chats; but I remind myself that she betrayed my trust by putting herself in this position.

I know that I need to tell Alan and then we need to confront Alice together, but I don't feel like I have a plan yet. It isn't a good excuse for my lack of intervention, but she does seem to be exercising some judgment with these boys, or men rather. The text messages are all similar to the first one with Derek – they don't talk about anything of any importance, in fact, they hardly talk about anything at all. When one of the guys suggests that they meet or even suggests that they talk on the phone, she ends the whole thing and moves on to someone else.

From what I can gather with her friends, they are all doing the same thing with the guys they have met on the site. It's hard to decipher everything from the snippets of the conversations that I read, which is clearly supplementing the conversations they have at school, but I think they are having a contest to see who can attract the most men.

I should still be furious with Alice, and of course I am! But I will admit that I am relieved to see that the girls don't have any intention of pursuing these men.

I'm going to follow Alice online for a few more days and then I will tell Alan and we will figure it all out together. One way or another it has to come to an end because it is taking up hours of my day – stalking is very time-consuming.

The phone rings and I see that it's Olivia calling. I shut down all of the open programs on my computer, paranoid that she will know what I'm doing even over the phone.

"Hi Liv!" I say.

"Are you busy?" she asks.

"Not really," I say, closing my laptop to emphasize the point more to myself than to her. "I was just finishing up some work, but I got a lot of work done over the weekend, so I'm feeling pretty good. What's up?"

"Can I come over? I really need to talk," she says and now I can hear that her voice sounds unusual.

"Of course, come right over. Is everything okay?"

"No, it's not okay, I did something really bad," Liv says and she starts sobbing.

Chapter 33 – Laura

I stare outside and watch the snow fall over the backyard, covering everything as far as I can see with an enormous white blanket. Each tree-branch twinkles as if covered with brilliant crystals. I can no longer see the distinction between the driveway and the grass and even the outline of the pool cover is starting to fade as the world becomes white.

I know that I will grow tired of the snow soon – it will become a burden, it will grow black with dirt and grime from the streets, it will become the norm instead of a novelty. However, right now it is magical. On this Friday afternoon it has brought the town to a halt and we are now sequestered in our homes, commanded to enjoy the brilliant snow from their warm confines. Michael even called to say he is closing the office early and sending everyone home because the weather channels are predicting a possible blizzard – maybe we could have a blizzard every Friday.

Claudia and Jody both asked if they could leave early to avoid the storm and I was pleasantly surprised that Robin asked if she could stay for the weekend instead of driving home. Once I knew about the storm I tried to prepare myself for three days with all four kids, but I've been so tired lately, I had trouble imagining how I was going to survive. I told Robin she didn't have to work at all and she was welcome to stay, but she's so wonderful, she told me that she "wouldn't dream of leaving me alone with them" and that she would be happy to stay for the weekend – she's definitely a gem!

I've put a fire on in the living room and put out wine and cheese and crackers for when Michael comes home. And Robin and I made hot chocolate and put out the ingredients for s'mores on a silver tray on the hearth. I can't believe how much I'm looking forward to our Norman Rockwell-esque evening at home!

I only wish I hadn't taken that third pill right before Michael called. I have such a nice warm, tranquil feeling right now, but I'm worried by the time he gets home and I have a glass of wine it will go from tranquil to sedentary.

It feels like even more of a waste considering the unsettling conversation I had with Dr. Singha this morning. I'm sure that I'll be able to find a way around it, but I can't believe he told me this is the last time he could refill my prescriptions for two months and that he could only refill my Xanax for 45 pills! I thought that one of the benefits of seeing a doctor who doesn't take insurance, charges $500 a visit and an additional $150 every time he calls in a refill is that I wouldn't have to worry about problems like this. He said he would get back to me with the name of another doctor who I could see, but he cautioned that all doctors' prescriptions are being scrutinized more carefully now, so I might have trouble with any doctor writing my prescriptions.

I know that I should just ration the pills more carefully, but they make me feel so much better, and I know I would be miserable otherwise – and then what kind of mother and wife would I be? I'm sure it can't be that hard to find a doctor who understands that I have a medical need for these pills.

***

The weekend passed in a blur of snowy activity. Friday night was exactly the cozy scene I envisioned, but I only enjoyed a fraction of the evening before I fell asleep on the couch – even Cameron stayed up later than I did. I could hear my family laughing and talking around me as I came in and out of sleep- thank god Robin was there to help put the kids to bed. As Michael carried me upstairs, I tried to thank her, but I couldn't get the words out, my body felt like lead and I tried to open my mouth, but it felt sealed with glue.

Michael didn't say anything on Saturday morning, but I could tell that he was curious why I had fallen asleep at 7 o'clock the night before. I made an extra effort all weekend with him and the kids and played outside in the snow – building snowmen with the twins, sledding with Logan and making snow angels with Cameron. Michael worked most of Sunday and with all the roads cleared and beautiful sunny skies, I suggested that Robin leave on Sunday afternoon so she could have a little time at home before she had to come back. She seemed reluctant to leave, even after she took the $1000 in cash I insisted she have for her extra work over the weekend; but I insisted she go home, mostly so I could show Michael that I could take care of my own children for the night.

And now Monday morning is here. The week stretches out before me, appearing endless. I'm going over the days in my head trying to find something to look forward to, but each day is filled with school and kids' activities and committee meetings and appointments with my trainer and none of it feels like a worthwhile reason to

195

get out of bed. I remember that wine club is Thursday night, which would usually be the highlight of my week; but after last month I'm not sure I can face everyone again.

A commotion at my bedroom door disturbs my gloomy thoughts and I hear Avery and Emma whispering as only 6-year olds can whisper – I could probably hear them two rooms away with the shower running. I admit that at times I have trouble telling the twins apart when they are right in front of me, so I don't have a chance of distinguishing their voices now.

"We can't wake her. Remember, we're not supposed to wake her up," one of them says.

"But I need to ask her something," replies the other one.

"You can ask me, I'll probably know the answer." It must be Emma who says this – she is the most confident 1st grader in the world.

"You won't know. I want to ask her about the winter carnival," Avery yells in a whisper.

"Well, Robin told us not to bother her – don't you remember?" Emma whispers back.

"But she won't be up for hours – and she'll probably be back in her room when we get home from school," Avery complains.

"You should ask Madison – her mom knows everything about the winter carnival, and then we won't get in trouble. Come on – let's finish getting dressed, I can already smell breakfast!" Emma says with the authoritative air of a much older sibling.

"Okay, fine – you're probably right. Mom probably won't know anyway," Avery says.

I roll over to try and go back to sleep, tears soaking my 600 thread count Egyptian cotton pillowcase.

Chapter 33 – Danielle

I look in the mirror this morning expecting to see the same thing I've seen every day for the past 4 months, but today I look different. I'm not sure a stranger passing me on the street would notice that I'm pregnant, but there is definitely a firm swelling underneath my belly button that wasn't there yesterday. I don't know how it could have happened overnight, but undeniably it's there. I turn sideways in the mirror and cup my right hand underneath my tiny bump the way that all the women do in the pregnancy books and instantly it feels real in a way it didn't feel before.

I call out to Jim, who is still getting dressed in the bedroom, "come here and look at this!"

Jim walks into the bathroom midway through tying his tie and stares at me completely naked in the middle of our bathroom. "What am I supposed to be looking at? I have to be out the door in 4 minutes."

"Look at the baby," I say excitedly. "You can finally see it," I say and cup my bump again for emphasis.

"Oh, yeah. I can see it," he says without much enthusiasm, "but don't worry Dani, the rest of you still looks great – you still have the best ass I've ever seen," he says playfully hitting my backside.

"I wasn't worried, I was excited," I reply, slightly deflated.

"Oh. Well, can't I be excited that your ass still looks so good?" he says trying to be funny.

"You better hurry or you'll be late," I warn.

Jim gives me a kiss and then pats me on the butt again and he's gone.

I try to revive my enthusiasm from a few minutes earlier, but I can't seem to get excited about my belly again. I wander over to the closet and wonder if this new development means my clothes aren't going to fit anymore.

I manage to find a pair of low-rise jeans that still fit because they are so low they button underneath my new tummy. It looks like I won't have a problem with tops for a long time though since it's still January and I will be wearing bulky sweaters for several months. Although I could wear something tight on top; I'm not sure why I'm still hiding the baby from everyone other than immediate family when I'm almost 17 weeks pregnant. I think it's time to start telling people. I'm going to go buy some maternity clothes today that show off my little baby bump and then I'm ending my silence – just the thought of this plan brings back some of my earlier delight.

***

Over $4000 and five hours later, my closet is full of the latest maternity clothes. I didn't realize how fashionable the clothes had gotten – I was thinking I would be in shapeless smocks, but I must have remembered pictures of my mother from my baby book and somehow neglected to notice the thousands of pregnant women on the streets of Manhattan.

I know I bought more than I need right now, especially considering my size, but the woman in the store was so helpful and genuinely excited for me; and once she had me put on the fake belly to see what I would look like in a few months, there was no turning back.

Megan and Kyle both have big tests to study for, so they asked to have dinner early and then be excused to their rooms – I definitely wasn't going to fight them on this idea. Jim won't be home until close to 8, but I am going to wait for him so we can have dinner together like we used to do. I select a new red v-neck sweater, that doesn't feel very maternity, but it is the first fitted top I've worn lately and I love how it looks hugging my stomach. The maternity pants are the real change, because they are comfortable, but I didn't buy anything yet with those hideous panels. The woman in the store told me I would be back when I was bigger and I would want them, but I can't imagine it. Tonight I'm wearing a pair of black skinny pants that look just like normal pants, but they're comfortable and adjustable; I look exactly like me, but a pregnant, maybe even sexy, version of me – I hope Jim notices.

***

We are halfway through dinner and it feels almost like it did in the beginning. Jim noticed my outfit right away and told me how great I looked, and now we are enjoying our meal and discussing his latest case and something that happened to Megan at school today and it's starting to feel like things might fall into place.

"We should probably book our tickets for Hawaii soon," I say between bites of halibut.

"Actually, I was going to talk to you about that," Jim says.

"What is it? You still want to do the race, don't you?" I ask.

"I do."

"Well, we can't wait too long. We would want to fly first class anyway, but now that I'm traveling for two, I'm definitely going to want to be in first class for that long of a flight," I give Jim a big smile and wait to hear his response.

"I'm still going to Hawaii, but I don't think it makes sense for us both to go," he says this very calmly and slowly.

"But it's a couples' triathlon, we both have to go. You can't go by yourself," I say before I realize what is about to come next.

"I'm not going by myself. I asked Amanda if she would run in the race with me," he says sheepishly – he might as well have said, "I asked Amanda if she would have sex with me."

"Amanda? She's in terrible shape," I argue, knowing that this isn't the point.

"Actually, she's been training for the last year, since about the time you left the office – you wouldn't believe it if you saw her. Anyway, it's really not a big deal, I don't want you getting upset about it. It's not like you are going to be in condition to race next month anyway," Jim says as he picks up his fork and continues to eat his dinner.

I am so mad I can feel how hot my face has gotten; it must be the same color as my sweater. I try to keep my voice down so I don't disturb the kids upstairs.

I take a deep breath before I speak, "Jim, I have continued to train at least 5 days a week since I've been pregnant with the sole purpose of competing in this race together. We may not win, but I can certainly compete. My doctor even told me that she has never had a patient like me – she has cleared me for the race and the long flight and she said she couldn't imagine doing that for anyone else."

"Sorry Dani, I didn't realize it meant that much to you. But I already asked Amanda and I think we actually have a chance of winning. Besides, who is going to take care of Kyle and Megan if we both go?" he squeezes my hand as he pushes his chair back from the table and clears his dishes to the kitchen.

I sit at the table, speechless. I cannot believe how easily he just dismissed me. When I met him I was attracted to the control he had over everyone at the office and the tales of his ruthlessness in the boardroom. During most of the time we dated and were engaged, I couldn't believe that someone so attractive and powerful would be interested in me; somehow I never realized until now that it's because he's a complete asshole – what have I done?

Chapter 34 – Olivia

Gretchen has said almost nothing for the past hour as I've sat at her kitchen table pouring my heart out. I'm not Catholic, but I imagine this must be similar to confession – I list off all of the terrible things that I have done and the other person just listens and occasionally nods or says "mmm-hmmm." We are sitting in Gretchen's cheery yellow and white kitchen, with the sun beaming off the snow outside, but I think it would be more appropriate to be huddled in the corner of a dimly lit church – the cloudless sky and butcher-block table aren't suitable for confessing infidelity.

I imagine Gretchen is waiting until I am done to tell me what a mess I've made or at least to give me a disapproving look; so far she has refilled my tea, gotten me more tissues and listened intently to my moans and snivels.

I reach the end of my story when I finish telling her about everything that happened with Chris last week and that thankfully my 'night away' with Charlie was ruined by the blizzard, but he's adamant that we make up for it soon.

Olivia takes a minute when I am finally done talking, and then she says, "I can't believe Chris is such a prick! To be honest, I never loved him, but I never would have thought he was that much of an ass! I'm sorry you had to go through that."

"Sorry? I'm the one who screwed up here. I've risked my marriage for a complete jerk – who cares about Chris, I deserved that."

"No you didn't. We'll talk about that in a second, but I think you're more upset about what happened last week than you realize. What you just told me sounds horrible. Even if you shouldn't have been there, you don't deserve to be treated like that," Gretchen says.

"Thanks," I say quietly, although I'm not convinced.

"So it's totally over, right?" Gretchen asks.

"Yes. Of course it's over!" I say, horrified at the thought of ever talking to Chris again.

"Okay, good. So that's it. It's over and you just move on," Gretchen says matter-of-factly.

"But, what about Charlie?" I ask

"What about him?" Gretchen says bluntly as she takes a sip of her coffee, which must be ice-cold by now.

"I have to tell him," I say.

"You definitely don't have to tell him. You can't tell him," Gretchen insists.

"But I can't keep this from him. How am I supposed to look at him every day for the rest of our lives knowing that I cheated on him and never told him?" I ask her.

"First of all, you only kind of cheated on him. You changed your mind before anything really bad happened. But more importantly, what good would come from it if you told him? You're going to stop feeling guilty for about a second, then he's going to be miserable and hurt and angry and then you're still going to feel guilty only you'll have brought Charlie into your mess too. How is that better?" Gretchen asks.

"Well, when you put it that way, it doesn't sound better. I just can't believe I can move forward if I don't tell him," I say miserably.

"That's the only way you can do it. You have to promise me you won't tell him. I know Charlie and he is going to be so upset if you tell him. It's actually selfish to tell him, because then you feel better and he feels worse, right?" Gretchen tries to reason.

"So I just pretend everything is normal?"

"Well, what have you been doing for the last few months? Has Charlie suspected anything?"

"I don't think so. I've been so wrapped up in my own little world, I'm not sure what he thinks, but I guess he doesn't think that anything's different," I speculate.

"So you keep doing exactly that. Only now, you don't have anything to hide, and soon you'll forget all about Chris and everything will go back to the way it was before," Gretchen says confidently.

I'm not sure I want everything to go back to exactly the way it was before. I shouldn't have ever gotten involved with Chris, but I think if things were all perfect, then I never would have been tempted in the first place. But it's more important to fix the mess I've made, so I'll have to worry about that later.

"You make it all sound so easy Gretchen, forgive my asking, but do you have any personal experience here that I don't know about?" I ask in a jovial tone, but I'm actually quite curious considering her tone of authority on the topic.

"Not me, but Alan's sister. A few years ago she had an affair. It was much more involved than you and Chris. Anyhow, she ended the affair, but then she confessed everything to her husband thinking he would be happy she was being honest or something like that; however, he did not appreciate the honesty. He left her and then they had this horrible divorce and a custody battle – the whole thing was really ugly. So, I think the moral of the story is not to cheat, but if you do and it's over, you don't need to tell the other person!"

"Hmmm, I'm not sure a lot of people would support that moral, but I can see it as a cautionary tale," I say.

"So, you promise me you aren't going to tell Charlie? If you're upset or you need someone to talk to, you just call me, whatever you need, but nothing good will come of it if you tell him."

"Okay, I promise, I won't tell him," I tell Gretchen. But I still feel unsettled knowing that I will be keeping this secret the rest of my life. Until this whole disaster with Chris started, I never kept a secret from Charlie. He knew everything that happened, even the tiny things that he didn't want to know - like when I ran out of deodorant and had to use his, or when the guy at the salad place gave me an extra diet coke and I didn't give it back.

Maybe this secret is my punishment – the secret and the guilt are the price I will pay.

"And Liv, try to remember, you messed up a little, but this doesn't make you a bad person, okay?"

Gretchen leans over to give me a hug and I can't stop picturing myself on Chris's lap, with my shirt off, ready to do anything. I would like to believe Gretchen, but I'm not sure she can definitively say that I'm not a bad person.

Chapter 35 – Gretchen

This week has not gone as I expected.

The blizzard last Friday ruined all of my plans for the weekend, and I am still trying to catch up on things I couldn't get done when we were all stuck home for three days. And then Olivia dropped that bombshell on me on Monday morning. I'm hoping that I had the right reaction and was a good and supportive friend, but truthfully I am still in shock. I can't believe she would cheat on Charlie! And I stand by my advice that she shouldn't tell him, but I can't imagine hiding that big of a secret from Alan.

Although that might be a bit hypocritical, since I am currently hiding the secret about Alice from him, and now I am hiding this secret about Charlie and Olivia. I'm pretty sure he would kill me if he realized that I knew his best friend was being cheated on, and I was keeping it from him.

I was planning to tell Alan about Alice and the horrible dating site over the weekend, but she was here the whole time with the snowstorm, and I wanted her to be out of the house so Alan could have some time to digest the news. But now there has been complete silence on her site, and with all communications with her suitors for the last 4 days. I'm sure it is wishful thinking, but what if all of this nonsense is done and all the girls have come to their senses and it's just over? I know I still need to punish Alice, but maybe I can handle it myself with her and not even involve Alan at all.

Then last night Alan comes home and tells me that he got a call from the Chicago Tribune. He kept saying, "it's still early," but I haven't seen him this excited about work in years. He was so animated telling me about the phone call he had with the editor in chief of the Tribune, it was hard for me not to be excited for him, even though I can't ever imagine leaving Westchester. I naively asked if it would really make sense to leave the New York Times, implying that Chicago would be a step down, but he assured me that this job would be a huge promotion and he would be working directly for the editor in chief of the Tribune, something that would never happen for him at the Times. I could see the stars in his eyes as he imagined himself running the whole paper one day. He was quick to remind me of how 'perfect' this was for me too since I work at home and could do my job anywhere. I didn't bother to tell him that it doesn't happen exactly that way, I'll wait until we are further along to have that discussion.

Obviously I want Alan to have great success in his career, and I know he hasn't been happy at work for quite some time; however, the idea of moving to Chicago makes me ill. I don't know a single person in the entire state of Illinois.

I have lived in New York for all 41 years of my life, only leaving Westchester County for four years to travel to Syracuse for college and then I returned home to White Plains – I wasn't even sure I could handle the move to Rye when Alan and I got married.

I know I need to wait and see what happens with the interviews, but for his sake I am terrified if he doesn't succeed and for my sake I am terrified if he does.

I want to call Olivia and ask her opinion on the meaning of the inactivity on the dating site, and I really want to confide in her about the potential of a move to Chicago, even though Alan told me not to say anything. But, I imagine she has enough to worry about without dumping my problems on her as well, and she is probably particularly stressed since she is hosting wine club tomorrow night. She's not a gifted actress, but hopefully she can busy herself playing hostess so no one will notice that she's a wreck.

I know I need to motivate to get work done, especially since I got a lot less done over the last few days, but I am having trouble finding the proper inspiration this morning. I look outside at the dark clouds and the stick-figure trees – the snow looks dirty and unkempt from hours of snow angels and snowball fights. To temporarily improve my mood, I cut myself an unnecessarily large piece of banana bread and put it on a pretty blue toile plate and refill my coffee in a matching mug. I slowly make my way to my little office and settle in for several hours of work before my second job starts at 3 o'clock.

***

When Alan gets home, I am in a considerably better mood. I got through all of the books for the local florist today and even got started on the budget for the pet store – a lot more progress than I thought I would make. And even more encouraging was that there was complete silence on Alice's match.com site and no texts on the topic. I'm planning to wait a few more days and then I can tell her I know what she's been doing, and I'm glad she stopped and we can determine a reasonable punishment without ever having to tell Alan.

"Where are the kids?" Alan asks when he comes in, giving me a quick kiss on the cheek.

"Alice is in her room doing homework, and Natalie and Ethan are watching TV. You're stuck with me," I say.

"I want to be stuck with you," he grins. "I have some exciting news."

My stomach drops, but I try to keep the smile on my face, "What's the news? Is it about the Trib? I thought you weren't talking to them until sometime next week?" I say casually.

"That's just it! I wasn't supposed to talk to them again until next week, but they called again today and asked if I had a few minutes to talk, and of course I said yes, and we ended up talking for almost an hour. And then, you won't believe this, but they want me to come out to Chicago next week, isn't that great?" Alan practically yells.

"Wow. Um, yeah that's great. It's so quick."

"I know, right? On the phone today, they said that if this happens they would want me to start in a month, can you believe it? I mean I know you and the kids would probably need a little longer to move out there, so I would go first and then you could get stuff settled here and come join me," he says.

"You've got it all figured out, huh?" I say, with more of an edge to my voice than intended.

"What's that supposed to mean?" Alan asks.

"It just sounds like you've had two phone calls and you've decided that you are packing up our whole family and moving us across the country without even asking anyone's opinion," I say with my arms folded across my chest, my body language adding to my sentiment.

"Nothing's happened yet. And is it so wrong if I am excited about something? The first good thing that has happened to me at work in years! This could be my chance for a huge career move - to finally be recognized for my work - and to finally make some money. Aren't you sick of being poor?" Alan says.

"Oh good lord Alan, we aren't poor," I say dismissively.

"Fine, we aren't actually poor. But we are poor compared to all of our friends. I'm tired of having less money than everyone else. Doesn't it bother you that your friends are so much wealthier than we are? They live in bigger houses and go on better vacations and have fancier clothes – and none of them have to work like you do," Alan says angrily.

I reply calmly, "you know, it used to bother me a lot. When I first met all of them I was envious of their houses – and sometimes I still am. And of course it would be nice to take more vacations, or honestly to take any vacations. But I don't like fancy clothes or shoes or jewelry. And I love our house – it is the perfect house for us – what would we do with 10,000 square feet? We would get lost. After I got to know most of these 'rich people' as you think of them, I've realized that they have all of the same problems as we do; actually I think they have more problems, and they definitely aren't happier than we are. I want you to be happy at work and to be proud of what you are doing, but please don't make any decision because you think we need more money, especially not if you think it's because *I* need more money," I exhale after my monologue and look at Alan to see if he's actually heard what I've said.

He doesn't say anything for a minute and I wonder if he's gearing up for a big fight, or if he's just digesting what I said. When he speaks again it is in a much quieter voice. "Okay, your point is taken. But, I still want to see if I can get this job in Chicago. I need to know that someone still thinks I'm good at my job," he holds up his hand in a stopping motion, "besides you Gretchen. I know that you love it here, but maybe you'd love it there too? Can you just let me see if I get the job and then we can discuss it?"

"Okay," I concede, "go to Chicago next week and knock 'em dead and then we'll deal with it."

"It'll be okay," Alan says. "I promise, as long as we're together, I promise it will be okay."

Chapter 36 – Danielle

"What's wrong?" Megan asks me as I am driving her home alone from school; Kyle is staying late for basketball practice, but thankfully getting a ride home from a friend.

"What do you mean?" I answer.

"I'm 15, not stupid. Did something happen with you and my dad?" she asks.

"Why would you ask that?" I ask her, trying to figure out what gave us away. It's not that she's wrong, it's just that I thought we had been doing a good job of acting normally – I guess I should stop waiting for my Emmy to be delivered in the mail.

"You and Dad are both acting really weird. I don't know what happened. If I knew what happened, I wouldn't have to ask, would I?" Megan skipped the 'duh' after her comment, but it was implied.

"I guess not."

"So what's wrong? Is it about the baby? Is there another woman?" she taunts.

"Megan! That is none of your business," I shout at her, much louder than I mean to.

"Sorry, sorry. I was just kidding," she says, slouching down in her seat next to me.

Now I don't know what to say after my overreaction, I'm obviously not making this look any better by screaming at her.

"Sorry for yelling, it must just be the hormones," I say sheepishly. If all else fails, blame the pregnancy – I've quickly learned that no one knows how to challenge a pregnant woman.

Maybe honestly is the best policy – or at least partial truths. "Your dad and I just had a little fight. It happens, all married couples fight sometimes."

Megan gives me a look as if to say, 'don't you remember I'm the child of divorced parents who went through an ugly marriage and uglier divorce – I know about fights.'

"Right," I continue, "so we had a little fight about the triathlon we were going to run in Hawaii and decided that it made sense for him to go without me and I will stay home, and then we can do the race together next year after the baby is born." I hope that it sounds like this was decided mutually, although I may still be too bitter to make that sound realistic.

Megan makes a noise I can't decipher – I'm going to choose to believe it is her way of accepting my story and ending the conversation.

We ride the rest of the way home in silence. We pull into the garage and Megan gets out of the car, and then before she goes into the house she turns around and says, "sorry my dad can be such a dick sometimes," and then she's gone.

I stand there with the car door open, still in total shock. Just when I think I know a little bit more about her, I realize I don't know her at all.

***

It's wine club again tonight. I don't know if I'm officially a member of the club, or if everyone is just taking pity on me because I still don't have a lot of friends here, but I'm fine with either option. I suppose tonight is when I will tell everyone that I am pregnant – it's either that or I wear a gigantic poncho and just let them think I've gotten fat.

I'm not sure why I'm nervous to tell people. Jim and I have been married for close to a year now, I'm almost 30, there's nothing unusual about my pregnancy. But I'm probably worried that they will wonder how Jim feels about having another baby when his kids are so much older. And even more worried since many of them *know* Jim that they know exactly how he feels, which I should have realized sooner.

I put on the same black pants I wore last week to try and impress Jim, it's only been a week, but my belly is significantly bigger than it was then and the pants look even more flattering. I choose a black and white striped sweater with ruched sides that act as neon arrows pointing to my bump – I could definitely still wear a non-maternity sweater, but I'm trying to let the sweater speak for itself so I don't have to do all the talking.

I look in the mirror to evaluate the overall 'look' - I contemplate asking Megan's opinion, but I'm not sure how that will be received. I look at myself from the front, and then turn sideways and then from the front again. I still have trouble believing that is a little person inside of me, but each day it gets more and more believable. Every other part of me still looks the same, except my short hair might be a little bit thicker. I reach up to touch my cheekbones and my neck, and reassure myself that there isn't extra padding that wasn't there yesterday. I'm fine with gaining weight, but I don't think I can deal with losing my cheekbones or getting a double chin, as shallow as that may be.

I'm glad that Jim isn't home yet when I leave. I know that we need to address what's going on, and avoiding each other does not count as dealing with the situation; but I am not in the mood to deal with him right now.

***

I've never been to Olivia's house and I'm looking forward to seeing her home. I imagine that everything is organized and orderly, just like she is. I am picturing labeled storage boxes everywhere, the upscale ones that I've seen in home catalogs, and anything that is out in the open will be meticulously displayed – like canisters of flour, sugar and coffee.

I pull into her circular driveway and park behind an unfamiliar car. There are already at least 8 cars here – I'm not the last one here, but considering I'm likely not an official member of this club, I don't want to be the first to arrive.

I take a deep breath and give my belly a pat for good luck, which is almost impossible to feel through my heavy down coat, and I head for the door.

The front door is cracked open, so I let myself in and put my coat on the front hall bench. I don't think anyone has noticed I am here yet, but I can tell I was already wrong on my approximation of Olivia's house. It is significantly smaller than Laura's house (but everyone's house is), and although it is smaller than my house, it is still spacious, and the first word that comes to mind to describe it is - perfect. It is rustic and warm, with oversized rooms and beautiful, inviting fabrics. The first floor is almost completely open-plan and I can see her living room, dining room and family room from the hall, and I can even glimpse into the kitchen where everyone is gathered. I think about the rooms I have just re-decorated in Jim's house and how pristine they look, but they feel so cold compared Olivia's house, more like a museum than a home.

I walk through the living room, brushing my hand along the back of the sofa, the brushed velvet feeling as soft as I knew it would. I quietly enter the kitchen amongst the raucous laughter created by ten women carrying on five separate conversations, fueled by multiples glasses of wine. I stand there for a minute before anyone notices me and then Olivia sees me and motions me over to the group with her free hand while she finishes her conversation.

I slide in between Olivia and Stephanie and try to catch up on their conversation. It's about school, that much is easy to interpret, but I can't tell which of their children they are referencing. I look for an entry into the conversation, but it seems easier to wait until they are done and nod along until then.

"Sorry to bore you!" Olivia says, "we were just discussing the new teacher at the lower school. She's taking over for one of Julie's teachers who just went out on maternity leave, and it's a bit of a change in the middle of the year. Can I get you a glass of wine? Red or white?"

Here's my chance, "actually, I'll have sparkling water if you have some. I can't drink for the next few months."

"Really? What's wrong?" Stephanie asks.

I take a step back so that they can see me better and I use both hands to rub my little belly and say the line I've only said to a few, select people, "I'm pregnant."

As I hoped would happen, both women scream and then hug me.

"That's so exciting!" squeals Olivia.

"How are you feeling? When are you due?" Stephanie asks.

The rest of the group notices the commotion and soon I am the center of attention and everyone is gathered around me asking questions, touching my belly, telling me how amazing I look, and sharing their own pregnancy stories. I know this doesn't erase all of my issues with Jim at home, or with my new status as permanent step-mom; but for a minute I get to bask in the glow of pregnancy I've previously only heard about.

My house is eerily quiet. The twins and Logan are at school and Jody took Cameron to his Friday morning baby class – I think it's gymnastics, but it might be music. I should feel bad that I don't know this, but I feel bad about too many other things right now to let that one worry me.

Everyone has left me alone in peace and quiet, because they believe that is what I want, but being alone doesn't make me feel any better. I don't know if Claudia told the kids that I wasn't feeling well, or if everyone can just sense it, but this past week everyone is on their best behavior - a new unwritten and unspoken rule. I want to put up a fight and tell them that I miss the bickering and the laughing and the screaming, but I can't seem to find the energy.

Michael has been in London for the past 5 days and got back late last night. It shouldn't be too much different than when he works late at night, but I hate sleeping in our big bed alone, and then waking up alone, and doing it all over the next night. He crawled into bed last night just after midnight and curled up next to me. I instantly felt better, even if just for a few hours. Although, when he left at 5am this morning (jet lag he said) I felt like I lost a limb, the pain was almost unbearable.

Now I find myself at the kitchen table, still in my nightgown and robe, nursing a cup of coffee, and I decide it is time to look at the texts that have been buzzing through on my phone all morning.

Gretchen: Where were u last night? We missed u!!

Danielle: You missed big news last night ☺

Sharon: Call me – we need to talk about final numbers

John: Want to do a session today? Hope you feel better – you must be really sick to cancel on me ☺ Let me know and I'll come by!

The only text I was hoping for isn't there – the one from CVS letting me know that the doctor called in my prescription.

I should reply to my friends, it's nice of them to notice my absence at wine club last night and check on me. I called Olivia at the last minute yesterday and told her I wasn't feeling well, but I'm not sure she believed me. I'm mildly curious about the news to which Danielle is referring, but not curious enough to engage in a discussion.

I don't even know what numbers Sharon is talking about, so there is no point in responding to her. It must be about this god-awful winter carnival next week. I haven't even made it to the last two meetings, so I wouldn't think she would have any questions of substance for me, but that doesn't seem to be the case. Sharon could run this thing blind-folded with both hands tied behind her back; she only wanted me involved because I have a lot of connections at school and in town, and she's self aware enough to realize that most people don't like her.

I have to text John back. If he is pursuing me, then things must be bad. I thought I had an appointment with him last week, but I must have cancelled it. I know I've seen him since I've been back from vacation, but I can't remember when.   I know I would have more energy if I had a training session; I'm sure that's my problem, I just need some exercise. Although an hour in the gym, doing burpees and kettle bells and handstand push-ups with John yelling at me the whole time sounds miserable. Maybe I'll get back to him after I lie down.

I wander back upstairs, conveniently still in my nightgown, and crawl back into my unmade bed. I know I took something a little while ago when I woke up, but I'm worried that I am now 'too tired' to fall asleep, so I take a bottle out of the middle drawer of my nightstand and take one more pill to make sure I can rest. I promise myself I'll return those messages when I wake up.

***

I feel a hand on my shoulder gently shaking me awake. It smells and feels like Michael, but I know that it can't be him this early in the day. Oh God, unless it's already evening and I slept all day. I try and open my eyes, but it's taking longer than I would like to unfurl my eyelids and orient myself.

"What time is it?" I ask, my voice sounds thick and raspy in my ears.

"It's 11:30," Michael says.

I sit up quickly upon hearing this; my head hurts from the rapid change in elevation. "I slept all day?" I ask in confusion – the room darkening shades and silence in the house are not helping with my sense of time.

"No, Laura, it's 11:30 in the morning. I don't know how long you've been asleep." He never calls me Laura, so that's unusual, and he's talking to me the way he speaks to the kids when he is trying to explain something very complicated that they might not understand.

"Wait, what are you doing home? Is something wrong? Did something happen at the office? Are the kids okay?" I was so disoriented when I first woke up that I didn't realize how abnormal it is that Michael is home in the middle of the morning on a weekday – I can't remember this ever happening before.

"The kids are fine, but I think something *is* wrong," he says gravely.

"What's wrong?" I ask, suddenly concerned.

"I got a call from my doctor telling me that he wouldn't be able to refill my Percocet prescription from my knee surgery unless I came in to see him; although he was very concerned that the pain was suddenly bothering me two years later," Michael pauses in his story and stares at me.

I hug my knees to my chest and bury my head on top of my knees; I know it is the ultimate in childish thinking, but right now I'm hoping that if I can't see him, somehow he also won't be able to see me.

Michael goes on, "I told the doctor that there must have been some sort of mix up at the pharmacy because I didn't call in a refill for that prescription, but he was very clear on what happened. He told me that my wife had called and insisted that I couldn't admit how much pain I was in, but she could tell how bad it was, so she wanted to make sure I had the pills so I could stop being such a hero."

My face is burning with shame and embarrassment. I don't know how I thought Michael wouldn't find out about it. I honestly thought the doctor believed me and was going to call in the pills. He actually told me that was what he was going to do! But instead he must have hung up the phone with me, and immediately called Michael – I am so stupid!

"Laura, my beautiful girl. What is going on?" Michael asks. But now he doesn't sound mad, or condescending, he sounds worried, and even scared.

"Sweetie, please talk to me. What's wrong?" I hear the strength in Michael' s voice begin to waver.

I can't look at him; I am too ashamed of what I've done to even begin to answer his question.

"Please just talk to me. If there is a problem, we can fix it," he pauses as if hoping I will say something, but then continues. "I know I haven't been around very much. I noticed that something was wrong in December, but then we went on vacation and everything seemed so good that I assumed it was better, or maybe I just wanted to think that it was better," he sighs.

"But I can't help you if you don't talk to me. I love you. You know I would do anything to make you happy. Please, just say something." Michael's voice catches as he says "please" and I think he is holding back tears, I can't take it if he cries, he's always so strong, I don't know what to do if he starts crying – especially if I'm the one that's making him cry.

"I don't know what's wrong," I whisper, "but something's wrong, I mean everything's wrong and I don't know how to fix it," I say and start weeping. At first the tears come slowly, hot and salty running down my face, but then they turn into uncontrollable sobs and I am crying so hard I can't catch my breath. Michael wraps his arms around me and holds me while I shake and cry, soaking his shirt with tears. I crawl into his lap so that he can hold me closer and he rubs my back and whispers soft 'shushing' noises in my ear, the way my mom used to do when I was a child.

Before I can lose my nerve, but still without making eye contact, I say, "I think I have a problem."

"What kind of problem?" Michael asks in a cross between his husband and mr-fix-it boardroom voice.

"I think I have a problem with pills." I don't know what's going to happen next, but a 50-pound weight has just been lifted from my shoulders; I almost start crying again with the relief that someone else finally knows.

Chapter 38 – Olivia

Every time my phone buzzes, I fear that it is Chris texting me. I don't know what he would say, or why he would want to talk to me, but I still panic with each vibration. Over the past few weeks I've actually thought about changing my phone number; but I don't know how I would explain that to Charlie, and I've had this number for 12 years, so it would be a huge pain in the ass to change it now.

Although I cannot imagine what I would say to him if he called, or if god forbid, I actually ran into him somewhere, I have still envisioned the conversation countless times, continually revising my lines. In some versions of my daydream, I yell at him and tell him what an absolute pig he is, in others I cry and tell him how much he hurt me and ask how he could do this to me, and there are some episodes where I have little emotion, but I want him to explain in detail his Jekyll and Hyde personality.

I'm sure that he has moved on to someone else and is casually flirting with her, making her think she is falling for him, waiting to set her up for his degrading sex act. But part of me wonders if he is really like that with everyone, or if that was some special Madonna-Whore thing he reserved just for me. I knew he had always liked me, even when I was young and newly married, but I dismissed it. I'm probably giving myself too much credit and blame to think that he has been pining for me for all these years and was hurt to think I had cheated with other people, just not with him – now I'm actually making excuses for his behavior, what is my problem?

There are days when I go hours without thinking about him at all, or more importantly, I don't think about what I did to Charlie. But then there are days when it is all I can think about. I am sitting in the viewing room at ballet watching my beautiful daughter dance, and all I can see are images of Chris's penis flashing in front of my face. I'm sure that everyone around me can tell what I'm thinking about, but when I glance over, the mom on my right is busy knitting her scarf and the nanny on my left is furiously texting away on her phone.

Thankfully, Charlie seems oblivious to my erratic moods and fantasies. February is always a busy time at work and he has been working long hours and traveling more than usual. When he is home at night we talk about the girls, or his job, or local gossip. We've only had sex twice since 'the night' with Chris, and somehow I managed to hold it together both times and act normally. Charlie even apologized to me over the weekend for our recent dry spell because he's been too busy and too tired – I am trying to listen to Gretchen's advice, but I don't know how much longer I can keep up this charade!

**

Today is Valentine's Day and Charlie and I are going out to one of our favorite restaurants. He told me that he has a surprise for me as well, but just hearing that makes me feel guilty. I bought him a new watch that I know he wants. It is a Raymond Weil ceramic watch that costs significantly more than we usually spend on Valentine's Day gifts, but apparently men are not the only people who give gifts out of guilt.

I asked Taylor to come early tonight so that I could go get my hair blown out before I get dressed. I am also wearing Charlie's favorite dress to dinner tonight – it is a simple black silk dress, but it is very short and low-cut enough to be appropriate and revealing at the same time. There are a lot of dresses in my closet that I prefer to this one, but I know that this is his favorite, and I think that is the least I can do.

Charlie should be home any minute now. I was so worried about being late, that I have been dressed and ready for 30 minutes and now I am just sitting on the bed, no longer sure how to act natural. I can hear the girls down the hall playing an animated game with Taylor, now I just need to wait to hear the front door open; I hold my breath and wait, my heart pounding so loudly I can hear each beat in my ears.

Moments later, I hear the door open and then screams of "Daddy" as the girls rush to the front door to greet him. I wait patiently and then Charlie appears at the bedroom door. I stand up from my seat on the bed and do a little spin to show off my look for the night.

Charlie gives an appreciative whistle and says, "Liv you look beautiful!" He crosses the room and pulls me close to him, catching me off guard with a long, deep kiss – not our usual greeting.

"Happy Valentine's Day!" I say, a little too loudly.

"Happy Valentine's Day sexy lady. What time do we need to leave for dinner?" Charlie asks.

"Probably in about 15 minutes. Or we could just go now and get a drink at the bar first."

"That's too bad," he says quietly, "I was hoping we had time to work up an appetite before dinner," and he leans down and starts kissing my neck and then I feel his hands start to unzip the zipper on the back of my dress.

"We can't," I say abruptly and take a step back, reaching around with both hands to zip up my zipper.

"Um, I'm pretty sure we can," Charlie says, trying to regain the mood. "I don't think they'll care if we are a few minutes late – and I promise I won't mess up your hair, don't think I didn't notice," he smiles.

"It's not the reservation, it's not my hair," I sigh as I sit down on the bench at the end of our bed.

"What's wrong?" Charlie asks, seemingly understanding that the window of opportunity for sex is gone.

"I don't know where to start. It might be better if I never even told you this, but I have to tell you. I can't live like this anymore and I think you deserve to know."

"Whoa, whoa. What are you talking about? You can't live like what anymore? Are you leaving me? What the hell is going on?" Charlie is clearly agitated, probably already thinking through worst case scenarios based on what I said, but unfortunately he isn't that far off.

"No, I'm not leaving you. I would never leave you," I tell him.

"So what's going on, I don't like the sound of this," he says.

"Well, something happened with Chris," I volunteer, although I know it is ambiguous and feeble, it is the best I can do.

"What do you mean something happened? Did you sleep with him? What are you trying to tell me here Olivia?" Charlie says, his voice getting louder and angrier.

"No, no, I didn't sleep with him. But..." oh God, how do I tell him this, what am I supposed to say - I hooked up with him, I'm not 13, shit, I did not think this through.

"But what? What the hell happened?" Charlie isn't yelling yet, but I can tell that he is close.

Oh God, here it goes, "I kissed him, a few times, and then I fooled around with him, but I didn't sleep with him. It was horrible, and he was awful and I stopped it before anything really bad could happen."

"Oh well good for you," he says, his voice dripping with sarcasm. "Am I supposed to be proud of you?"

"No, that's not what I meant, I just meant, well, just that I came to my senses before anything else happened and I realized how wrong it was." I am stumbling over my words and can barely look at Charlie.

"So, when did this happen? How long ago was it? Was it just the one time?" Charlie is looking at me with rage in his eyes.

"It was a few weeks ago, but I don't think it matters, what matters is that it's over." I am now desperately wishing I had taken Gretchen's advice.

"Well, I don't think you get to decide what matters? I'm just finding out about this now, so if it's okay with you, I still have a few more questions about my wife almost sleeping with some other guy," he says through clenched teeth.

"There's really not much to tell you," but I know I am lying as I say this, "you can ask me questions if you want, but I don't think that is going to make you feel better," I say hopefully.

"Let me decide what makes me feel better. Okay, so I do have a few questions for you, let's see, first question, did you touch his dick?"

And it went from there. For the next two hours, Charlie and I went back and forth in yelling and tears and me apologizing over and over again. It was excruciating telling Charlie about Chris and watching him get more incensed by the minute as he grilled me with detailed questions about what we said to each other, where he touched me, why I did it, etc.

Finally, Charlie seems to have exhausted his list of questions – the inquisition has ended. He isn't as angry anymore, he just looks sad and defeated - I wish he were angry again.

"I'm going to go to Westport for the night. I'm going to stay with my brother," Charlie says standing up and walking across the room toward his closet.

"No, no, please don't do that. You can stay here. I can sleep in the guest room tonight if you want and then we can talk about this in the morning. Please, Charlie, you don't need to leave," I plead with him.

"I don't think I can be around you tonight," he says as he comes out of his closet with his overnight bag and starts pulling clothes out of his dresser to pack.

I don't know what path to take, whether to cry and beg him to stay, or to acknowledge his need for space and let him go with dignity. I opt for the latter, hoping that is what he wants me to do.

"Will you be back tomorrow?" I ask hopefully, noticing that he has packed more than one day's worth of clothes.

"I don't know Olivia," he says. I wince as he continues to use my full name. "I need some time to think about this. You've just shattered my entire world, so I honestly don't know how long it's going to take me."
I nod in agreement, while the tears flow down my cheeks. "Can I call you tomorrow?" I ask, like a desperate teenager.

"I'll give you a call when I'm ready. I'll call the girls tomorrow. Please tell them that I had to go on a trip for work – there's no need for them to be involved in this," he says bitterly.

And then he's gone. Now it's almost 10 o'clock on Valentine's Night and I am still wearing this damn dress, alone in my bedroom, maybe the first night of my life as a future divorcée.

I change out of my dress and put on flannel pajamas, not even bothering to brush my teeth or wash my face; I'm sure my skin will look terrible in the morning sleeping with all of this make-up on, but that will be the least of my problems.

I know the kids are asleep. I hope that Charlie paid Taylor before he left, and that she is not still sitting downstairs waiting for me, but I don't have the energy to check. Lord knows what she thinks happened here tonight and what she is going to tell her parents when she gets home.

I reach over to turn off the light on the night table; sitting on the table is Charlie's unopened, over-priced guilt gift. I was sure I had no more moisture in my body to produce tears, but the tears begin to flow again and I cry myself to sleep, only hoping tomorrow will be a better day.

Chapter 39 – Danielle

"Happy Valentine's Day Mom," I say cheerfully into the phone.

"Happy Valentine's Day sweetie!" my mom says back. "How are you feeling? Is everything okay?"

"I feel really good. Everything's fine," I assure her.

"Oh good. I just haven't talked to you in over a week. Remember when we used to talk every day," she says with that special kind of guilt only mothers can manufacture.

"I know mom, I'm sorry, things are just so busy here. I'll call more, I promise," I tell her. Although things *are* busy here, especially with Kyle's and Megan's schedules, that is not the reason I have not been calling my mom. I don't want to lie to her, but I don't want to worry her by telling her that things aren't great with Jim, and I know that the more often I talk to her, the harder it will be to keep it from her.

"Have you had any more doctor appointments recently? Is there any news? You looked so cute in the picture you sent the other day," she gushes.

"I have an appointment in a few days. It's my 20-week ultrasound, which I guess is pretty important. The doctor told me to expect it to take almost an hour. They check every little thing about the baby to make sure it's okay. I promise I'll send you a picture of the little alien when I have it," I joke, knowing she does not like it when I refer to her future grandchild as an extraterrestrial.

"I can't believe how much everything has changed since I was pregnant, it's amazing! I wish I could be there with you," my mom says.

"I told you that you could come anytime you want," I tell her, hoping that she continues to refuse the offer - not knowing what I will do if she accepts.

"I know, I know. I wish I could, but I think we should stick to our plan. You'll come down here during the kids' spring break while they are away, and then your dad and I will both get to see you. Besides, I wouldn't want to step on Jim's toes."

"Oh, I'm sure he'd be fine with it," I say, knowing that he won't be anywhere near the radiology department on Tuesday, "but you're right, we'll keep our plans the way they are."

My mom and I talk for a little while longer, mostly talking about the baby. She still doesn't understand why I don't want to know if it's a boy or a girl - she's confident I will change my mind once I have to start decorating the nursery.

Before we hang up, I promise that I will call more frequently and she reiterates her excitement. It's wonderful that my mom is so enthusiastic, as well as my new friends, and even Kyle and Megan – if only Jim were anywhere near as committed to this baby, this pit in my stomach might disappear.

***

I am meeting Jim at a local restaurant for dinner for Valentine's Day. He suggested a restaurant in the city, one of our old favorites, but I didn't feel up to the trip.

I'm going to make an effort tonight to put my anger and resentment behind me, and give Jim another chance. I've tried to put myself in his shoes recently and it must be a huge adjustment to be a new dad again after 12 years. I told him when we met that I wanted kids, but the hypothetical and the reality are quite different. I am experiencing that as well with his children; I knew I would be a step-mom, but I thought it would be a title in name only, I didn't realize that I would be called into duty.

I may have made some hasty decisions, but it's too late to turn back now. I need to have a fresh start with Jim. I will rediscover all of the reasons I fell in love with him in the first place and then everything will be okay. My positive mindset is making me feel better already. The mood in the house has been too negative since Jim told me about his plans for the Hawaii trip, and I have been fueling that with my own destructive energy; that can't be good for the kids, and that certainly can't be good for the baby.

I'm sitting at the table, anxiously awaiting Jim's arrival; I wish I could order a glass of wine but I know that I would get disapproving glances from people at the other tables and I can't handle the judgment. I am facing the restaurant's front door so that I can see Jim when he arrives. The door keeps opening and couples enter with their arms wrapped around each other, husbands' taking their wives' coats, partners kissing while they wait for the maître d' to seat them – everyone is more in love tonight than usual, and those without the tolerance for these types of displays, or even worse, without anyone at all, wouldn't dare dine out at a restaurant such as this on February 14th.

I glance at my watch for the twentieth time in as many minutes to confirm what I already know - Jim is late. I take out my phone to make sure I have not missed a text or an email or a call from him telling me that he is running late, but I have not missed anything. I don't have a single new email or call or text because everyone I know right now is out celebrating Valentine's Day.

The waiter comes over and politely asks me again if I would like anything to drink. I order a second club soda, with a lemon this time for variety. I'm sure Jim has a good reason for being late and not letting me know – he must be stuck somewhere and his phone died, or maybe he lost his phone. Oh my god, maybe he is hurt, or he was in an accident! I try to erase some of the nasty thoughts that have gone through my head, as I realize that something could be wrong.

Thirty-six minutes after our reservation time, I look up at the front door to see my husband walk inside, seemingly uninjured and in perfect condition. He hands his coat and briefcase to the woman at the coat-check and scans the restaurant until he sees me at the table; he gives a half-wave and then starts to walk toward me.

"Sorry I'm a little late," Jim says as he pulls out his chair to sit down.

"You're over a half hour late!" I say, exasperated with him, already forgetting my commitment to a fresh start.

"Really? I must have lost track of time. Sorry about that," he says, without remorse.

"Where were you?" I ask.

"A few of us went out for drinks after work," he says nonchalantly.

"On Valentine's Day? Who goes out for drinks on Valentine's Day?" I ask, aware of the pointless nature of the question, but unable to let it go.

"I guess I do," he says matter-of-factly, looking around for the waiter to order a drink.

His comment stings me. He left me sitting by myself for thirty-six minutes without even a text letting me know he was running late, and now he won't even let me be mad about it. I pick up my menu so I have something to look at other than his face. I picture what would happen if I just got up right now and walked across the restaurant, got my coat, and walked out the door. Would he chase after me? Would the other diners stare and then talk about us for the rest of their meal? Would Jim be humiliated and realize how upset I must be feeling? I wish I could find out the answer, but I am glued to my seat. I will my legs to move, to display an act of protest, but I know I'm not going anywhere – that just isn't me, or at least who I am now.

After Jim and I place our orders, and the menus have been removed, we are left with each other. Jim breaks the silence by reaching into his inside suit jacket pocket and pulls out a small blue box, tied with a white ribbon. I hate myself a little bit right now, because just seeing that blue box makes me feel kinder toward him. It is the best and worst marketing in the world, but Tiffany has created a Pavlovian response with those little boxes. I know I am not alone, because I see women at the tables around us have noticed Jim's gesture and are trying not to be obvious, but they too are curious to see what treasures might be inside.

"I really am sorry I was late," Jim says, "Happy Valentine's Day Dani." And he hands me the box and gives me a soft kiss on the lips.

Other than a couple gifts when we were dating, and my massive engagement ring, I actually have very few pieces of jewelry, so I really am quite excited to open the present, even though I am trying to contain my enthusiasm and make sure Jim knows that this does not mean all is forgiven.

I open the outer box, then the soft blue pouch inside, and let out an audible gasp.

"Do you like it?" Jim asks.

I am speechless. But clearly not in the way Jim thinks. It is a brooch. It is a fucking brooch! It is a diamond and sapphire seahorse brooch! It may be the ugliest thing I have ever seen. I am 29-years old, not 95 years old! Did he actually think I would ever wear this? Does he know me at all? Did he even buy this, or send someone to get this hideous piece of jewelry for me? Does he even know me at all? And then I remember. I have only met Linda a few times, but the last two times I saw her, she was wearing a brooch (or a fancy pin, as my mom would say)

on her dress. It looks like tonight is not the fresh start I
envisaged – I think I'm going to need a different plan.

Chapter 40 – Gretchen

"I'm sure it wasn't that bad," I say to Olivia as she sits across from me at my kitchen table, recounting to me the events from last night after she ignored all of my advice.

"No, I promise, it really was that bad. It was like I didn't get just how big of a deal it was until I said it out loud to Charlie. And then it was awful. It was worse than awful. I don't think I could have kept it from him forever, but maybe you were right, maybe that was better. I don't think he's ever going to forgive me," she says hopelessly.

"He will. I know he will. Charlie loves you. He just needs some time," I reassure her, hoping that I am right.

"Mommy, I'm bored," Julie says wandering into the kitchen.

"I know sweetie, we'll go home soon, just a little while longer," Olivia tells her daughter.

"Don't worry about it. I'll ask Alice to play with the girls. She won't mind," I tell Olivia.

"I'm sure she has better things to do," Olivia says.

"She can spare a little of her time, I promise," I assure her, as I yell up to Alice. I'm still not convinced that the situation with Alice has been resolved, but I feel like Alice owes me, even though she doesn't know it yet, so I feel no guilt in requiring her to do some free Saturday morning babysitting.

Alice begrudgingly comes downstairs and takes Elizabeth and Julie into the family room.

"Thank you Alice!" Olivia calls after her. "Thanks Gretchen. I could use a little more time being sad in here before I have to be happy for them for the rest of the weekend."

"Are you going to call him?" I ask her.
"He called this morning, but as soon as I picked up he asked to speak to the girls, and I could tell by his tone that he did not want to talk to me. Julie took the phone in her room and I could hear her giggling with him and then Elizabeth came in and they were laughing and being silly. I was eavesdropping from the hall like a naughty child, which I guess I am, and then Julie came back and gave me my phone and said "Daddy had to go," and that was it. So I don't think I should call him, it will probably just piss him off."

"I'm sure he'll be home tomorrow. He'll probably just spend the weekend with his brother and then he'll come home and you guys will talk about it tomorrow night. He'll go get drunk with his brother tonight and realize that he misses you, even though he's still mad, and he'll come home," I tell her confidently.

"I hope you're right. Okay, tell me something, anything, to take my mind off of this. You must have some news or gossip, there must be something we can talk about other than my miserable life," Olivia moans.

I definitely have news to share, but I don't think Olivia wants to hear it right now. Alan had a great week in Chicago and is now waiting for his formal offer to be the next Executive Editor of the Chicago Tribune. I know that it is a huge step up from his role as Business Editor at the Times and I am thrilled to see him this excited, and that someone is finally acknowledging his years of hard work; however, I don't know if I'll survive the move. Making new friends at my age, starting over with new schools and new social groups and even new grocery stores! I certainly have gossip that will take Olivia's mind off of her own problems, but I think it may push her over the edge.

Instead I choose a different path – the tried and true path of gossiping about others. "Can you believe that Danielle is pregnant? That must be quite a shock for Jim."

"Oh, I know! Actually, I heard from Stephanie that he's not happy about it, but I'm not sure how she knows that. But, what did he expect? He married that young girl and then he didn't think she was going to want a baby? It's his own fault, if he's that stupid. I just feel bad for her. I don't think this is what she expected at all. She has Kyle and Megan full-time now, and she is going to have the baby. And I don't know Jim very well at all, but from what I've heard, he's not very involved as a dad," Olivia says, engaged in the conversation, happy to have moved on to someone else's troubles.

"We used to be friendly with Jim and Linda, a long time ago, when Alice and Megan were little. I actually never liked either of them very much. I wasn't surprised when I heard they were getting divorced, nor was I surprised when I heard that he was getting re-married to a 20-something girl from his office only a few months later. But I was surprised when I met Danielle because she seems so nice and normal! I can't understand why she would throw away a successful career as a lawyer and her whole life in the city, for someone like Jim!" I'm actually surprised that Olivia and I haven't had this conversation sooner since we've clearly both been thinking the same thing for months.

"He *is* really good looking," Olivia offers, "and he is in amazing shape. I prefer my men a little larger and more cuddly, but I did see him running one day with his shirt off and he could be on the cover of one of those men's fitness magazines."

"I wonder if he's really good in bed?" I speculate aloud.

"Eww, gross. I don't want to think about him in bed," Olivia says.

"I'm just thinking that he must be really good in bed, to get a cute, young girl like Danielle when he's 45. But the honeymoon phase always wears off - hopefully she enjoys it while it lasts," I say.

"I think she has a while before that happens. And maybe he'll be different this time around," Olivia suggests.

Just then, Julie and Elizabeth run screaming into the room, Julie is in tears.

"She bit me!" Julie screams, pointing at her sister.

"Did not," Elizabeth yells back.
Julie then holds up her arm and shows Olivia the complete set of teethmarks on her forearm that are so

pristine they could almost be used for dental identification purposes.

"Elizabeth, apologize to your sister. We will deal with this at home."

To me she says, "Okay, I think this must be my cue to leave."

Alice walks sheepishly into the kitchen. "Sorry Mrs. Somers. I was watching them, but then my phone rang, and I got distracted for just a minute. I'm really sorry."

"It's okay Alice, it's not your fault," Olivia says to her.

I am annoyed at Alice, but getting mad at her won't do any good now, and most likely Elizabeth would still have bitten Julie even if Alice was right there – Lizzy bites when she's mad, it's a well known fact.

Olivia makes her way into the front hall and starts to put coats and hats on the girls and gets herself ready to leave.

"Thanks for talking Gretchen. I really do feel better. I may need to call you again in a few hours when I have another meltdown, but for now I'm okay," Olivia says with a weak smile.

"You're more than welcome, so happy I could help," I tell her.

"Oh, by the way. I meant to ask you if you've heard anything from Laura. I called her after wine club and she never got back to me, and I haven't seen her at school or anywhere all week. I know you see her more than I do, but I just wanted to check and make sure she is okay," Olivia asks.

"Actually, I was going to drop by her house in the next day or so, because I haven't heard from her either. I got one text from her last week, but it didn't say much and that is all I have heard from her. She might just be busy getting ready for winter carnival, but I'll try to stop by. Thanks for reminding me!"

"Okay, well let me know what you find out. And I'll call you later if I need another counseling session," Olivia jokes.

"I'll be here, but I might have to raise my hourly rate!" I tell her and give her a big hug.

I watch as Olivia takes each of her daughter's hands and walks carefully down the front path to her car, all of them bracing against the blustery February day. I'm sure that Charlie will forgive her and everything will be fine, but I am so happy I am not in her shoes right now.

Chapter 41 – Olivia

I'm curled up on the couch on Sunday night, watching re-runs of Law & Order, when I hear the front door open. Presuming it isn't a burglar who has found a key to our home, it must be Charlie coming home after the weekend with his brother – just as Gretchen predicted.

I don't want to appear too eager, although maybe I should appear eager and jump up and run to the door to greet him, but instead I maintain my position on the couch and pause the TV so I can give him my full attention when he opens the door.

"Hi there," I say quietly as Charlie walks into the front hall.

"Hey," he says, standing in the hall with his coat on and his bag over his shoulder.

"I missed you," I tell him.

"Liv, I don't think I'm ready to be home yet, I just came back to get some clothes for work tomorrow, I didn't bring any of the right clothes with me," Charlie says.

It feels like I got punched in the stomach. I knew he was mad, but I can't believe he isn't coming home.

"I think we need to talk about this," I implore, "I don't think it will help if you aren't here."

"I'm not ready to talk yet, I still need some more time by myself, okay?" he says.

"I'm so, so sorry," I say and start to cry, "it was stupid and I'm sorry, but I love you so much, and I need you, please don't leave," I sob.

"What would you do if our places were reversed? How would you feel if I had been carrying on with someone at work for several months, and came close to sleeping with her? What would you do?" he asks in a calm, rational tone.
I don't know why I hadn't put myself in his position before now. I don't know how I would react if I found out all of the things Charlie just found out about me. I would be furious if I knew he almost slept with some girl, but I would probably be more hurt to find out that he had feelings for someone and had kept it all a secret from me for months, while he fantasized about her and I existed in a state of naiveté.

He must take my silence as an answer, as he heads up the stairs towards our room. I follow him, not willing to give up, even though I know it is a losing battle.

"Is there anything I can say or do that would make you stay?" I ask him.

"Liv, you broke my heart. I'm not saying this can't be fixed, but it isn't going to happen overnight."

"Okay," I say reluctantly, relived to hear him say that it could be fixed.

I sit on our bed as Charlie packs and unpacks his bag; I try not to notice how many sets of clothes he is packing. I pretend that he is packing for one of his trips, and that this is a regular Sunday night, even though the crushing feeling in my chest lets me know otherwise.

"What were you looking for? Is there something I wasn't doing?" Charlie asks me as he zips up his bag.

I consider my response carefully before I answer, as this is something I have thought about hundreds of times in the last 48 hours. "I was looking for the old Olivia. The Olivia that was smart and sexy and funny and didn't have kids or drive an SUV or organize stupid school events with local Moms and pretend they were the Olympics," I tell Charlie.

"Well, congratulations I guess," says Charlie.

"But, that's not me anymore. I want to be a mom with two kids and a wonderful husband. I love my life. I went looking for something that didn't exist, and I shouldn't have taken you, or this, for granted, but the old Olivia didn't realize how lucky she was," I tell him, tears slowly streaming down my cheeks.
"I'll give you a call later this week," Charlie says and he's out the door and gone again.

Chapter 42 – Danielle

"Are you sure you don't want to know if it's a boy or a girl?" the ultrasound technician asks me as I am lying on the table in the dark, examination room, the only sound is my baby's rapid heartbeat pulsing through the speakers. The room is illuminated with a glowing image of my alien baby on the screen – my perfect alien baby according to the technician and the results of the last hour of measurements and tests.

Jim and I said that we wanted it to be a surprise, but Jim is in Maui right now with Amanda and I am alone with a belly full of cold, sticky jelly.

"Actually, I changed my mind. I do want to know," I tell her, excited and surprised by my own change-of-mind.

"It's a girl!" she says, beaming at me, as if she had something to do with it.

"A girl? Are you sure?" I don't know why I'm questioning her, but I want her to tell me again before I'll believe it.

"Yes, Mrs. Walters, it's definitely a girl. Congratulations!"

My first thought is that I can't wait to tell Megan, because I know she wants a little sister. Then I think how excited my mom will be to hear the news, next I decide that today is the day I will announce my big news on Facebook, especially since I can tell everyone it's a girl! And lastly it occurs to me that I should probably call Jim...

***

I've been spending a lot less time on Facebook because it depresses me, and because I have nothing to share, but today is going to be my triumphant return.

I put on a pair of over-priced Seven for all Mankind maternity jeans with a fitted black sweater and boots and spend half an hour in front of the full-length mirror trying to get a picture that is fitting for my announcement. When I'm happy with the proper mix of pregnant, cute and athletic, I post the photo and add this comment:

Baby Girl due July 2nd – Just over halfway there and everything is great!

Within a minute I have 15 likes and 5 comments. As the minutes tick by, the responses go up exponentially, from people I haven't heard from in years – high school friends, college friends, law school friends. I know that it doesn't mean anything, but it's nice to have my ego pumped up, even if only from distant connections through social media. I can just hear Jim now telling me how juvenile and superficial it is; but his voice is getting quieter and quieter in my head. I know I don't have to worry about Jim seeing my post on facebook since he would never waste his time with something so trivial.

While I'm watching the responses come in, I scroll through my friends' posts to see what I have missed recently. Just in the past twenty-four hours, there are dozens and dozens of posts about drinking and parties and clothes and vacations and complaints about late nights at work (perhaps Jim isn't totally off-base with his views of the site). I'm scrolling through so quickly that I almost miss it, but lucky for me, I don't.

Kate Greene is a girl that I used to train with at my gym in the city, and apparently she is also in Hawaii for the race. She has posted a picture of herself and a few friends relaxing at the pool after the first-day of warm-ups, and in the background of her photo is Jim with Amanda at the poolside tiki bar – with his tongue halfway down her throat.

I know I should be upset, or angry, or hurt, but I actually feel relieved. From the moment I met Jim I have made a series of bad decisions and now I can finally get my life back. It won't be exactly the same, I remind myself, as I rub my hand across my belly, but maybe this is what was supposed to happen. Maybe Jim wasn't a mistake, because without him I wouldn't be having my baby girl. I smile just thinking about the pictures I saw of her this morning; I really should stop calling her an alien - she's beautiful. I know it won't be easy, and it certainly isn't how I thought it would happen, but thinking about my life as a single mother, back at work as a lawyer and without Jim, just feels right.

But just in case my plan doesn't work as smoothly as I hope, I save the incriminating picture as insurance.

***

I promised Laura and Sharon that I would volunteer at the winter carnival tonight, even though I still don't understand what happens at the event, or how a school that costs $40,000 a year to attend could possibly require fundraisers. As promised, I reviewed a few vendor contracts for Sharon in December, and now she asked that I come sit at a table at the door to make sure that everyone has the proper wrist bands when they arrive. I'm still not sure how I got stuck with *any* role in the event, when I know there are hundreds of parents attending, but Kyle and Megan are too old for the festivities and Sharon and Laura must assume I have nothing better to do – which unfortunately isn't wrong.

It is mass chaos when I arrive at the school. I'm sure those familiar with the territory know where to park and how to navigate the barricades – there are cars parked in most of the no-parking zones, but I assume *I* will get a ticket if I decide to park there. I park four blocks away and walk back to school, clutching my down coat tightly to my body and cursing the miserable northeast winters; I will never adjust to this season, no matter how many years I spend here.

As I get closer to school, I see the manifestation of Sharon and Laura's hard work (and hordes of other type-A parents). There is a full-size ice-rink on one of the lawns with hockey games set up at one end, and what appear to be professional figure skaters at the other end. Inside the giant tent, I catch a glimpse of carnival games that would rival the Six Flags theme park in Dallas. I let myself in to the main entrance of the school, slightly concerned at the lack of security, and follow the noise through the halls until I find the gym. The gym is set up with all of the food stalls, and a babysitting area, and a DJ is setting up on the stage to ensure the children never experience a lull in the festivities.

I look for Sharon amongst the crowd and find her snapping at the custodian about the inferior job he did setting up the tables.

"Excuse me, Sharon, I just wanted to check and see where you wanted me?" I ask politely.

"Oh, right," she says, embarrassed to be caught yelling at the support-staff." Do you see that table right in the middle by the doors? Just go over there are have a seat. There is a list of all of the people who have already paid, and a cash box, and a box of wrist bands. I'll be there in a second to explain it in more detail," she says. And with that she excuses me and goes back to micro-managing the table-layout.

I wander over to the entrance area, wishing for the hundredth time tonight that I had not volunteered to help! I sit down at the table and start looking through the lists of names, not surprised that they are almost all complete strangers.

"Hey Danielle! I didn't know you would be here!" says a familiar voice.

I look up to see Gretchen standing right in front of the table, smiling down at me.

"Hi Gretchen!" I reply, genuinely pleased to see a familiar face.

"How did they get you to do this? They had to drag me to this and all of my kids go to school here!" she laughs.

"Laura roped me into it back in November and I never seemed able to say no. By the way, have you seen her?" I ask.

"No, I haven't. But I'm sure she'll be here tonight. She's the co-chair of the event, she couldn't miss it?" Gretchen says, but it's more of a question than a statement.

"Speaking of Laura, well not really, but I mentioned something to her a while ago, and she told me not to say anything, but I 've always felt weird not saying anything to you about it," I say to Gretchen.

"What is it?" Gretchen asks, clearly curious.

"So Megan mentioned something to me about your daughter Alice. I don't want you to take this the wrong way, and I know that I am new at this whole step-mother thing and I don't know Alice at all, but it has bothered me ever since she said it," I'm babbling now and starting to wish that I hadn't said anything, but I can't change course now.

"Danielle, what is it?" Gretchen says, her tone a little more serious.

"So Megan told me that Alice and her friends are involved in some online dating thing with older men," I tell her.

"Thanks for telling me Danielle. I actually know about it. It's all over now. The girls were involved, but they aren't anymore. I'm not saying that it's okay, but we're figuring out what to do about it," Gretchen tells me, slightly annoyed that I've intervened.

"Are you sure that it's over?" I ask her.

"Why would you ask that?" she asks me, really annoyed now.

"Look, I know that this is none of my business, and I can tell you don't want to talk about it; but Megan actually told me yesterday that the competition ends tonight and the girl who wins is the one who actually goes through with it with the guy she met online. I think Megan probably knew more about it, but she wouldn't tell me anything else – it's a lot better than it used to be, but we're not quite best friends," I say, trying to lighten the mood.

"Oh shit. Shit, shit, shit. I have to get out of here. Can you tell Sharon I had to leave?" And with that she turns and runs out of the gym.

Chapter 43 – Laura

"What are your plans for today?" Michael asks as he is shaving at his sink and I am brushing my teeth at mine.

I spit out my toothpaste and rinse my mouth before answering, "I'm going to take Cameron to his music class this morning, then I have a training session with John and then I need to get ready for the winter carnival tonight. I need to be at school to help set up by 3."

"Aren't you supposed to go see the doctor today?" he asks innocently, even though he already knows the answer.

"I moved my appointment to tomorrow. I went yesterday, and I couldn't fit in the appointment with the carnival tonight. I'm going to go first thing tomorrow morning, I feel good, I promise," I stress to Michael.

"You remember how important he said it was that you went every day, right? We all agreed that you could do this as an out-patient, but you can't start cancelling appointments or it isn't going to work," he says.

True to form, Michael has become an expert on prescription medication addiction in the last two weeks, as well as rehabilitation and recovery. It is just his nature to tackle a problem head-on and find the solution.

It has been a rocky few weeks, but Michael has made it easier than I could have imagined. I feared his judgment and disappointment, but he was more disappointed in himself for letting the problem get out of hand without noticing. He took the first week off of work and we went to a clinic in the city where I stayed for five nights and Michael rarely left my side while I talked to doctors and therapists and got the pills out of my system. I know that the normal course of treatment would have had me in a room with another druggy and Michael would have been nowhere in sight, but he found a place where he could be there the whole time and I never had to see another patient. I didn't ask how he did it; I didn't even want to know.

For the past week I have tried to resume my normal life, but I'm not sure when everything became abnormal, so stepping back in isn't as seamless as I hoped. Michael has been going in to work a couple hours later and coming come earlier. I know he is doing it because he is worried about me, but just having him around has made me feel stronger.

We agreed on out-patient care, which means I meet with the doctor for a 2-hour therapy session every day. I'm hoping this doesn't continue forever, since it makes it a lot harder to get back to a normal schedule when I have to fit in two hours of therapy a day; but it was a lot more convenient than any in-patient options, so I wasn't going to argue.

"Maybe you should call the doctor and you could do a phone session before you go to school?" Michael suggests, ever the problem solver.

"Okay, I'll try and do that," I say to appease him, knowing that it is unlikely.

"You're just doing such a great job and I want to make sure you don't backslide," Michael says, coming over and giving me a big hug and a kiss on the top of the head.

"I promise, I feel really good. I'm going to work-out today and the doctor said that's really good. And I'll be busy at school, so that will keep my mind off of everything. Do you think you will be able to make it in time for the carnival?" I ask.

"Actually, I don't think I can make it. I have a dinner tonight with new clients and I really shouldn't miss it. I was going to skip it, but I don't think that's such a good idea. I'll try to be home around 9, okay?" Michael says.

"Sure, that's fine," I tell him, trying not to let him hear my disappointment, "That's probably about the same time I'll get home anyway."

***

I put all of the other mothers to shame during Cameron's music class. There are nannies busy checking their phones, most of the moms are engrossed in conversation with each other, at one point they are "shushed" by the instructor for speaking too loudly and one mom is so bored or tired she actually nods off during the class. But not me – I am supermom today. Cameron is snuggled in my lap and we sing every word of every song. When the maracas are passed around, I grab four of them and we each shake them in perfect rhythm as if we have been practicing for hours each night. Cameron and I take our turn on the oversize drum in the middle of the circle and we get to go a second and then a third time, because no one else is paying attention. At the end of the class,

Cameron wraps his arms around me and says, "I love you momma," loud enough that all of the other mothers can hear, even over their screaming, whining children who are begging for stickers and complaining about giving the castanets back to the instructor.

Robin or Jody usually come to these music classes, but I'm definitely going to come back. I don't know why I didn't want to come before, but I feel great as I walk out of class holding Cameron's little mittoned-hand while we walk to the car. I spent an hour with my son, who loves me, and although I know it's not a competition, I definitely did a better job than any of those other nannies or moms. I feel happy and smug as I head home to meet with John.

The day continues smoothly and before I know it, it is 3 o'clock and I am in the car heading to school to help get ready for the biggest school fundraiser of the year. I never got the chance to call the doctor today, but I feel better than I have in weeks and I will see him tomorrow morning, so I can't imagine it will make a difference if I miss one day.

When I arrive at school the organized chaos is well underway. There is a giant tent set up on the main lawn, several commercial trucks parked in the parking lot, and people everywhere carrying things – I don't know what they are carrying, but everyone I see is carrying something and they are all running around like they are about to miss the last flight off the island. I park in one of the last open spots in the visitor lot and hurry inside to find Sharon.

I freeze the second I walk inside. I don't know how I could have been so thoughtless. I never considered all of the people that I would have to see here today. I don't know how I could have planned on coming to this event and forgotten that I would have to face all of those people from that disastrous wine club in December and the other women that I have been ignoring for the last few weeks while I work on my own issues. I promised Sharon I would come today, and one of the things I told Michael and the doctor I would work on was being more engaged, since they were worried I was spending too much time alone; but I don't think I can handle this level of engagement.

"Laura, I'm so glad you're here! Where have you been?" Sharon calls out as she walks across the gym toward me.

I knew Sharon was expecting me, but still I feel trapped. "Sorry I'm a little late, I must have lost track of time," I answer awkwardly.

"Is everything okay? You don't look like yourself," Sharon presses.

"Um, everything's fine. I have to go," I say quickly as I see Kristen and Stephanie coming over – I have no idea what I'll say to them if they make it over here.

I grab my purse and walk quickly out of the gym and down the hall to the girls' restrooms at the end of the 1st floor. I walk inside, relieved to see that it is empty, and I let myself into the last stall and lock the door. I take a few deep breaths and try to remember what the therapist told me – any of the calming phrases or mantras, but nothing is coming to me.

All I can think of is how good I would feel if I took a few pills right now. I know exactly what it would feel like when the drugs kicked in; my arms and legs would start to get the tiniest bit warm and then loose and then my whole body would feel lighter, almost like I could float. I told Michael and the doctors that I didn't have any pills left, but I do have a few left for an emergency. I must have known deep down that tonight could be bad, because I put two pills in the inside zipper pocket of my bag, just in case. I didn't have any intention of taking them, it just felt better to put them in there – a security blanket of sorts. But now that I'm here, I don't think I can go back out there without them, I don't think I can face those women on my own – it's just too hard.

Chapter 44 – Gretchen

It doesn't occur to me until I am halfway to my car that Natalie and Ethan are still at the carnival. It's not as if they aren't supervised. Half of the parents from school are there setting up right now; but I should probably tell someone that I left. I quickly text Olivia:

Gretchen: had to leave. problem with alice. please watch N & E!! thanks and sorry!!

Thankfully she writes back just as I am starting the engine:

Olivia: okay – will do. Charlie is coming, so he can watch my girls. hope all fine with alice – lmk.

I read her text twice to make sure I saw it correctly, but it does say that Charlie is coming to the carnival. As far as I know, he still hasn't come home and it has been almost two weeks, so if he's leaving work early to come to the carnival that must be good news. I wish I could write her back and investigate further, but I'll have to be a good friend later when I have more time.

I didn't think anything of it this morning when Alice told me that she was going home with Annie after school. I agreed when she told me that she was "way too old for the little kid carnival" and was happy that she would have somewhere to go after school to do her homework and hang out until Alan picked her up after work. Now I wonder if she had an ulterior motive in going to Annie's house, or if she even *is* at her house.

I race through the exclusive streets of Rye, not paying a moment's notice to the multi-million dollar homes or the beautifully landscaped grounds, evident even under 6 inches of snow. Annie lives less than 10 minutes from school, but of course today I hit every red light and there are cars at each and every four-way intersection when usually I would be the only one on the road.

I pull up in front of Annie's stately all-brick Georgian Colonial and try to take deep breaths as I walk down the long pathway to the front door, not knowing what I will find when I get there.

Annie's mom answers the door shortly after I ring the bell. "Oh hi Gretchen, can I help you?" she asks, sounding and looking confused.

"I'm looking for Alice, is she here?" I ask, already knowing the answer.

"Um, no. Annie is at Kelly's house today. I think Alice might be there too, do you want me to call her?" she asks helpfully.

"Oh no, no, don't worry about it. I must have misunderstood Alice this morning when she was leaving for school, and my phone is totally dead, I think she did say she was going to Kelly's. It's just one of those days!" I laugh, hoping that I sound convincing.

"Oh, I totally know what you mean! Don't worry about it. When you see Annie, tell her I'll pick her up around 6, okay?"

"Okay, no problem," I call out, already halfway up the path to my car.

Kelly lives on the other side of Rye, but this town is so small that nothing is too far away. She actually lives only a few houses down from Danielle and Jim. There must be some irony in that, or maybe it is just one of God's funny little tricks.

I am desperate to get to Kelly's house and finally figure out what is going on, and possibly even stop one of these girls from making a terrible mistake? But I'm also worried about what I'll find there and worried that this will change my relationship with Alice forever. I know I should have addressed this problem sooner, but I buried my head in the sand because I didn't want to acknowledge the little girl stage of her life is completely gone. I think she skipped about three stages in between, but even though she's doing it too fast, and doing it all wrong, she is still growing up and moving on, and doing it all without me.

As I turn the corner onto Kelly's street, I see something colorful against all of the white snow, perched on one of the Adirondack chairs on Kelly's front lawn. As I get closer, I see that it is actually a person sitting on the chair, hunched over (probably because it is 25 degrees outside), but once I am almost at the house, I can see the person is wearing Alice's coat and hat.

I slow down and park across the street. I take a minute to regroup before I get out of the car; two minutes ago I was prepared to knock down the front door and start charging into bedrooms looking for lecherous old men, but it appears I need less adrenaline to deal with the situation – and maybe an extra hat and pair of gloves!

If Alice hears me approach, she doesn't alter her position to show it. I brush off a pile of snow from the chair next to her and sit down.

"Are you okay?" I ask Alice calmly, starting with the most important question.

"I guess so," she replies, her voice hoarse as if she's been crying.

"What does that mean? Are you hurt? Did something happen?" I ask, starting to lose my composure.

"No, I'm not hurt. I'm just embarrassed. And mad at my friends, and mad at myself. And you're here, so I'm guessing I'm in trouble," Alice finishes.

"I'm going to need to know everything, but before we go anywhere, I need to ask if everyone inside is okay. Are there any men there? Is anyone in trouble?" I ask, feeling like an after-school special.

"Oh God, mom, no, there are no men there," Alice says exasperated, "and other then being total bitches, they're all fine," Alice says.

"Okay, let's go sit in the car, because it's freezing out here, but we aren't going anywhere until you tell me everything," I tell her, slowly finding my anger now that I know she is all right.

"Can we at least move the car to another street so we aren't sitting in front of her house?" Alice asks.

"Fine," I tell her, heeding her request.

I move the car around the corner, turn off the ignition and un-buckle my seatbelt so that I can turn in my seat and face Alice in the passenger seat.

"Okay, I want the whole story. And you know that I know a lot of it already, so if you leave something out, I'll find out and then you'll be in even more trouble. So, tell me everything. Now."

Alice does not join me in unbuckling; she maintains her position staring straight ahead out the windshield, into the darkening sky – although it is only 4:45 in the afternoon, it is winter in the northeast and daylight is scarce.

"You remember the thing in the fall with Kelly and the match.com guy?" Alice starts.

"Yes," I tell her. But what I want to scream is, "of course I remember, are you kidding me?!?"

"So, Kelly did end up finding out about it, and she wasn't mad at all, she thought it was great. She loved that all of these older guys thought she was hot. But, she said that as payback, we all had to put our own profiles up on the site and she would make it a competition to see which of us was the hottest," Alice pauses in her story.

"So who were the girls that did it? And why did you do it? Just because she told you to?" I ask foolishly.

"Annie and Kate and I all did it. And I know you won't understand, but Kelly is impossible to say no to, she's like the queen of the 8th grade. Kelly and Meredith said they would start spreading all of these lies about us if we didn't do it. And it really didn't seem like such a big deal," Alice sees the look of shock on my face at her comment, "I know mom, I know, it was stupid, okay. Do you want to hear the rest?"

"Yes, I want to hear everything. I'll try not to say anything until the end, but I can't promise," I tell her.

"So we put the same kinds of profiles on the dating site that we had done for Kelly, and Kelly actually put hers back up as well because she said she was going to 'win' by getting more guys or something like that."

"Can I ask a question?" I interrupt.

"Sure."

"What is the point of the competition?" I ask.

"That's what I'm getting to. So at the beginning it was just the girl who got more likes on her site. And then Kelly changed it and said that we actually had to start texting or messaging with the guys, and the girl who got the guy to say the sexiest thing in the text would be the winner."

"Oh good god Alice!" I yell out.

"Mom, you said you would let me finish," Alice complains.

"You know that these are real people, right? These are real men?? And you are really a teenager? Just barely –

you're more like a child!" I tell her, disgusted to hear the story first-hand, even though I knew most of this already.

"I know, mom, I know. It's awful. I realize that now. So, I actually stopped doing anything after that. It got too weird and so I just stopped texting anyone and I didn't go on the site anymore. I told the girls I was doing it, but I really wasn't. And then Kelly decided the last part of the contest would be that someone had to actually meet one of the guys. Well, I obviously wasn't going to do it, but Kelly wanted everyone to meet here this afternoon and she claimed that she was going to bring this college guy she met here today, and I'm really not sure what she was going to do, but she said we all had to be here," Alice stops the story there and looks at me, almost asking permission to end the tale.

"So what happened today?" I ask, trying not to sound too eager, but dying to hear how this ended.

"It was awful. It turns out the whole thing was a big joke, only I was the only one they didn't tell. The other girls put their profiles up for like a minute but then they took them down right away. I was the only one who actually had my picture up on that disgusting site, and there were men dad's age who were 'winking' at me – it was so gross! And then I was actually texting with guys from the site, and I told Kate what we said in the texts and she told Kelly and then Kelly and Meredith read them out to everyone this afternoon and everyone was laughing at me," Alice is distressed as she re-lives event from earlier this afternoon.

"Why would they do that?" I ask, genuinely confused.

269

"I don't know, because they're all really mean!" She pauses, and starts again, "Because Kelly thought the thing before was all my idea, so she was mad at me. And she told Annie and Kate to do it, and they listened to her, and I'm stupid, and I followed along too," Alice says.

"Wow. I really don't know what to say right now. I had a lot prepared, but I'm not sure any of it applies. Don't think there won't be repercussions for lying and for all those things you did online, but for today you may have had enough," I tell Alice.

"Thanks for coming mom," Alice says quietly.

"I'll always come get you," I tell her and reach over to squeeze her hand as we head back to school together.

Chapter 45 – Olivia

I'm just about to take the girls outside to the skating rink when I get Gretchen's text asking me to watch Natalie and Ethan. Obviously I tell her that it won't be a problem, but now I actually have to find both of them in this maelstrom. I'm hoping that they are both still in the gym and they haven't left for the skating rink or the outdoor tent; the carnival is getting more chaotic by the minute and although I'm sure that they are both fine, I'm not convinced I'm going to be able to find them.

I hold Julie and Elizabeth's hands tightly as we make our way through the gym, which, thanks to many other parents' hard work, now resembles a gigantic ice castle. Thankfully, I spot Ethan in line for cotton candy and my job is halfway done.

With massive cones of fluffy spun sugar in each of their hands, I march Ethan, Julie and Elizabeth over to the babysitting area. Julie and Ethan half-heartedly protest, but they are too engrossed with their treats to put up a good fight. This is only my second year at the carnival, but whoever came up with the babysitting area within the carnival is an absolute genius. There are four high-school students who sit in one corner of the room that is blocked off with gymnastics mats, and parents can drop their kids off and then pick them up as many times as they want for the length of the carnival. It is the most low-tech element of the entire event, yet in many ways, the most essential.

Unconstrained, I am now able to search the gym more thoroughly and determine that Natalie is not here. As I head out toward the exit, I notice that Danielle is at the ticket table.

"Danielle, I need to ask you something," I call out to her as I walk toward the table.

"Oh, hi Olivia. Sure. Let me just finish up here and I'll be right with you," Danielle answers, seemingly overwhelmed by the long line in front of her table – a casual observer would think this was a sold-out concert rather than a school carnival.

While one ticket-buyer pauses to re-assess her raffle ticket purchase, Danielle takes the opportunity to speak with me, "What can I do for you Olivia? I had no idea how crazy this would be!"

"I just wanted to ask if you had seen Natalie. Gretchen's daughter? Gretchen had to leave for a little while and she asked if I could watch her kids for a little while she was gone, but I can't find one of them," I admit to Danielle.

"No, sorry. I haven't seen her daughter. To be honest, I don't think I've ever met her, so I don't think I can be much help. I did see Gretchen run out of here though, hopefully everything's okay," Danielle says gravely.

"Oh, everything's fine," I tell her, although I have no idea if it is, and I'm not sure why Danielle cares so much.

"Oh, by the way Olivia. Your husband is here. He just bought his ticket a few minutes ago, but it's so crowded in here, I'm not sure if you've seen him yet," Danielle informs me.

"Oh, right. Thanks, I'm sure we'll find each other," I say, hoping my voice does not convey the trepidation I feel at seeing my own husband.

I wander outside to the tent, knowing that I have a 50:50 chance Natalie will be here or at the skating rink – with my recent luck, I'll be wrong. I wander between the game booths, hoping to recognize her group of 3rd grade friends, but I have not spent much time beyond the walls of kindergarten, so all of these big kids look the same.

There is a group of girls clustered around the skee-ball machines (one of my personal favorites), and I recognize Natalie's brown French-braided head in the sea of blonde hair.

"Natalie! Natalie! Over here!" I call out.

Natalie picks up her head to look around and see who's calling for her, but she doesn't respond.

"Natalie! Over here! It's Mrs. Somers. Olivia. Can you come here please?" I call to here, not wanting to get any closer to her group, trying to remember at what age girls are completely embarrassed by all adult behavior.

"Oh, hi Mrs. Somers!" Natalie calls out, as she comes running over. I guess 8 is too young for complete embarrassment, or else Gretchen has just raised a well-mannered child.

"Hi Natalie. Your mom had to leave quickly to go get Alice, and she asked me to keep an eye on you while she is gone. I have Ethan with Julie and Elizabeth over in the gym. But, I guess you aren't going to want to come with me if all of your friends are here?" I ask, knowing that I don't sound like the adult in this conversation.

"Amy's mom is right over there. She is watching all of us. Please don't make me leave," she pleads.

"Don't worry, I won't do that," I tell her, as I try to figure out how I am going to watch all 4 children, when one of them won't come with me, *and* handle seeing my husband for the first time in over a week. "Okay, you can stay here for the next 45 minutes, but then you have to come meet me in the gym. Is that a deal? Meet me at the front ticket table." I tell her.

"Okay, that's fine," Natalie says, slightly disappointed, but unwilling to fight with a grown-up who isn't her mom or dad.

The outdoor walkway is only 25-feet long, but I'm still freezing without my jacket. The overheated gym feels great when I walk back inside, but it does nothing to help prepare me for seeing Charlie immediately upon entry.

"Hi Liv," Charlie says, "I've been looking for you and the girls, but this place is ridiculous, it took me 15 minutes just to do one loop around the gym!" I'm trying to read the subtext in his words, but I think he is being relatively straightforward so far.

"I know, it's kind of incredible how many people come to this, but I guess it's good for the school – it's only our second year, I'm sure we'll get used to it after a while," I laugh, and then wonder if Charlie is thinking that he won't have to get used to it because he is leaving me – god I hate feeling like this.

"I guess. Anyway, where are the girls? I'm so excited to see them!" He doesn't state the obvious - that he hasn't seen them in over a week because he has temporarily moved out, and left us, and it is all my fault; but I'm sure it's in there somewhere.

"They're over in the far corner with the babysitters. Gretchen had an emergency with Alice, so she asked me to watch Natalie and Ethan, and I just put the kids in there for a few minutes while I went to go find Natalie. Oh, and I did find Natalie, but she was with other kids, so I left her there, but she is going to meet me in 45 minutes," I jabber on to him, feeling the need to excuse all of my behavior and assume he is judging every decision I make.

"Okay then. I'm going to take the girls over to skating if that's okay with you? Should I take Ethan too?" Charlie asks.

"Sure. Actually that would be great," I answer, wondering why he isn't more annoyed, but then I remember we are at school surrounded by friends and neighbors, and he likely doesn't want anyone to know that we are having problems.

I watch Charlie walk toward babysitting, and then see Julie and Elizabeth run toward him. He effortlessly picks up both girls and swings them around, unbridled joy on both of their faces like I haven't seen once in the daily routine over the past week. Charlie leads the girls outside, with Ethan racing to catch up, and I let myself out of the gym and down the hallway toward the bathroom.

To my disappointment, the bathroom is not completely empty – there is someone in the last stall. It's probably for the best, because it will keep me from dissolving into a blubbery mess. I grab the counter with both hands and take a close look at myself in the mirror. I look exactly as I did a few months ago, the same bright turquoise eyes and long lashes, dirty blonde hair and perfectly arched brows to match. Although when I look closer, it's possible I've aged several years just in the past few weeks. I think there are lines around my eyes and mouth that I never had before – probably from crying and frowning too much. I practice smiling and frowning in the mirror to see which makes the lines worse – according to this mirror, I should maintain no facial expression in order to look my youngest.

I stop making faces in the mirror when I remember that I am not alone in the bathroom. I glance at the occupied stall, noting that whoever is in there has been in there for several minutes. I instantly recognize the Prada ankle boots and the leather pants.

"Laura, is that you?" I ask, already knowing the answer.

Chapter 46 – Laura

I'm still clutching both pills in my hand, when I hear the bathroom door open and someone walk in. I wait to hear the stall door open and close, but nothing happens. I peer out between the crack in the stall to see Olivia staring at herself in the mirror, her face five inches from the glass, smiling, frowning, grimacing, raising her eyebrows; it looks like she's warming up for an improv show. I have to put my hand over my mouth to keep from laughing and revealing myself.

"Laura, is that you?" Olivia suddenly asks.

Oh shit. I thought I was being so quiet, how did she know I was in here? I look down at my feet and realize it must be the shoes. I've only worn these boots a few times, but Olivia loves shoes and she made it very clear that she loved this particular pair, but she could never justify buying them.

"Hi Olivia. Yes, it's me," I answer, glad to have the door in between us as a shield.

"Is everything okay?" she asks.

"Yes, I'm fine. I just wasn't feeling well for a minute, so I came in here, but I'm sure I'll be better soon," I answer, looking down at the pills in the palm of my hand.

"Oh good. I needed a bit of a break too. I'm wondering how long I can stay in here before I have to go back outside," Olivia says.

"Oh? What's wrong?" I ask her, surprised to hear that there is anything wrong in Olivia's well-designed, under-control world.

"Honestly, pretty much everything. Charlie and I are in a huge fight, well I'm not sure you can call it a fight, he's mad at me, I'm not mad at him. He has been sleeping at his brother's house for the last week. And he's here tonight and I don't even know how to talk to him anymore. My own husband – isn't that ridiculous?" She asks, but I think it's a rhetorical question.

I am stunned. I picture Olivia as super-woman, sometimes I even envision her wearing a cape. She had this amazing career that she chose to give up to spend time with her kids, and now she does everything with them without any help; and of course I assumed she and Charlie had the perfect marriage, because whenever I see them together they always seem so happy. I'm going to have to alter my entire opinion of Olivia.

I put the pills in my pocket and unlock the door. Although I would happily stay behind the comfort of the stall, Olivia's confession, combined with her small stature, make her seem like a vulnerable child. I don't think we've ever exchanged more than a perfunctory hug or kiss on the cheek, but when I wrap my arms around her, she hugs me back tightly – clearly in need of comfort. It feels good to be useful, and to know that I can provide support; I don't always need to be the one on the receiving end.

Just then the door crashes open and Kristen comes in breathless.

"Olivia. Thank God. We've been looking all over for you! You have to come now, Julie's hurt. The ambulance is on the way, but you need to come!" Kristen says between breaths.

"What? What happened? Where is she? What's wrong?" Olivia is asking questions, but she is already running out the door.

"Wait for me, Olivia. Let me help," I call out as I run down the hall after her, all thoughts of pills and fears of seeing people completely removed from my thoughts.

Chapter 47 – Olivia

I run through the halls of the school, asking Kristen the same questions over and over again, even though it's clear she doesn't have the answers. Luckily Kristen does know of a shortcut to the field outside, so we do not need to cut through the gym; I couldn't fathom slowing down now to excuse myself and squeeze past parents and children happily waiting in line for snow cones.

Kristen, Laura and I push through an exit door on the school's lower level that leads directly outside. A blast of cold air hits me as we run onto the field, but I barely notice it, my only thought is getting to my baby.

As I get closer to the ice rink I see that everyone on the rink is huddled in a circle. At first I wonder where Julie is, and then it hits me that she must be in the center of the circle, the reason for its formation. I hear sirens in the distance, and they start to grow closer as I reach the edge of the rink. I hear ambulance sirens every day and take them for granted, sometimes I'm even annoyed when those sirens mean I miss the green light or I'm two minutes later than I would have been without them. Now I realize how selfish I have been. Not just with Chris, but in general; right before I step onto the ice I make a pact with God that I will be a better, more altruistic person, if only Julie is okay.

I take a step onto the ice and I can see Julie lying on the ground, her body looks so small in her pink puffy ski pants and matching jacket. The school nurse and a man I don't recognize are crouched down on the ice next to her, blocking my view and keeping anyone from getting close to her. I try to walk carefully in my boots, but it's hard to balance caution with my desire to race to Julie and hold her little body. Charlie turns around just as I am getting close to the circle of onlookers and he takes two giant steps towards me and picks me up in a massive bear hug, it is the last thing I expected.

"Oh Liv, I'm so sorry. I don't know how it happened. I looked away just for a second, and then she was down," he says between choked back sobs.

"What happened? I don't understand? Kristen couldn't tell me? Please just tell me what's going on? Why can't I go see her?" I beg him.

Charlie puts me back on the ground and then takes a deep breath before he begins, "Julie and Ethan were skating and then Ethan said he wanted to practice hockey, so I said I would play with him at the other end of the rink where they had the hockey stuff set up. I guess Julie wanted to play hockey too, or just to be with me, but the next thing I knew she was down at our end of the rink and there were a lot of bigger kids down there with us. I turned my back for just a second to pass the puck to Ethan and then when I turned around someone had skated into her and knocked her over..." Charlie pauses.

"I still don't understand. She falls all the time when she ice skates, why is this so different?" I ask, annoyed and confused.

"Liv, she got hit really hard and she hit her head on the ice when she fell. She's unconscious now from the fall," he explains quietly.

"Oh my god, my poor little girl," I stammer, trying to process what Charlie's just said.

I had not noticed the paramedics arrive while we were talking, but suddenly there are three uniformed men quickly, but carefully, making their way onto the ice with a stretcher. I've seen this happen countless times in movies and on TV, and I've watched the occasional stranger at an accident scene on the side of the road, but I never thought much about it since it was so far removed from my life. But now it isn't a stranger. I watch the giant men secure my firstborn on a back board before they transfer her to the stretcher. In an instant, one of them has hooked her up to an IV and someone else has covered her with a blanket. I think the entire performance took 4 minutes – clearly a well-choreographed dance.

It is only when they start to roll her off the ice toward the ambulance that anyone remembers that Charlie and I are even there.

"Are the parents here?" asks the blonde-haired paramedic, who must be the most senior member of the team, but I still can't believe he is more than 30.

"We're right here!" Charlie and I call out in unison.

"Okay, please come with us. You can ride with your daughter if you'd like," the paramedic tells us, already starting to load the stretcher into the ambulance.

"Wait, Charlie! Where is Elizabeth?" I ask him, amazed that I had not thought to ask this earlier.

"One of the moms took her inside. I'm sure you would know who it is, she knew me, but I couldn't remember her name," Charlie says.

"I'll take care of her, don't worry about it," Laura says passionately. I forgot that she came with me from the bathroom; she must have been standing here the whole time.

"Thank you so much," I say to Laura, desperately meaning it.

"It's the least I can do," she says.

"Oh wait! We are also supposed to be watching Ethan and Natalie for Gretchen. She had some sort of problem with Alice, so she had to leave. Can you find them too?" I ask, but I am already climbing into the ambulance beside Julie.

"I'll take care of it. I won't let you down," Laura says.

The paramedic slams the doors shut and Charlie and I are left staring at each other with our knees jammed awkwardly against the stretcher and the other equipment and our beautiful, motionless little girl lying between us.

I couldn't bring myself to ask before, but now that we are here, speeding toward the hospital, I have to ask, "Is she going to be okay?"

The paramedic who is riding in back with us looks over and says, "Ma'am, we're doing everything we can. We'll know more when we get to the hospital."

Charlie reaches over Julie to take my hand and says, "She's going to be okay, I know it Liv. It's all going to be okay."

***

We arrive at the emergency entrance to Greenwich Hospital, and it is impossible for me not to remember that this is the exact same entrance I came through five years ago when I was in labor with Julie. The mood is entirely different tonight as we pull up with sirens blaring and a team of doctors waiting the second the doors open. Charlie and I sit quietly as the doctors and paramedics shout back and forth to each other about Julie's stats and a recap of the injury.

Julie is rolled away from us before we can protest and the one remaining doctor leads us inside the hospital and directs us to the waiting area. I collapse onto the leather couch (only Greenwich Hospital would have leather couches in its waiting area instead of the hard molded plastic chairs found in every other hospital in the world), the events of the afternoon finally catching up with me. Although I realize this is the first time Charlie and I are alone together, I don't have the energy to obsess over our marital problems right now, they will just have to wait.

Charlie sits down next to me, his leg pressed right up against mine.

"Liv, can we talk about this?" he asks.

"I don't think I can talk right now. I just need to find out how Julie is doing and then we can talk about us, okay? I can't take anymore misery right now," I tell him.

"Okay. You don't have to say anything. But I just wanted to tell you that the instant I knew something happened to Julie, all I wanted was you. I just knew that if you were there, everything would be okay – I knew I would be okay, and I knew Julie would be okay. I need you Liv, I love you," Charlie hesitates.

"I love you too. And I'm so sorry…" I try to apologize again, but Charlie cuts me off.

"I know you are. And I'm still hurt and upset, but I know you love me. I've thought about what it would be like without you this last week, and it doesn't work without you. The girls need you, and I need you. I know you were looking for something else that you were missing, but I'm not missing anything," Charlie says.

"I'm not either," I tell him, my eyes wet with tears, "I thought I was missing something, but now I know that I'm not. I wish I had never taken you or our family for granted - it's just too fragile. And now our little Julie…" I wrap my arms around him and bury my head in his massive shoulder, grateful to have my embrace unequivocally returned for the first time since my confession.

I could stay wrapped up in Charlie's arms for the rest of the evening; but he can't protect me from the reality of Julie's situation. Thankfully I have received texts from Gretchen and Laura letting me know that I don't have to worry about any of my other responsibilities:

Gretchen: so sorry about Julie! Keep me posted! Do you need anything? Am home now with all 3 kids. Alice fine, will tell you later.

Laura: I hope Julie is okay – please let me know as soon as you have news. Lizzie is home with us and playing with kids – she is great, she can sleep here if you want, just let me know.

I have dozens of other texts as well from parents at school that saw or heard what happened, but I can't read those now.

***

At 9:30 that night, the doctor comes out and yells into the waiting room, "Julie Somers, the family of Julie Somers?"

Charlie and I almost trip over each other trying to get off of the couch and race to the doctor to hear what she has to say.

"We're here," I call out as I speed-walk the 15 yards across the room to where the doctor is standing.

"How is she?" Charlie asks as soon as we reach the doctor.

"Hello Mr. and Mrs. Somers, I'm Dr. Jackson. I'm the pediatric neurologist who has been observing your daughter."

"Hello," Charlie and I both say as we shake her outstretched hand.

"So, can you please tell us how Julie is doing? Can we see her?" I ask.

"Yes, you can see her. She hasn't woken up yet, but all of her vital signs are good. We did an MRI and everything looks fine. We won't know more until she's awake, but..." Dr. Jackson says.

"But what?" Charlie interrupts.

"I was just going to say that the longer she is unconscious, the more concerned we will be, but it's also a good way for the body to rest after a trauma. If you'd like, you can see her. You can follow me," Dr. Jackson tells us.

As we approach Julie's room, I clutch Charlie's hand, unsure of what we will find inside. I try to prepare myself for seeing my little girl in that big bed with all the machines.

As the doctor opens the door to the room, I hear a little voice say, "Where are my mommy and daddy? Do you know my mommy and daddy?"

I push open the door and see Julie's bright blue eyes looking around the room trying to assess the situation.

"Mommy! Daddy!" Julie cries out when she sees us.

"Well, this is an exciting development," Dr. Jackson says, as she goes around to the side of the bed to check something on one of Julie's monitors and to speak to the nurse who was in the room when Julie woke up.

"So what does this mean?" Charlie asks the doctor. I'm too busy crawling onto the bed and smothering Julie with kisses to ask any questions.

"Well, we still want to keep her overnight for observation, and there is a chance of concussion, but based on her behavior now and her test results, I think she's going to be just fine," Dr. Jackson tells us.

"I know we're all going to be just fine," I say to Charlie and Julie, and especially to myself.

Epilogue - Olivia

"Do you think she'll be surprised?" I ask Gretchen.

"Probably not. When Danielle called today to check on the timing, I could hear in her voice that she knew this wasn't a regular wine club," Gretchen says, as she continues setting the table with alternating light pink and purple napkins.

"Well, we needed an excuse to get her back to Rye. Even if she isn't actually surprised, I hope she enjoys our attempt to throw her a surprise baby shower," I say, as I bring in two more trays of appetizers to add to the dozen already in the living room – I may have gone overboard on the food.

"She'll be surprised that I don't pass out," Laura says nonchalantly as she comes in from the kitchen carrying three bottles of champagne. "Don't worry, these aren't for me," Laura jokes.

I'm still amazed when I think about what Laura went through, and how none of us knew about it until after it was over. Shortly after the winter carnival, Laura admitted herself to a month-long in-patient rehab program. She told us that she had been having problems since the fall and that they had gotten worse and worse through the winter. She tried an out-patient program in February, but the temptation of being at home and engaged in her normal life were too hard.

Laura was gone for all of March and since she has been back, she has been a completely different person. In fact, her whole family has changed. Although she still looks like she could be on the cover of a magazine, her beauty is slightly less intimidating now that she lets her flaws shine through. She seems to have accepted her imperfections and those of her children and family and even embraced them, and it has made her a better friend and mother. She says that there are moments of struggle for her every day, but I would wager on her success – she's a survivor.

The doorbell rings and we all stare at each other.

"It can't be her, we still have thirty minutes," Gretchen says confidently.

"It's probably just one of the other ladies. We told everyone else to come at seven, so it must be one of them," I say to Laura and Gretchen as I walk toward the door.

I open the door to find Stephanie hidden behind an enormous present and 7 other women on my doorstep.

"Hurry, let us in!" someone calls, "I think I just saw her car!"

I step back to let everyone inside, "the present table is over there," I tell the ladies, pointing to the side table in the family room that I have covered with a pink lace tablecloth for the occasion. Although I would never describe myself as 'girly', once I started decorating for the baby shower, I couldn't seem to stop; there wasn't enough pink, lace, or baby paraphernalia in the store to satiate me.

"Olivia, everything looks beautiful!" Stephanie gushes, after she places her gigantic present on the floor next to the table, and comes over to survey the room.

"Thanks! I know Danielle has other friends in the city, but I wasn't sure if anyone else was throwing her a shower, so I wanted to make sure we did something for her. I may have gotten carried away," I smile as I assess the transformation of my house over the past 24-hours.

"Julie and Elizabeth must be thrilled – it looks like little-girl heaven in here!" Kristen interjects.

"They would be, but I won't let them near anything until the party is over. They think I'm so mean!" I tell everyone.

"So where are they now?" Kristen asks.

"Charlie and Alan took the kids out for dinner and then they are all having a sleep-over at Gretchen's house. Lucky Gretchen," I say and smile in her direction.

"I'm thinking I may just sleep here and let the dads handle it. I'm sure they won't notice if I don't come home, right?" Gretchen laughs.

Kristen follows me as I wander into the kitchen to make sure the oven is pre-heating for the desserts and to start putting the cocktails and mocktails on trays so that they will be ready to bring out into the living room.

"Olivia, can I ask how Julie is doing? I know it's been two months, but I just wanted to check," Kristen asks cautiously.

"She's doing great. And thanks for asking. The doctors have checked her several times since the accident, but she had absolutely no permanent damage. She was so lucky. Well, we were all so lucky. She complains that I hold her too tightly now, but I think that's the only consequence,"

"That's a miracle - and so wonderful for all of you. You and Charlie were so great that day," Kristen says.

"That's not quite how I remember it," I laugh.

"No really, you both were wonderful. You're so lucky to have each other."

"Yes, we absolutely are," I agree.

***

The doorbell rings again; this time it must be Danielle.

"Okay, everyone get ready to yell "surprise", Gretchen whispers loudly enough that Danielle likely hears from outside.

I open the front door and Danielle is standing at the front door looking pregnant and radiant. I lean forward and stand on my toes to give her a hug as 10 women behind me yell "surprise."

"Oh my gosh! You didn't have to do this!" Danielle says, as she walks inside and sees all of the tell-tale baby-shower clues, especially the cake on the table that says 'Happy Shower Danielle.'

"Do you like it?" Laura asks hopefully.

"I love it!" Danielle answers. "It's really too much, you didn't have to do anything for me. I don't even live here anymore," Danielle says a little sheepishly.

"We wanted to!" I tell her. "Besides, we like buying baby stuff, it makes us feel young."

"You are young," Danielle tells all of us, but it isn't incredibly convincing.

"Come sit down and eat something! You look like you are wasting away. You know you are eating for two, yes?" Gretchen says, as she leads her over to the couch.

Danielle sits down in the middle of the couch and we all take our seats around her on the surrounding chairs and couches, eager to hear about her life away from Rye, and away from Jim.

"So how have you been?" Gretchen asks.

"Good. Everything is really good," Danielle answers.

"And you feel good? I mean you look amazing! I can't believe you are due in a little over two months!" Stephanie gushes.

"So, everything's just good? No more details?" Laura inquires.

"Okay, okay. I'll give you the whole story. I'm sure that what you have all imagined has actually been far more interesting than what has actually happened, but I can tell from looking at all of you that you aren't going to be satisfied with my one-word answers," Danielle teases.

"Let's get some drinks first before we get started!" Gretchen demands.

"I'm coming, I'm coming," I yell out, running to the kitchen to get the trays of drinks, "I was distracted, sorry!"

"Okay, that's better," Danielle says after taking a sip, "nothing like some pink lemonade to go with some juicy gossip – ugh, I can't wait for two more months to be over," she groans.

"Okay. Here's the story with all the details. I promise it's not as exciting as you think," Danielle tells all of us, but we are all leaning in close, doubtful of her promise, if the truth is anything like the rumors that have been flying around town.

"First, I'm sure you'll be disappointed, but I didn't get half of all of Jim's money. I heard that story too, but sadly that one isn't true," Danielle says and we all laugh.

"So the night Jim got back from his trip to Hawaii, I confronted him about the girl he took with him. At first he denied that anything had happened, but he eventually confessed to sleeping with her in Hawaii and then told me that he had slept with someone else even before the trip," Danielle pauses as the whole room gasps.

"I know. He's a giant asshole. Anyway, I was about 99% sure that our relationship was over before then, but that was pretty much the nail in the coffin. I told him I wanted a divorce and that I was going to move back to the city and I think he was mostly just relieved. I'm still trying to remember what I saw in him at the beginning, other than the obvious," we all laugh when she admits this, since we've all thought that Jim's physical appearance is the only thing she could have ever seen in him. "I think it was the authority too. He's quite impressive to watch when he's commanding a room."

"So what happened next?" Stephanie asks, anxious to hear the rest of the story.

"I stayed in the house for a few more days while I looked for an apartment in the city and we tried to figure out our plans for separation. Amazingly, Jim was a lot nicer once he knew that he was going to be a free man again. He should never have gotten married after Linda – I think I was just supposed to be a fling, but he got carried away. We do have a pre-nup, but it is very generous, especially with the baby coming, so I was able to find an apartment pretty easily. I'm on the upper west side in a two-bedroom, two-bathroom, one block from Central Park. I was completely moved in by the second week of March, so now I'm settled, and starting to get the second bedroom ready. This will help a lot!" Danielle says, as she gestures toward the table overflowing with gifts.

"That's great sweetie. I'm so glad that you're doing okay. But, what about Jim? Will he be involved? Are you going to be okay as a single mom?" Laura asks, not shying away from some of the tougher questions that we are all thinking.

"I honestly don't know what will happen with Jim. The divorce will be final soon – he was able to fast-track it somehow. He says he wants to be involved with the baby, but I don't believe him. But I'm really okay with it if he isn't. I know you think I'm crazy. But I've found a job starting in October, and they will let me work 3 days a week. It's at the firm where I did my first summer internship in law school, and they were thrilled to hear from me," Danielle pauses to take a sip from her drink and grabs a California roll from the table.

"Wow. I'm so impressed. You really do sound like you have everything together," I tell her, surprised at how different she sounds from a few months ago.

"I know I was a bit of a mess this past year. I feel like I have been a mess ever since I met Jim. But that's not who I used to be. Now I feel exactly like myself again. Oh, well with one obvious exception," Danielle rubs her basketball-like baby-bump affectionately.

"So what will you do with the baby when you go back to work?" Laura asks, again with the hard questions.

"My mom is going to come for the first three months that I'm at work. Ha! I can tell by your faces that you think I'm really crazy now! We'll see how it goes, but I think it will be good for us. And then I'll hire a nanny like everyone else. Honestly, the only part of all of this that has been hard has been saying good-bye to Megan and Kyle – I think they've gotten hit the worst," Danielle says sadly.

"Are they still with Jim? I feel so bad for them if they have to move again!" Gretchen says.

"They are staying with Jim for now because Linda and Bill are still out West, but Jim's not home very often, so he hired an au pair to drive them around and be there when they get home from school. I've only seen them once since I've moved out, and I guess they're doing okay, but I know Megan is really mad at both of her parents. I think she is counting down the days until college – unfortunately she still has three years left," Danielle laments.

"Okay, well enough of the inquisition, we have sufficient answers for one evening. I think it's time for a toast!" Gretchen says, raising her glass.

"Yes! Here's to the new mommy-to-be!" I say raising my glass.

"Cheers!" everyone says together, clinking glasses and taking generous sips of their champagne, and pink lemonade for Laura and Danielle.

"Gretchen, can you help me in the kitchen?" I ask her. "Ladies, please eat and drink! We'll open presents soon," I say as I turn to walk to the kitchen with Gretchen following behind.

"What is it?" Gretchen asks.

"I actually wanted your help with the little cakes, but I also had a question for you."

"Ask away," she says, taking the aluminum foil off of the tray of cakes that we need to assemble.

"So Charlie told me that Alan is interviewing for a job in Chicago. I knew that he had been there a few times for work, but I didn't realize they were for interviews. You would tell me if there was something going on, right?" I ask her in a serious tone.

Gretchen sighs loudly.

"Oh no!" I practically yell, "What does that mean? That doesn't sound good!"

"No, no. I promise, everything's fine. Well, now it's fine. It's just been a long couple of months. I'll give you the short version of the story. Alan has been miserable at work for a long time. Then he got an amazing job offer at the Chicago Tribune and wanted us to move there. When everything happened with Alice at school, he was even more intent on the move – he insisted that we needed to move her from this poisonous environment. I couldn't imagine moving, but I was having a hard time arguing with the economics of the job offer and the opportunity for a fresh start for Alice..."

I am too impatient and I cut her off, "so what's going on? Are you moving or not? I have to know how this ends?"

Gretchen continues, "I actually went out to Chicago two weeks ago to look at houses with Alan. Did you know how much more you can get in Wilmette than you can in Rye for the same price? Anyway, right after we got back, Alan's boss called him in and somehow he had found out about the job offer and he said he didn't want to lose him, and he basically apologized to Alan for overlooking him and offered him a huge raise and promotion if he stayed at the Times. And then it felt like fate, because we found out that night that Kelly's family – you know the horrible girl in Alice's class? – her family is moving to Chicago! What are the odds of that? So Kelly will be out of Alice's life, and one of the other mean girls is actually transferring to Rye Country Day, so I think the dynamics at school will be drastically different next year once they are gone," Gretchen stops to take a sip of her drink.

"Please tell me that I am connecting the dots correctly and this means that you aren't going anywhere?" I ask impatiently.

"Yes, you are correct. And that's why I didn't say anything. I guess I'm not surprised that Alan told Charlie – it's funny what men talk about. Anyhow, Alan just couldn't turn down the offer at the Times. So I guess all's well that ends well, right?" Gretchen asks.

"I think it's better that you didn't tell me. I don't think I could have handled all of that. I have had enough excitement this year to last a lifetime," I tell her.

"That was exactly my thought," Gretchen says, smiling back at me.

THE END

Rachel Cullen is a graduate of Northwestern University and NYU Stern School of Business. She worked in consulting and marketing in San Francisco, London and New York and currently lives in Westchester, NY with her husband, 3 children and her dog Cocoa. *The Way I've Heard It Should Be* is her first novel.

Made in the USA
Columbia, SC
29 July 2019